'You've been spying on me?'

Ethan released Deirdre's hand, shook his head and wandered across the room.

Deirdre's skin heated. 'Of course not.'

'But you've been giving my father information about me.'

'That's not true. I assist in running his office and help care for the twins—'

'My kids?' His head snapped around. 'You've seen my kids?'

'Yes,' she whispered. 'They're beautiful children.'

The longing in his eyes affected her like a punch to the stomach. She should have known the moment she saw those exquisite babies, had looked into those thick-lashed hazel eyes, that Ethan had fathered them.

He lifted her chin with his fingertip and peered into her eyes, saw the moisture gathered there. Was he seeing betrayal...or love?

Dear Reader,

Welcome!

For those of you waving kids off to school after the end of the holidays, take a trip down memory lane and enjoy Susan Mallery's *Surprise Delivery*—although I do hope none of you gave birth in a lift as Susan's heroine does!

Cathy Gillen Thacker is kicking off a new miniseries with *Dr Cowboy*, featuring the first of the **McCabe Men**—four sexy brothers about to head up the aisle... So look for those every couple of months.

There's also one of Lindsay McKenna's trademark strong, silent warrior men to distract you, and there'll be another one next month, and another one in Desire™ the month after that. What more could a woman want?

Well, terrific stories from wonderful writers like Diana Whitney, Christine Flynn and Jean Brashear perhaps? We hope so.

Happy Reading!

The Editors

The Fatherhood Factor

DIANA WHITNEY

SILHOUETTE
SPECIAL EDITION®

First published in Great Britain 2000
Silhouette Books, Eton House, 18-24 Paradise Road,
Richmond, Surrey TW9 1SR

© Diana Hinz 1999

ISBN 0 373 24276 X

23-0009

Printed and bound in Spain
by Litografía Rosés S.A., Barcelona

DIANA WHITNEY

A two-time Romance Writers of America RITA Award finalist, *Romantic Times Magazine* Reviewers' Choice nominee and finalist for Colorado Romance Writers' Award of Excellence, Diana Whitney has published more than two dozen romance and suspense novels since her first Silhouette® title was published in 1989. A popular speaker, Diana has conducted writing workshops, and has published several articles on the craft of fiction writing for various trade magazines and newsletters. She is a member of Authors Guild, Novelists, Inc., Published Authors Network and Romance Writers of America. She and her husband live in rural Northern California, with a beloved menagerie of furred creatures, domestic and wild. She loves to hear from readers.

To Diane Henderson,
a dear friend, a wise soul and a precious person.
May your karma choose wisely.

Chapter One

"You're closing the office?" Stunned, Deirdre O'Connor set the platter of fresh-baked shortbread on the doily-draped credenza. Her heart shuddered, skipped a beat. Her palms iced in fear.

"'Tis only for a few months, child, a single semester at university." Across the quaint, antique-studded parlor smiled Deirdre's mentor for the past five years and her friend for as long as she could remember. Cotton-haired, wreathed in wrinkled wisdom, Clementine Allister St. Ives eased out a breath, rolled her thick shoulders with an apologetic shrug. "Time will pass before you know it."

Panic swelled quickly, trembled through a voice Deirdre no longer recognized as her own. "It's sorry I am about Professor Owani's health problems, but surely someone else can absorb his course work, someone who doesn't have to close down a thriving law practice to move halfway around the world.''

Clementine's soft cluck of reproach made Deirdre cringe. ''Listen to yourself, child. 'Tis not the wilds of Borneo, after all.'' Easing herself into the old rocker from which she had greeted clients for nearly five decades, Clementine absently massaged her swollen knuckles. She sighed, gazed out the mullioned windows trimmed with authentic Irish lace. ''Honolulu is lovely, they say. I've always wanted to visit. 'Twas never enough time.''

''There still isn't! I mean…'' Embarrassed by the un-intended edge in her voice, Deirdre cleared her throat, coughed away a trace of brogue that tinted her speech at vulnerable moments. ''Your calendar is full through spring, with clients and court dates—''

''On my desk, dear, there's a list of colleagues who will be taking over for me.'' At seventy-two, Clementine's gait had slowed, but her crafty mind was still sharp, and she juggled a daunting schedule with amazing vigor. The quirky, wonderfully spry woman had once served as legal advocate for Deirdre's immigrant parents and their eight children. She'd since become Deirdre's dearest friend and confidante.

The thought of losing her even for a few months was devastating. ''You've a speech scheduled for the San Francisco Family Law Association meeting next month. You can't be leaving them in the lurch like that.''

''Geoffrey McIntyre has a whole drawer full of dried-up speeches. Nothing that old coot loves better than a captive audience.''

''But…counseling sessions! They can't possibly be rescheduled in time—''

''Already done, child.''

Deirdre's heart closed like a fist. "Your genealogy courses at City College?"

"Did I mention my assistant just received his credentials? Fine lad, that one. Full of vigor and enthusiasm, he is. He'll do fine on his own." A tubby tomcat leapt up to rub its furry forehead against the age-dimpled chin of its mistress. Clementine stroked the purring animal with obvious affection. "Ah, 'tis worried, you are? Not to fear, my pet. You'll not be left behind."

That the cat would not be abandoned was no surprise to Deirdre. Animals were precious, like children. She still missed her own beloved calico, a sweet-natured feline whose death had grieved her deeply. When she'd also lost the husband she'd adored, Deirdre's world had gone black. It was Clementine who'd eased her back into the light, who'd offered solace and friendship, and had kept the dragon of loneliness from devouring her whole.

Once again she felt the dragon's breath on her back. And it frightened her.

Loneliness was a state of mind, Deirdre supposed, a weakness to which she had refused to capitulate by enmeshing herself in a career that was more a vocation than a job. Intellectually she understood it. Emotionally she was unprepared for the shock of it, the fear of being alone again. Totally, completely alone.

"'Tis time you took a bit of life for yourself," Clementine said, as if reading Deirdre's thoughts. By any standard, Clementine was an amazing woman, with a leprechaun grin and lilting Irish chuckle, eyes twinkling with humor and warm with ancient wisdom. "A beautiful world out there, lass. A world of beauty and excitement, all waiting for you to take it for your own."

A question bunched in Deirdre's throat, caught by a wave of emotion. She didn't want time for herself, didn't want to venture beyond these protected walls. This was her world. This was her life.

Deirdre's gaze circled the familiar room. Brocade wing chairs accented by crocheted doilies, an antique sideboard on which fresh pastries and beverage were served to "guests," as Clementine referred to her clients, and the old-fashioned floral wallpaper studded by framed diplomas from the prestigious universities from which her uniquely brilliant employer had garnered a wealth of post-graduate degrees. Old-world charm scented by sweet lavender and potpourri filled the stately Victorian manor that had been a home to Deirdre, a respite from the emptiness of life without the husband she'd adored.

"Your salary will of course remain in effect while I'm gone." Shifting in the chair, Clementine inspected her with unnerving acuity. "You work too hard, my dear. I can't remember the last time you took a vacation."

Deirdre absently smoothed the rolled edge of a crocheted place mat on which the platter of fresh shortbread cooled. "Two weeks is a vacation. Six months is—" she sucked in a breath "—a long time."

"'Tis but a blink of God's eye, child."

That offered little solace. "Perhaps you could use an assistant in Hawaii, someone to help organize the paperwork."

"The university has already seen to it."

"A personal secretary, perhaps, someone to keep your schedule, scrub your bathroom, take your clothes to the cleaner, anything." She hated the desperation in her voice, but was helpless to suppress it. "Clementine, please, I have to keep busy, to be of some use to somebody—"

"Santa Barbara is lovely this time of year."

That took her aback. "Santa Barbara?"

"'Tis a magnificent place, where the ocean shines blue enough to shame the sky, and sunsets blaze with such magnificence that grown men weep with joy." A sly gleam flickered in the woman's eyes, then was gone. "My friend Horace lives there. Have I ever mentioned him?"

"Not that I recall."

"Horace P. Devlin. Crusty old codger, but his wife is a lovely person." Chuckling, Clementine tickled the cat's chin as it batted at the half-moon granny glasses dangling at her matronly bosom. "Going through a difficult time, they are, trying to care for sweet twin grandbabies and run a law office at the same time."

"Twins are a handful." The acknowledgment was heartfelt and born of experience, since she'd helped her weary mum raise two sets of twin siblings in her own expansive family.

Heaving a sigh that was only a tad theatrical, Clementine shook her head. "At wits' end, they are, needing someone to help with the babes, and keep up the office, as well." She gazed out the window with feigned befuddlement that didn't fool Deirdre for a moment. "But where could one find a person with such experience, someone with the warmth of an angel, the patience of a saint and the mind of a scholar, someone who just happens to be available for...oh, the next six months or so? 'Tis a puzzlement indeed."

Deirdre was intimately familiar with her beloved boss's mode of operation, and recognized a setup when she saw one. "Ah, so that's the plan."

Clementine managed to look appropriately startled. "Why, whatever do you mean, child?"

"You're wanting me to assist your friends in Santa Barbara."

"What a splendid idea!"

Deirdre's head was spinning. This was all going much too fast. Instinctively she knew there was considerably more to the story than she'd thus far been told. "I don't understand. Why are the Devlins raising their grandchildren? Where are the twins' parents?"

"The mother rests in God's arms."

"I'm so sorry." A twinge of sadness twisted her heart. "And the father?"

"A wee custody dispute." Clementine flicked her wrist as if batting an annoying insect. "Nothing you can't handle."

The sly woman's clandestine agenda became crystal-clear, much to Deirdre's horror. "Oh, no, I'll not be involving myself in such a thing."

Before Deirdre could turn away, Clementine leapt from her chair with surprising agility, disrupting the snoozing cat, unceremoniously dumping it from its warm napping spot. "Think of the babes." Clementine touched her arm, pleading. "Those dear, sweet innocents so desperately in need of stability in their lives. 'Tis for the children, Deirdre. They need you."

She wavered, caught by the sad image of tiny toddlers thrust in the midst of a crisis between people they loved most. She knew then that she would go, that she must go. She also knew on some level that the decision would change her life forever.

For the children, of course. It was always for the children.

"Dublin?" Crouching, Deirdre peered beneath the bedframe on which a bare boxspring and mattress had been dumped by a team of inefficient movers. She stood, checked a closet packed with a tumble of unpressed clothes straight from the packing crate. "Here, kitty, kitty, kitty."

She blew out a breath, swiveled around a stack of half-unpacked boxes to the living area of the small, one-bedroom duplex. "Dublin, sweetie…meow, meow? Not nice to hide from Mommy."

She tilted her head, listening for an answering mew that never came. A twinge of real panic needled into her chest. The kitten, barely six months old, had been a gift from Clementine before she'd left for Hawaii last week. Dublin was a gray-and-white bundle of brimming curiosity and whiskered mischief that had pounced, bounced, darted and dashed its way into Deirdre's heart from the moment she'd laid eyes on the tiny creature as it peeked out from a gift-wrapped kitty carrier.

During the chaos of moving Deirdre had kept the kitten safely tucked in that carrier, releasing it to explore its new environment only after the movers had left. Now she frantically tore through the small living space, calling and searching until her gaze fell on the front door, which had been left open to catch a wafting sea breeze through the screen. The screen door was locked in place, although there were claw marks in the fabric where the tiny animal tested his climbing prowess.

There was another flaw, one that nearly stopped Deirdre's heart. A corner of the protective screening had been torn away, pushed outward as if something small had crawled through it onto the front porch shared with the neighboring unit. An ominous tuft of white fur stuck to the metal frame.

"Oh, no." In less than a beat Deirdre was out the door, and down the porch steps. "Dublin? Here kitty, here kitty, kitty!"

Pausing in the driveway, she shaded her eyes to study

the unfamiliar area. Mature oaks lined the rural street on which a few small homes were situated on large lots. The duplex itself was a homely rectangular building divided lengthwise into two separate apartments.

A covered porch along the entrance revealed twin doors flanked with identical windows, and porch steps on each side leading to the pair of driveways abutting both the right and left side of the narrow property.

Deirdre's dusty old coupe was parked in her driveway. On her neighbor's side an older-model sedan sat with its hood up, surrounded by a scattering of tools.

Across the street, perhaps two hundred yards from the duplex porch, stretched the railroad tracks upon which trains rumbled with unnerving frequency. In the three hours since her arrival, four of the metal beasts had roared past like seismic claps of thunder. A wilderness of weeds studded the railroad property, along with a few pitiful eucalyptus trees clumped along the tracks. The salty tang of ocean freshened the air, lifted the fine hairs fringed above her brow. The sea was close by, as Clementine had promised, less than a quarter of a mile beyond the undeveloped acreage abutting the tracks.

A blur of movement caught her attention. A man sprinted through the weeds with contagious tension.

Deirdre heard the telltale rumble at the same moment she saw a flash of white on the tracks. ''Oh, God, Dublin!'' Terror and nausea nearly doubled her over. A gasp, an adrenaline surge, and she sprinted forward, screaming her kitten's name.

Not that it mattered. All sound was drowned out by the deafening roar of the oncoming train, and the shrill blast of its whistle.

A pair of perky eyes peered over the metal track rail. Feline ears twitched. The earth trembled. An air horn shrieked. "Dublin!" A hot-metal stench burned her nostrils. She ran faster, faster. The ground rolled beneath her feet. Yellow cat eyes widened. "Dublin!"

The train sped closer, so close she could see the engineer's frantic expression, feel the blast of hot air from the engine.

Too late. It was too late. "Dublin!" she shrieked, a moment before the sprinting man suddenly dove and rolled right in front of the speeding engine.

Deirdre jerked to a stop, frozen with fear as the ground vibrated beneath her feet, and boxcar after boxcar clattered past. Her stomach lurched, her knees nearly buckled. She was certain that neither her beloved kitten nor the brave soul who had tried to save it could have possibly survived.

Tears spilled over, dust whipped her face. Hot wind and horror, numbness and shock. She couldn't move, couldn't breathe. Boxcars whizzed past. Time stood still.

When the faded old caboose finally zoomed by, a gasp caught in her throat. She nearly fainted with relief.

On the other side of the tracks, a dark-haired man cuddled the terrified but apparently unhurt kitten in his arms.

Man and cat were so completely absorbed with each other that neither noticed they were being watched. The man stood slightly askance, a profile of strength that seemed paradoxical to his tenderness with the tiny animal.

Deirdre couldn't hear what the man was saying, but could tell by the gentle way he brushed his cheek against the kitten's head that he was soothing the animal's fear, speaking in gentle tones. The little cat responded by butting its forehead against his chin, a gesture of affection that elicited a masculine smile so unexpected and dazzling that it took her breath away.

As the train rumble faded, she caught a shrill mew, followed by a mellow voice, a whisper of tenderness that sliced straight into her heart. "Shh, little guy, I know that was scary, but you're okay now." He paused, smiling as the kitten laid a soft paw on his face in a gesture that looked very much like a grateful feline caress. "You're very welcome."

Dublin gazed up adoringly, and mewed.

"Is that so?" The man chuckled. "I hope you've learned your lesson. Railroad tracks are not good for kitties." Still cradling the tiny animal as if it were something precious and fragile, he turned to cross the tracks.

The moment he saw Deirdre, his entire demeanor changed. His eyes widened in surprise, narrowed quickly as he arranged his expression into one of nonchalance. Squaring his shoulders, he shifted his grasp on the kitten, balancing it in his palm rather than hugging it to his body. "Your cat?"

She nodded, struck mute for some reason she chose not to explore.

He shrugged, moved forward in a distinctive don't-mess-with-me swagger that Deirdre recognized instantly. Her own five brothers had used a similar change of stance as a protective mechanism when they felt threatened or embarrassed, or to conceal vulnerability. Clearly this man wished to distance himself from the softhearted alter ego that had hugged a panicked kitten as if it had been a frightened child.

As he approached, she noticed that he studied her without looking, also another habit her brothers had displayed, that unique male ability to inspect people from the corner of their eyes without attracting attention.

Deirdre, however, regarded him directly. Not a tall man, he was nonetheless sturdily built, with muscular shoulders rippling beneath a sweatshirt smeared with black grease, and dusted with loose dirt and gravel from his gymnastic shoulder roll. A few dried leaves and weed stems clung to the sleeve, and to the tousle of coffee-brown hair shagging around his ears. She suppressed an urge to brush them away.

But it was his eyes that drew her, a speckled tone of hazel and gray fringed with thick, dark lashes that were incredibly erotic. Although her own lashes were also dark and longer than his, they were too sparse to accent the faint blue of her irises, and tended to poke up in little spikes that made her look perennially surprised.

This man had eyes to die for.

And those eyes were now focused directly on her. "Keep a better watch on him."

"Excuse me?" It took a moment for her to yank her gaze to the mewing kitten he held out. "Oh, of course." Gathering the furry little animal to her breast, she breathed a sigh of relief, smiling as it nuzzled beneath her chin. Tiny whiskers tickled her throat, a cold nose brushed the edge of her jaw. "Dublin, my sweet, sweet boy, you scared the life out of me." The kitten trilled softly, massaged her shoulders in a feline version of a claw hug. "I don't know how to thank you, Mr....?"

Apparently he hadn't expected her to look up so quickly, because she caught the warmth in his eyes a moment before he blinked it away. "No problem." He spun and strode toward the street fast enough for his boots to spit gravel.

Tightening her grip on the kitten, she hurried after him. "It's truly grateful I am. I've just moved in, you see, and am not familiar with the area." Breathing hard, she was nearly running to keep up with him. "I'm not usually so careless, but there was this wee hole in the screen, and Dubby found it, and—''

When he stopped at the street, she nearly ran into his back. She skidded, stumbled, had barely righted herself when the man crossed the pitted asphalt, heading straight for the duplex without so much as a backward glance.

She stood on the weed-encrusted curb, feeling a bit slighted. Dublin mewed as if to console her. "Hmm? Yes, quite right. Not a particularly social type at all."

A soft squeak made her smile. "Ah, your hero, is he? A very brave man indeed, although I suspect he's a touch embarrassed at having been caught playing kissy-face with a kitten." The cat widened its eyes. "The male ego is a fragile thing," she murmured, glancing for traffic as she crossed the street. "You'd not be knowing that, wee one that you are. Aren't you glad you won't be plagued with such hormonal nonsense?" Dublin hissed. "Hmm? Still perturbed about that little operation, are you? Well, it was for your own good. Doesn't make you any less of a cat."

Chuckling, she hugged the kitten fiercely, so grateful for its safety that she could have wept with joy. As she crossed the patchy grass toward her side of the duplex porch, she saw her kitten's rescuer appear from the neighboring driveway carrying what appeared to be a roll of duct tape in his left hand.

He entered the porch from his side, barely glancing at Deirdre as he strode to her front door, which was barely five feet from his own. He squatted to inspect the torn screen.

Deirdre's mouth was suddenly dry. "Can it be fixed? I mean, if it can't I'll have to leave the solid door closed, but it seems a shame to waste that lovely ocean breeze." He ripped a sticky length of tape, used his left hand to tear it off after notching the edge with his teeth. Undeterred, Deirdre chatted on. "I'm told the shore is close enough to walk in less than a verse."

Still crouched, he angled a glance upward. "Less than a verse?"

"Oh, my mum judged distance by the number of canticle verses one could recite on the journey. A habit from her own childhood in the Irish countryside, where feet were the primary mode of transportation, and folks considered walking time an opportunity for the devout to catch up on daily prayers." Something flickered in his gaze, but clouded over before she could identify it. As she stood over his crouched form, she noticed a thin scar running from the base of his jawline to just below his ear. When he turned back to his work, she saw the scar also extended to his nape, where it disappeared into the ragged neck of his sweatshirt. "Anyway, I'm looking forward to long walks on the beach at sunset. Perhaps you could show me the best route."

He didn't look up. "A block north, cross at the intersection, follow the path down the embankment until your feet get wet."

"Oh. Well, that sounds simple enough. Have you lived here long, Mr....?"

A twitch of annoyance rippled the small scar at his jaw. Clearly he wasn't prepared to introduce himself, nor did he enjoy small talk. "A couple of weeks."

"Really? So you're new in town yourself. Perhaps we could find our way around together. I'd be pleased to fix you supper sometime. As a reward," she added quickly when he shot her a suspicious look. "For saving dear Dublin. I'm ever so grateful." She hadn't expected him to reply, and he didn't. Deirdre was nothing if not persistent. "So where is it you've come from, Mr....?" She waited a beat, then moved on. "Ah, guessing games. I love them. Let's see, you've a touch of sun on your face and hands, red but not tan, as if you've come from a place where sunning oneself is not a community pastime. Thrifty with words, you are, so I'd be thinking the northeast if you displayed the distinctive accent of those hardy souls. The northwest then... Seattle, perhaps." She shifted the kitten, feeling proud of her powers of observation. "Am I getting warm?"

"Not even close."

Deflated, she shrugged. "Would your powers of observation be better then?"

"I'd say so."

"Prove it." The conversation was inane, she knew, but she was reluctant to end contact with this intriguing man.

"Okay." Taking her challenge, he glanced up, allowing his gaze to linger on her face for a beat longer than comfortable before sliding the length of her with an unhurried leisure she found unsettling. "San Francisco," he announced, then returned to his task while Deirdre gaped in astonishment.

"How did you know that?"

The hint of a smile touched the corner of his mouth. "Pale skin, dewy from foggy mornings, a Golden Gate sparkle in your eyes—" his gaze dropped to her hips, slipped slowly to thighs revealed by the cling of khaki slacks a bit too snug, thanks to her indulgence of sampling her own home-baked treats "—lush thighs, soft but well-muscled by hiking hills and valleys. Shoes worn more at the toe than the heel, soles ground away by concrete, hence the observation of city sidewalks rather than rural landscape. Steep city terrain equals San Francisco."

"Go on with you," she murmured, as astounded by the effect his leisurely inspection had on her heart rate as she was by the accuracy of his observation. "Blarney, it is, straight from the leprechaun's lying stone."

"Am I wrong?"

"You know you're not wrong." The knowing gleam in his eye had told her that. "But I'm not buying those tall tales about worn shoes or foggy mildew on my earlobes." She crouched to his level, nudged him with her shoulder. "C'mon, now. Tell us the truth. How did you really know all that?"

A wisp of amusement touched his gaze as he swallowed a smile, then offered a brusque nod toward her driveway. "I read your car."

"My car?" She followed the gesture to her dusty old coupe, where her focus fell first on the parking sticker for the underground lot across from Clementine's Victorian law office, then slipped to the license plate holder that proudly announced the San Francisco dealership from which she'd purchased the car years earlier. "Ah."

"You sound disappointed."

To her horror, a strained giggle rolled from her throat before she could stop it. "Truth be told, I rather enjoyed your flights of fancy."

"Reality is always a letdown." The edge to his voice caught her by surprise, as did the flash of pain a moment before his eyes went blank. Hunching over, he continued his work as if she no longer existed, smoothing one strip of tape on the base of the torn screen, then ripping off another strip for the side. He flinched slightly as the tape roll slipped from his grasp.

Earlier Deirdre had noticed him favoring his right hand, which seemed to be stiff and inflexible. "Have you hurt yourself? Your hand," she explained when he gave her a disbelieving stare. "It seems to be bothering you. Did you injure it when you rolled over the tracks?"

"No."

"It should be X-rayed, just to make sure. I'll pay of course—"

"No." The word was issued with enough force to make her blink.

Deirdre felt her smile tighten, but was determined to remain friendly. This man was her neighbor, after all, and had saved her kitten's life. "My name is Deirdre," she said cheerfully. "Deirdre O'Connor."

He stood so suddenly, she took an involuntary step back. "Needs rescreening. Call the landlord."

"The landlord? Ah, and who might that be?"

He regarded her with mild suspicion. "Marc Rosenblum, the man you pay rent to."

"I don't pay rent." She felt the telltale prickle on her cheeks, and knew she was blushing. "That is, the rent is being paid, of course, but not by me."

He hiked a brow.

"It's not what you're thinking," she blurted, certain she was glowing like neon. The combination of nerves and embarrassment loosened her tongue, and thickened her Irish brogue until it was dense enough to slice. "'Tis strictly business, don't you know, and not a bit of the hanky-panky you'd be guessing."

The corner of his mouth twitched. "Ethan."

Her breath slipped out all at once. "Ethan," she repeated, enjoying the feel of it on her tongue. "A strong name. It suits you."

He shifted the roll of tape to his left hand. "I'll call the landlord and have it seen to."

"That's kind of you." When he turned away, she touched his arm to stop him. He froze, staring at her fingers on his wrist, then flicking a startled glance upward. There was something stunning in his gaze, something profound and compelling.

For a moment, neither of them moved. Only when Dublin shifted suddenly in her arms did Deirdre retrieve her hand to steady the restless cat. "Could I offer some refreshment, a sip of something cool perhaps, and a bite of pastry—?" He shook his head, which for some inexplicable reason made her talk even faster. "It's the least I can do, what with you saving poor Dubby here from such a fierce fate. I don't know how else to thank you."

"Don't worry about it."

"Perhaps another—" his apartment door shut in her face "—time." Deirdre stood there a moment, clutching her cat and feeling silly. Finally she called out, "It was lovely meeting you, as well," then returned to her own side of the duplex to continue her unpacking chores.

Safely ensconced in self-imposed isolation, Ethan shrugged off a pang of regret for his gruffness. He heard movement through the separating Sheetrock, the scruff of something heavy being dragged across the hardwood floor, the lilting murmur of her voice as she spoke aloud, either to herself or to the tiny animal he had first seen scampering across the road toward the railroad tracks.

A burst of melodic laughter filtered through the thin wall, startling him. It was a lovely sound, bubbling with a delight that penetrated his cynical shell. He couldn't afford any distraction, not even the pleasant diversion of a beautiful woman with hair like shining midnight, and eyes twinkling like brilliant stars.

He flipped on the television to drown out the sounds from next door, then retrieved a beer from the fridge, using the crook of his arm to steady the can while he popped the top.

Holding the beer in his left hand, he settled into an easy chair, automatically scooping up the rubber exercise ball that was always within reach. He palmed the ball in his right hand, flexing his numb fingers around the hard rubber. His gaze focused on the flickering television screen, but his mind was lost in thought, memories of the past, visions of the future, thoughts of a wounded warrior preparing for the most important battle of his life.

He willed his numb fingers to tighten their grip on the rubber ball, was pleased when they offered slight response. It was a small improvement, not nearly enough.

Sweat beaded his brow, slipped down to sting his eyes. He blinked it away, concentrating as his hand curled with enough force to stimulate the damaged nerve along his wrist. A sharp pain skewered up his forearm, as if a hot poker had been inserted beneath the skin. Ethan didn't blink. He didn't mind the pain. In fact he reveled in it. Pain was life. Life was hope.

His hand was responding, his strength and control increasing every day. The process was slow, tedious. Time was his nemesis. Ethan's time was running out. The past circled like a sworn enemy, concealing a future rife with uncertainty. Years of blood, sweat and tears had prepared him for this quest. Losing was not an option.

He moved to the window, eased an opening at the side of the drapes. It was there again, the dark sedan with tinted windows. It slowed, veered to the curb across the street and parked.

Ethan flexed his jaw, curled his fingers around the rubber sphere and squeezed. He needed control, he needed strength. He needed to retrieve all that had been stolen, to replace the ball with a gun and take back what was his. No one would stop him.

No one.

Chapter Two

Armed with a map and Clementine's handwritten directions, Deirdre drove to a three-story professional building just off Pacific Coast Highway. Ivory stucco with a red-tiled roof, the architecture fit neatly into Santa Barbara's historic Spanish style but lacked the quaint charm of Clementine's quirky old Victorian. The law office of Devlin & Son was on the second floor.

Juggling a container of butter cookies she'd baked as a gift for her new co-workers, Deirdre stepped from the elevator into a quiet, carpeted hallway and made her way to the proper suite. Before she had a chance to shift her parcel and reach for the knob, the door flew open and a red-faced woman in a flannel business suit huffed out.

The woman jerked to a stop, eyed Deirdre up and down. "Are you the new legal assistant?"

"Yes."

She laid an empathetic hand on Deirdre's shoulder. "Be afraid," she murmured. "Be very afraid."

A guttural shout rattled the maze of burlap-covered office partitions. "Johnson! Where are those blasted transcripts?"

The woman shuddered once. "You haven't seen me," she whispered, then shouldered her handbag, spun on chunky heels and practically sprinted for the elevator.

"Johnson!" The owner of the booming voice strode around an upholstered partition like a fat rooster, a rumpled beach ball of a man with squat legs, a jowled face, bushy brows rolled into a hideous frown and a shock of gray-streaked hair plastered against his bulbous skull as if glued with petroleum jelly. Tie askew, shirtsleeves rolled up to the elbows, the man Deirdre assumed to be none other than Horace P. Devlin himself looked more like a harried private eye out of a potboiler detective novel than one of the most respected probate attorneys in the state.

Two manila folders were tucked under one arm; the third file was open, allowing him to riffle loose papers while marching toward the deserted reception desk. "Get Judge Nielsen on the phone," he barked without looking up. "Reschedule the Ames deposition for Friday. Get me the Rodriguez file...." He flipped a page, muttered a mild oath, then glanced toward the desk, and did a double take, as if just noticing that whomever he expected to occupy the desk was not there.

Uttering a bitter epithet, the rotund fellow spun around, his face redder than the splendid sunset Deirdre had enjoyed from the porch of her duplex last night. Blinking, he eyed Deirdre with a vaguely familiar intensity. A vein bulged at his left temple. "Where's Johnson?"

"If you're referring to the short blonde with wire-rimmed glasses and frantic eyes, she just left."

"The wimp." He closed the file he'd been reading, wiped his shiny forehead with his free hand. "You're O'Connor?"

Denial teetered on her tongue. "Yes." She shifted the plastic cookie container to extend her hand. "It's a pleasure to meet you, Mr. Devlin."

"You're late."

"Ah, I'm sorry. I took a wrong turn at that peculiar traffic circle, and—"

"Call the temp agency, tell them to send a receptionist that doesn't vomit every time the phone rings." Horace thrust the files he'd been carrying into Deirdre's outstretched hand. "Draft a codicil to Mrs. Henry's will, run three copies of the old lady's trust paperwork, get Judge Nielsen on the phone, and see if you can find what that flannel-suited airhead did with the Rodriguez file."

Hustling past at the same dizzying speed with which he'd entered the small reception area, Horace jerked to a stop at the edge of the partition to glance over his shoulder. Deirdre noted that he inspected her with the same intensity as Ethan had done yesterday, but without the subtle gleam of sensual interest.

"You're a big girl," he announced, as if Deirdre needed a reminder that her taller-than-average frame was arranged with better than waiflike proportion. "Clem didn't mention that."

Indignance overcame astonishment. "I'll try not to break your fine furniture with my substantial girth, Mr. Devlin. Will you be checking my teeth now?"

Horace didn't exactly smile, but the grooves in his forehead relaxed a bit. "No need. We don't offer dental insurance." With that, the arrogant attorney disappeared into the partitioned maze, leaving Deirdre to fume silently.

A bit of bully bluster might send the fainthearted likes of Ms. Johnson into a fit of vapors, but Deirdre had dealt with strident egos before. One didn't survive in a boisterous family of ten without learning to stand up for oneself.

It would be a cold day in the devil's house before a cantankerous old poop like Horace P. Devlin got the best of an O'Connor.

Deirdre rolled up her sleeves and went to work.

By noon, she'd tracked down the computerized document files, researched the office appointment calendar to reschedule the Ames deposition, located the elusive Judge Nielsen's number on a Rolodex that had been abandoned beside a puddle of milky-brown liquid on the coffee room counter and arranged for a new receptionist, one who would hopefully have a thicker skin than the previous six that had come and gone during the past three weeks.

The reception desk had been littered with investigator contracts, surveillance transcripts and a disarray of files, including the elusive Rodriguez folder. There was also a sealed brown envelope labeled "Subject X" that was clearly marked for Mr. Devlin's eyes only. A renewable work order for another week's worth of surveillance on the unnamed subject was clipped to the envelope, along with a note asking her to approve the contract and forward the signed original back to the investigator.

Secrecy, she'd learned, was a passion with a bilious boss who viewed courtesy as a waste of time, and barked one-word orders with drill-sergeant precision. Horace expected everything instantly, so she wasn't perturbed by his bloodcurdling shout as revised codicils requested ten minutes earlier were spitting from the printer.

"O'Connor!"

Snatching up a stack of files, she retrieved the still-warm codicil pages, proofed them on the move and juggled the documents into the proper folders as she crossed the threshold into hostile territory.

Hunched over a spartan metal desk heaped with dog-eared files, Horace held a telephone receiver to his ear while shuffling through a legal document nested amidst the clutter. "The revisions are complete," he barked into the phone. Responding to the challenge in his eye, Deirdre flopped the files in his overflowing In basket. He grunted into the receiver, snatched a hard candy from a heaping crystal bowl at the edge of his desk. "They'll be there in an hour."

Deirdre made a mental note to telephone a courier.

"Yes. Next week. Good." Horace roughly cradled the receiver, unwrapped the candy, popped it into his mouth and spoke around it. "I need the Jamison transcript." She dropped the document on his desk. He regarded it briefly, his brows bunched in annoyance. "It's not notarized."

"My Notary Public certification is expired. I'll make other arrangements."

A withering stare. "See that you do."

She neither blinked nor looked away. "Will there be anything else?"

Horace's private line rang. He snatched up the receiver, barked into the phone. "Devlin... Yeah... yeah... What do you mean you can't find him?"

Deirdre backed toward the doorway, had nearly made her escape when Horace fixed his beady gaze on her, jerked a thumb toward a guest chair in a silent command that she should remain. She sighed and seated herself.

"I don't care how many Rodriguezes you've hunted up, you haven't found the one I need." Horace retrieved the file Deirdre had just brought him. "The Rodriguez I'm looking for saved the life of one Nels Svenson four years ago in the aftermath of a single-vehicle auto accident. The bad news is that Svenson died anyway. Heart attack. The good news is that he lived long enough to remember the Good Samaritan in his will." Rolling his eyes, Horace leaned back in the chair, his voice heavy with exasperation. "I don't care how much trouble it is. Rodriguez has money coming— What?" Horace lurched forward. That worrisome vein bulged again. Deirdre was perversely fascinated by the rhythmic pulse at his temple, and realized that one could actually measure the man's anger quotient in vein-beats per minute. "Are you nuts? Of course the right one matters! You think every Rodriguez in the phone book is part of one big extended family? What kind of a detective are you? I don't pay you to pee on my foot and tell me it's raining. I pay you to find people."

He slammed down the receiver, helped himself to another candy and regarded Deirdre with surprising calm. He shoved the bowl toward her. "Have one."

"No, thank you."

"They're sugar-free." He shrugged as she narrowed her gaze. "I gave up cigars this year. Mother insisted."

A hint of smoke, faint and not particularly unpleasant, still clung to the furniture. Deirdre had noticed the humidors arranged on a polished teak bookcase beside a sparkling crystal ashtray.

Horace popped the candy in his mouth, tossed the wrapper into a nearby wastebasket. "So, are your living arrangements satisfactory?"

Although startled by the question, she kept her expression impassive. "The duplex is fine, thank you."

"The location is to your liking?"

"It is."

"Have you met your neighbor?"

"I have."

"Any problems?"

"None that I'm aware of."

He stared at her as if reading her soul. "You're a widow."

Instinct kept her gaze steady. "I am."

"For the past five years?"

"Yes." Just like a lawyer, Deirdre thought, to know all the answers before a question was posed.

"How long had you been married?"

"Eighteen months."

"You must have been a child bride." Horace broke the visual stalemate then, leaning back in a swivel chair that was worn around the edges, rather like the man himself. "Your husband drowned, didn't he? A boating accident."

A lump swelled in her throat. She did not want to discuss this, did not want to relive the heartache of losing Christopher. Vaguely aware of voices filtering from the reception area, Deirdre pulled herself upright, clasped her hands together to quell their trembling. "My professional qualifications are your concern. My personal life is not."

He regarded her as if she'd said nothing of importance. "Was it a good marriage?"

"That, Mr. Devlin, is none of your business."

A gleam flickered in his eye, admiration perhaps, or grudging respect. "Everything is my business."

The sound of scampering feet caught his attention, and his gaze brightened like sunlight off a mirror as a pair of identical, dark-haired toddlers sprinted through the doorway.

"Gwampa!" squeaked one of the tiny boys.

The other bounded past, arms outstretched. "Gampa!"

Horace's demeanor changed from brooding to beaming in the space of a heartbeat. The chattering children clamored onto his lap.

"We-we-we got *ice kweem!*" said the boy who turned *R*'s into *W*'s.

"Ice keem!" agreed the child who ignored *R*'s altogether.

Neither announcement was necessary since chocolate remnants were smeared on both grinning baby faces.

Horace quirked a brow in feigned fascination. "Ice cream, is it? And did you eat it all up?" Two identical heads bobbed in unison. Retrieving a handkerchief from his pocket, Horace dabbed both grubby faces with surprising expertise. "This is Timmy," Horace told Deirdre as he wiped the chin of the squirming child. "The calm one is Tommy." He chuckled at his own joke, since Tommy had crawled into the middle of the heaped desk, and was in the process of emptying files into a pile of disheveled documents.

Envisioning herself working until midnight to repair the damage, Deirdre leapt forward to scoop up the curious youngster and pry a wrinkled transcript from grubby little hands. "Let's see if we can find something more fun to play with than boring old legal papers, shall we?"

To her shock, Horace issued a thunderous guffaw that seemed thoroughly out of place in a man who had only moments before seemed incapable of amusement. "He's a pistol, isn't he?" Still chuckling, he shifted Timmy on his lap. "Boys, this is Deirdre. She'll be taking care of you on Tuesdays and Thursdays, while Gramma is working."

Since part-time nanny duty for the two-and-a-half-year-old twins had been part of Deirdre's agreement, the announcement came as no shock to her. Tommy's huge, hazel eyes gazed up with blatant adoration. "Dee-dwa pwetty."

Her heart melted. "Thank you, Tommy."

When she smiled at Timmy, the shy child buried his face against his grandfather's chest, and peeked through chocolate-coated fingers with eyes identical to his brother's.

Before Deirdre could do more than smile at the timid twin, a sweet fragrance wafted into the room along with a magnificent, stately woman who rushed forward with the same frenetic motion as the determined little Tommy, who tried to wriggle from her grasp to retrieve the document she'd taken from him.

"Mercy!" the woman exclaimed, jerking to a stop when she saw Deirdre. "You are even more gorgeous than Clementine's description!" Her eyes widened. "Oh, dear, there's chocolate on your lovely white blouse." She rushed forward to pluck the bucking toddler out of Deirdre's arms. The moment Tommy's feet hit the floor, he scurried away, and Deirdre was yanked into the fragrant embrace of a woman even taller than she, and more powerful than her slender frame would suggest. "We are so pleased to have you with us, dear. So very, very pleased."

"I'm, er, pleased to be here." Feeling rumpled and unnerved, Deirdre extricated herself, stepped back to get her bearings. "You must be Mrs. Devlin."

Her laugh was melodic and contagious. "Call me Nettie, dear. Everyone does. Except for the boys, of course."

A loving glance encompassed the toddlers, then lingered on her husband. "And Horace has his own pet names for me, don't you, my roly-poly muffin man?"

Horace's eyes warmed like golden lava. "Indeed I do, precious, but I shall try to contain myself in front of the children."

Nettie's cheeks pinked. Her nervous giggle was interrupted by the sound of a throat being cleared. All eyes turned toward the doorway, where a man in a business suit observed the chaos with mild curiosity. "I'm looking for Mr. or Mrs. Horace Paul Devlin."

Nettie stepped forward, her faced wreathed in welcome. "I'm Mrs. Devlin. May I help you?"

The man reached under his lapel, pulled an envelope from his pocket, then slapped it in her hand. "You've been served, ma'am. Have a nice day."

Deirdre was exhausted. Hard work had always been a part of her life, but she'd never ended a day so physically and emotionally drained. The Devlin law office was like Alice's Wonderland, where nothing was as it seemed, and chaos was the norm.

After the process server left, Deirdre had entertained the twins in the outer office to allow Nettie and Horace a private conference call with their attorney. What little she'd gleaned from the one-sided conversation indicated that the Devlins' estranged son, the twins' father, was demanding immediate visitation with the boys.

Oddly enough, the Devlins hadn't seemed surprised by that, nor had they seemed terribly upset. They were, however, subdued and concerned, but for reasons Deirdre suspected were deeper than the obvious. There was something bubbling beneath the surface of this sadly fractured family, something that Deirdre couldn't quite identify. It wasn't any of her business, of course. Her only assignment was to assist with the office, and care for the children on those days when Nettie performed office bookkeeping duties.

At least Deirdre presumed that was her only assignment. Considering Clementine's penchant for clandestine motive, one could never be certain the wily old woman didn't have a secret agenda for even the most innocent of suggestions.

Still, Deirdre was too tired to ponder that possibility at the moment. As she pulled into the parking lot of a small video store a block from the duplex, she looked forward to a relaxing evening enjoying the one movie that never failed to lift spirits and soothe rattled nerves.

The store was crowded, but she sidled through the packed aisles, humming to herself. When she found the section she sought, her heart soared. "The hills," she sang softly, "are— Oh, no." She found what she was seeking, only to realize that the video itself was not stacked behind the empty box. It had already been rented. She spun around, clutched the arm of a gangly adolescent restocking tapes nearby. "Do you have another copy of this?"

He squinted at the box. "Nope, just one. Not much call for old Julie Andrews stuff."

Horrified at the heresy, Deirdre shook the empty box at him. "I'll have you know that *The Sound of Music* is a musical classic, the most memorable film of this century."

He blinked. "I like *Star Wars* myself."

Her heart sank. "Thanks anyway." Replacing the box on the shelf, she trudged toward the door. No living hills, no panoramic vistas, no tearful smile and satisfied sigh.

A disappointing conclusion to what had been a most trying day.

Several customers were lined up at the checkout counter. She passed by them. A harried clerk flopped a video on the pickup point, beyond an alarm detector that signaled if someone passed through holding a tape that hadn't been properly checked out. Deirdre's eye went straight to the recently rented video, and her heart leapt like a happy trout. She snatched it up, hoping to talk the customer who'd rented it into making another selection, but when she spun around, she came face-to-startled face with none other than her grumpy but heroic neighbor. "You rented this?"

Ethan frowned, first at her, then at the video she clutched to her bosom. "Is that okay with you?" He plucked the tape from her hand, brushed past and went out the door.

She followed, chattering madly. "Actually, you won't believe this." A slightly maniacal laugh bubbled from her throat before she could stop it. "But *The Sound of Music* is my favorite musical of all time. I adore that movie. That's why I'm here. I was hoping to rent it."

In the parking lot, he paused to zip his jacket and tuck the video inside. "You came to the right place. Video stores are notorious for having movies to rent." Then he hunched into the wind, jammed his hands in his pockets and walked away.

She huffed out a breath and hurried after him. "The thing is, they only had one copy, and you got there first."

He paused at the intersection, angled a glance. "You snooze, you lose."

"Ah, but that's the beauty of it. We can share." The light changed, and Ethan crossed the street with Deirdre right on his heels. "I mean, there's no sense in me listening to the movie through those thin walls tonight, and you having to listen to the same thing tomorrow night. Why don't you just come over and we can watch it together?'' She shivered against the brisk ocean breeze, rubbing her upper arms to warm them. ''Do you like fresh potato-leek soup? It's my mum's recipe. To die for, it is. And steaming hot biscuits, so tender each bite melts like sweet butter on the tongue.''

''No, thanks.''

She huffed beside him, struggling to match his stride. ''I know I have no right to ask—I mean, you got there first, after all—but it has been such a tiring day, and my heart is just set on seeing that movie.''

He reached into his jacket and handed her the tape without slowing his pace.

Puffing, Deirdre stopped, clutching the plastic case. ''I guess you haven't got your car running yet,'' she called. ''Can I give you a—'' he turned the corner and disappeared ''—ride?'' She eyed the precious video, which had lost some of its luster. ''Well, Julie, just you and me.''

Feeling oddly let down for someone who had just achieved the reward she'd been seeking, Deirdre returned to the parking lot, retrieved her car and drove back to the duplex.

Twenty minutes later, she'd just given the thick, simmering soup a final stir when there was a knock at her door. Ethan leaned against the porch rail with windblown hair and cautious eyes. ''Homemade biscuits, or store-bought?''

''Homemade.''

He stepped inside.

Three hours later, feeling sated and more at peace than he had in many years, Ethan clicked the remote to rewind the tape while Deirdre bustled around the kitchen. "There is no doubt about it," she called out between clinks and clanks of manipulated utensils. "Andrew Lloyd Webber is the premier musical composer in the world today. I don't see how you can disagree."

He didn't actually, but had discovered the lovely Ms. O'Connor to be a lively conversationalist, and had enjoyed the spirit with which she argued her positions. It had been a pleasant diversion from the bleakness of his current situation.

Ethan didn't know what quirk of fate had propelled him to her door this evening. Certainly he hadn't planned it, but for some reason he chose not to explore too closely, he'd been inexplicably drawn to Deirdre's half of the duplex like a moth to the proverbial flame. There was something about her, something guileless and outgoing, a warmth that just crept right into a man's soul before he realized what had happened.

Deirdre's voice floated into his thoughts on a whiff of Irish. "And who would you be putting ahead of Lloyd Webber on the genius scale? Musically speaking, that is."

Ethan felt a strange pull on his lips, and knew he was smiling. "John Lennon."

She poked her head through the doorway. "John Lennon? Are you daft, man? He didn't compose musical scores for film."

Clicking the eject button, Ethan leaned from his position seated on the floor to retrieve the tape. *"Yellow Submarine,"* he said succinctly, and snapped the tape into its case.

"Oh, now I know you're pulling my leg!"

His eye automatically slipped to the shapely bare calf

exposed beneath the hem of a flowery, knee-length skirt. "Not at the moment, but I can oblige if you like."

She blinked, sputtered a laugh and disappeared back into the kitchen. "Well, I must admit I've a soft spot for Lennon's music myself, but you can't be putting a movie of teen idols belting Beatles tunes in the same league with *Phantom of the Opera.*"

"If Lloyd Webber was so proud of *Phantom*, why did he force the leading man to wear a mask?"

A trill of delighted laughter filtered from the kitchen, sending an army of goose bumps marching down Ethan's spine. "You've a point there, I suppose."

Leaning back against the sofa, Ethan crossed his ankles and patted his thigh to entice Dublin into his lap. The frisky animal needed no second invitation, and pounced at his fingers with predatory glee. Ethan let out a fake growl from deep in his throat, slipped his hand under the kitten's belly and rolled the creature onto its back to tickle its silky tummy. The kitten responded by wrapping all four paws around his hand, and trying to chew off his thumb.

"Saints preserve us, the man knows how to smile."

Yanking his hand away from the determined cat, Ethan glanced up as Deirdre emerged carrying a tray on which a porcelain pot and two cups steamed beside a platter of pale cookies sparkling with sugar crystals.

"It was a grimace," Ethan said, shifting while the kitten crawled up his chest. "Your cat revels in causing pain."

"Does he now?" With a smile a man could get lost in, she set the tray on the coffee table, then settled on the floor beside him. Ethan felt something akin to loss as she demurely tucked her shapely legs beneath her skirt, concealing them from view. "Do you take milk in your tea?"

"Tea?" He eyed the pale liquid in the cups, and felt the involuntary pucker twist the corner of his mouth. He'd rather sip day-old dishwater. "None for me, thanks."

Her head snapped up, eyes huge and startled, with lashes so long, they spiked nearly to the base of her brows. "No tea? But why?"

"I hate it."

"You hate tea?" She shuddered at the heresy. "I may have some coffee somewhere.... Give me a moment."

"Don't bother." He touched her arm to keep her from rising, then jerked back, stunned by the electric heat tingling his fingertips. Judging by the expression on her face, she'd felt it, too. Her lips softened in surprise, her gaze riveted on his as if seeing him for the very first time. It was as if she'd seen his soul, observed that private place where all of his secrets were stored.

Something inside him cracked, exposing a vulnerability that was unnerving, a whisper that this woman was special. Too special.

"I should be going," he announced, and stood so quickly, the cat hooked its tiny claws to hang from his shirt.

"So soon?" Deirdre stood, clearly bewildered.

"Thanks for dinner." He dislodged the determined kitten and headed for the door before he could change his mind.

Deirdre hustled after him, wringing her hands. "There's plenty of soup and biscuits. Let me fix you a take-home—"

"No, thanks." His body language held her back a step.

She wavered there, unsure and dazed by his sudden retreat. Guilt pricked him, but only for a moment.

A man could only take so much before he set his heart on a shelf and locked up his emotions. Over the past two years, Ethan had lost his wife, his family, his career and had nearly lost his life. Now he was a man on a mission, a quest too important for distractions of a heart he could no longer trust.

Gruffness was an effective shield against those who would get too close. He cast a dispassionate glance over his shoulder. "By the way, your clock radio is too loud. It woke me up this morning."

With that, he retreated from warmth into the familiar chill of a long and lonely night.

Chapter Three

"Scones?" Undaunted by Ethan's suspicious scowl, Deirdre lifted the corner of an embroidered tea towel to reveal a steaming platter of warm breakfast treats.

If his narrowed gaze was any clue, he was unused to such neighborly gestures and was mentally calculating her motive. Oven-warm offerings were simply a part of Deirdre's cultural programming, a nurturing need to eliminate any and all unhappiness that crossed her path. Acts of kindness had been scrupulously taught by her own beloved mum, who kept a freezer of casseroles to thaw at the first hint of a friend in need. The O'Connor motto was that happiness was infectious; sharing it was free.

If anyone needed a bit of free happiness, it was the man with the brooding eyes. "Blueberry," she announced. "Guaranteed to start the glummest morning with a fresh smile."

A westerly breeze brushed by her ear, wafting the bakery scent inside Ethan's screen door. He sniffed appreciatively, but hesitated. "I've already eaten. Thanks anyway."

"Nonsense. You've just finished your shower and haven't even been in the kitchen to start your morning coffee." She offered her sweetest smile. "Thin walls, you know."

His gaze skittered, perhaps with embarrassment at having his movements monitored, or with guilt because he'd also been monitoring hers. The latter image made Deirdre shiver with peculiar excitement.

Over the past days, Ethan had hovered in the shadows of her life, exiting the duplex at the same time she did, always managing to be outside when she arrived home from work. He avoided eye contact until spoken to, then would issue a brusque nod designed to imply that her presence was unimportant to him.

Of course, he also watched her from the corner of his eye in that masculine façade of feigned nonchalance that was as intriguing as it was irksome. On the one hand he seemed to crave human contact; on the other, he continually pushed it away.

A mystifying man, Deirdre decided. Still there was something touching about him, and the paradox of one who wasn't as strident on the inside as his demeanor would suggest. She knew that much about him. And she suspected he knew that she knew it.

"You should eat better, you know. You've lost too much weight as it is."

He covered a startled expression like a man used to concealing his thoughts. "Is that a professional or personal opinion?"

"Actually, it's an observation. Most men don't buy

pants so loose that the only thing holding them up is a belt and a prayer.''

A wary shadow crossed his gaze. ''Not that you're unattractive,'' she added quickly. ''Slim hips are quite becoming, especially with shoulders such as yours. You must work out a lot.''

The instant his lips thinned and his eyes narrowed, Deirdre realized that comments about his body, no matter how casual and complimentary, had touched a forbidden chord.

''Thanks for the insight, and the fashion advice.'' The edge on his voice made her flinch. ''I'll keep it in mind.''

As he stepped back from the doorway, she caught the screen with her free hand to keep it from closing. ''Oh, don't be scampering off to sulk.''

''Sulk?''

''Men sulk,'' she insisted cheerfully, releasing the screen when he took a step forward, propping it open with his shoulder. ''Women pout. It's a fact of life, you know.''

A gleam of amusement broke through only to disappear with the next blink. ''Actually, I was unaware of the distinction.''

''My brothers had sulking down to a fine science, they did. A pained expression, a stoic lift of the chin was enough to reveal that they had been grievously wronged but were much too manly to complain about it.'' As she spoke, she folded the tea towel back to offer a more tempting view of the steaming scones. ''My sisters and I, on the other hand, preferred a quivering lip and a long-suffering sigh. Our father simply couldn't resist.'' Pushing her lower lip out with a practiced tremor, she rolled her eyes upward as if heartbroken by insurmountable loss. She drew a broken breath, let it slip out all at once on a whisper of a sigh. At the same time she shuddered her shoulders, allowing her chin to quiver as if tears were imminent.

She suspected it was one of her finest performances.

As for the desired results, she wasn't certain, for Ethan was staring at her as if she'd lost her mind. It happened slowly, a tenuous smile twitching one corner of his mouth, then the other before finally grooving itself into the sharp planes of his face as if struggling to travel an unfamiliar path. He was not a man who smiled often, she realized, but he was smiling now. And it was dazzling. "That is the silliest thing I've ever seen."

She laughed. "If that's so, you must not spend much time around children."

His smile faded as quickly as it had bloomed, and a shadow of sadness slipped into his gaze. "No, not much."

"Ah, that's a shame. Children have such elastic expressions, and are always twisting their little faces into the most amazing shapes."

He didn't reply, but she saw the withdrawal of his focus shift into himself, as if his mind had traveled to another time and place.

Deirdre recognized an emotionally wounded man when she saw one. Ethan wanted to be happy. She could see it in his eyes. She also saw the telltale fear of a man who viewed happiness as fleeting, unworthy of trust.

"Ethan?"

"Hmm? Oh." He cleared his throat, refocused on the gift she held out and shook his head. "Thanks anyway, but—"

"Oh, go on." Tilting her head coquettishly, she lifted the platter to present a more tempting view, and teased him with a smile. "Indulge yourself. You know you want it."

Ethan's tongue moistened his mouth the way Dublin's did when Deirdre reached for the kitty treats. Still, he made no move to retrieve the platter of scones, so she switched tactics. "It would be cruel of you to force me to eat them all myself. You've room for a spare pound or two, but my poor hips are already the size of tugboats. I don't need them swelling up like the *Queen Mary*."

He blinked up in genuine surprise. "There's nothing wrong with your hips."

The statement was issued with such firmness that she wobbled back a step. A titter of nervous laughter slipped out before she could stop it. "Nothing a bit of exercise and a few months of starvation wouldn't cure, I suppose."

The screen door swung wide so quickly she barely swerved in time to avoid it. Ethan stepped onto the porch, scowling. "Women aren't supposed to be shaped like anorexic pencils. They're supposed to be shaped like…like you. You are perfect just as you are."

He meant it, Deirdre realized. God bless him. The man actually admired her ordinary, rounder than fashionable body. "Why, Ethan, my dear sweet man, that is probably the nicest thing anyone has ever said to me."

A glimmer of astonishment was blinked away in a heartbeat, replaced by an exquisite sadness. "I'm sorry to hear that," he said quietly. Then he retrieved the platter of scones, retreated into his house and closed the door in her face. Again.

Ethan ate like a starving man. Food hadn't appealed to him much lately. Deirdre had been right about that. He had lost weight. Since his future depended on pleasing his doctors, he'd forced himself to consume meals he didn't want for calories his body needed. He'd wondered if he would ever enjoy eating again.

Then Deirdre O'Connor had entered his life, offering magic morsels that made his mouth water for food just as her beauty made his mind want for something deeper, more profound. Something frightening.

A thump beyond the wall caught his attention, as did every movement from Deirdre's apartment. He scooped up a fourth scone, carried it into the living room and enjoyed it while leaning against their shared wall. Her laughter filtered through like cool buttermilk on a summer day. Refreshing, exhilarating, with a sassy hint of country tang. It made him feel alive.

"Dublin! Look what you've done now, naughty kitty."

He pictured her standing askance, slender hands poised on her enticing, voluptuous hips and feigned indignation in those gorgeous, china-blue eyes. She spoke to her kitten as if it were a small, furred person. Ethan liked that about her.

A thin mew barely registered through the Sheetrock, audible only to someone listening for it. He chuckled to himself, imagining the tiny creature gazing up with amber-eyed innocence and a "Who, me?" look on its face.

"I hope you're proud of yourself, knocking over a helpless plant. Look there, dirt all over my clean counters, and me late for work."

Gooseflesh dappled his forearms in anticipation of what would come next. Ethan knew this woman more intimately than he had a right to, knew her schedule, her movements, her quirks and idiosyncrasies because he had immersed himself in the sounds of her life. Late for work or not, Deirdre O'Connor would not leave a messy kitchen, not for an entire day, or even an entire hour. She would clean up immediately, and while she worked she would sing, sing with clear, resonate sweetness that brought a smile to his lips, and sometimes a tear to his eye.

Sometimes she sang show tunes from the musicals they both loved. Sometimes she'd sing old favorites from a bygone era, or croon an Irish hymn from another time. Hushed with anticipation, he waited.

He was not disappointed. Her voice flowed to his heart like warm butter on a cool tongue, melting softly with haunting charm. "Memory," she sang softly.

A pause, the wisp of a broom sweep, and her sweet voice slipped into his mind, and his heart. Ethan leaned against the wall, living the lyrics, immersed in the melody, the images of past youth, of beauty. A time of happiness, of being whole. His numbed fingers contracted, the scars along his arm tingled. He could practically feel the steel pins heat against his once-shattered bones. Ethan didn't feel beautiful. He didn't feel whole.

But Deirdre was beautiful—the most beguiling, desirable woman Ethan had ever seen. Her voice whispered through the walls, sweet and poignant, growing fainter as she moved farther away.

The lyric tormented him sweetly. He, too, could remember a time of happiness, a time of innocence. A time of hope. For that moment, with Deirdre's haunting voice caressing him like a lover's touch, the memory lived.

Moisture gathered in his eyes, just a hint but enough to annoy him. Worse, his heart felt as if it had been squeezed. Ethan told himself that it wasn't the woman herself who intrigued him, but the music that had touched his heart. He told himself that it was sheer coincidence they left the house at the same time, even though it meant he had to stand at the bus stop for an extra half hour every morning. He even told himself that her smile of greeting didn't affect him, didn't continue to circle his mind throughout the grueling physical therapy sessions that commandeered much of his time.

He told himself that the exquisite, desirable Deirdre O'Connor didn't matter to him, that she was simply a neighbor, no more no less.

Ethan told himself a lot of things. Too bad not one of them was true.

"My—my—my turn!" Tommy announced, snatching a small red car from his brother's hand.

From her vantage point at the Devlins' neatly tiled counter, Deirdre saw timid little Timmy's lip quiver as he considered the wisdom of confronting his boisterous twin. After a final longing gaze at the confiscated toy, Timmy selected a miniature sedan with chipped paint and cautiously guided the diminutive vehicle around strategically placed salt and pepper shakers, a startling contrast to the reckless squeal of his brother's shiny red speedster.

Deirdre smiled. Despite distinctly different personalities, the boys shared a unique bond, an emotional connection so intense that they frequently communicated without words, sometimes even without looking at each other.

It was a double-edged sword, that compelling closeness, a dependence upon each other that was constantly at odds with innate human need for individuality. Deirdre understood that, had watched the intricate drama unfold with her own siblings. The fraternal twins enjoyed a less intense kinship than did her identical twin brothers, whose love-hate relationship during their formative years had evolved into an enduring amity so profound that even their wives sometimes felt excluded.

As alike as the Devlin twins were, they were nonetheless distinctive, as was every child. The dark-haired, bright-eyed youngsters had become the highlight of Deirdre's life. Less than two weeks after her arrival in Santa Barbara, she found herself looking forward, with increasing enthusiasm, to "nanny" days in the Devlins' surprisingly modest home. She loved caring for them, loved everything about them, from Timmy's shy grins, to Tommy's wild antics that never failed to evoke gales of laughter. Deirdre cherished every moment.

"Want cheese samwich!" Tommy announced, with an executive power clearly inherited from his grandfather.

"I like cheese," Timmy ventured with a hint of apology, as if emulating his peacemaking grandmother's propensity for offering suggestions rather than issuing edicts.

"Then cheese sandwiches it shall be," Deirdre replied, reaching into the refrigerator. "How about some grapes to go with that, and a big glass of milk?"

"Want gwapes!"

"I like gapes."

Chuckling to herself, Deirdre set about preparing the children's lunch, glancing over her shoulder at an ominous crash. "Don't be so rough with the cars, Tommy, you'll scratch the table."

Huge hazel eyes angled a mischievous glance in her direction. "I—I—I Timmy."

Timmy blinked at the brazen usurping of his identity, but otherwise said nothing.

"Are you now?" Deirdre's brothers had frequently enjoyed switching places, much to the consternation of those outside the family who couldn't tell the two apart. "Ah, I see. I must have been confused then."

Tommy giggled, deliberately crashed the shiny red car into a salt shaker. "Uh-oh, look what Timmy did."

Deirdre carried two plates to the table, noting Timmy's horrified expression. "I didn't do it, Deeda, I didn't!"

"I know you didn't—" she winked at the befuddled child "—Tommy." Deirdre set a plate in front of each twin, enjoying the real Tommy's double take when he saw that the crust had been neatly sliced from his brother's sandwich, but not from his own.

Frowning, he pushed the plate away. "Don't like cwusts."

"Of course you do, Timmy. It's Tommy who doesn't like them."

The child considered that for a moment, then shrugged. "Okay, I—I—I Tommy."

Deirdre switched the plates without comment, and was wiping down the counter when Nettie arrived home, flushed and clearly distracted. She dropped her handbag on the table to greet the children. "Hello, sweethearts. Have you had a good day?"

"We got gwapes, Gramma!" While Tommy scooped up a handful of shiny green orbs to show off, Timmy took advantage of his brother's redirected attention to surreptitiously pocket the coveted red car.

"So you do, my precious, so you do." Nettie planted a kiss on each tousled head, then offered Deirdre a strained smile. "You didn't need to wash the breakfast dishes, dear, but I do so appreciate that you did." Heaving a sigh, she smoothed her rumpled linen jacket, touched the back of her hand to a forehead gleaming with nervous moisture. "It's been a most disturbing morning."

"I'm sorry to hear that." Since Deirdre knew that Nettie and Horace had spent time with lawyers discussing the subpoena their son had issued, she was hesitant to pry into their personal business, and settled on a polite, but less intrusive request. "Is there anything I can do to help?"

Sighing, Nettie glanced at the twins, who were engrossed in playing with the remnants of lunch. She gestured that Deirdre should follow her into the living room.

"It's Horace," she murmured as soon as they'd left the kitchen. "He refuses to allow the children's father to have visitation rights with the boys."

"Why?"

"Horace and our son are—" She struggled silently for a moment. "Estranged," she said finally.

"I know," Deirdre said, saddened by the rift in the family. "Horace mentioned that your son had made bad choices in his life."

"Was that all he said?"

"Yes." Actually, Deirdre's follow-up question had been met with enough hostility that she'd not broached the subject again. Although she admired Horace as a fine attorney, and had even learned to respect his rather blustering ways, she suspected that he would consider any choice he disagreed with to be a bad one, and presumed there was more to the story than she'd been told. "Horace never explained to me where the children's father has been all this time, or why the courts would even consider returning custody to a man who had abandoned them in the first place."

A pained glance, a sorrowful sigh. Nettie lowered herself stiffly onto a nearby chair, her gaze shifting in guilty avoidance. "Our son is a good man. The tragedies of the past aren't entirely his fault."

"He abandoned his children," Deirdre repeated. In her mind, she simply couldn't get past that.

"There were unfortunate circumstances." Again Nettie averted her gaze, studying her own knotted fingers twisting against themselves in her lap. "The children haven't seen their father since they were babies, that's true. They need stability in their lives now. It would be difficult for them to be taken from the only home they've ever really known into the care of a man who is a virtual stranger to them."

"Of course it would." Something pricked at her, something bothersome, yet too evasive to be identified. "But if he wants to see his children, to become part of their lives, wouldn't that be good for the boys? I mean, now that their mother is gone, God bless her—"

"Don't bless that woman," Nettie snapped with shocking hostility. She turned away, lowering her voice but not able to quell the anger in her tone. "I'm sorry. I know it's terrible to speak ill of the dead, but that woman was a terrible, sinful person. She destroyed our son, destroyed our family. Someday those beautiful children will learn what their mother did to them, and she'll reach out of the grave to destroy them, too. I won't let that happen."

A chill prickled Deirdre's spine, a whisper of prophecy. At that moment, she realized that there was more to her current assignment than met the eye. Clementine never did anything without clandestine motive. Deirdre should have realized that. For the past five years, she'd been the wily old woman's partner in crime so to speak, a behind-the-scenes facilitator of Clementine's crafty plans to reunite splintered families, create new ones and establish loving homes for children who desperately needed them.

Now she realized that she'd been placed squarely in the eye of an unfathomable storm without so much as a compass to guide her. The success or failure of a mission she didn't even understand rested solely on her own shaky shoulders.

It was troubling indeed.

Deirdre arrived home early that day. Ethan wasn't outside, as he usually was, either watering the lawn, or working on his car, or just pretending to fiddle with a loose nail on his side of the porch. Deirdre was surprised to realize that she missed the quiet camaraderie of seeing him there, of her cheery greeting and his curt nod.

The driveway vibrated as a train sped past, clattering the tracks on the other side of the narrow road. Deirdre had gotten used to the routine rumble, and barely noticed its passing as she exited the vehicle, relieved almost to tears at being home.

Home. The duplex had become more of a home to her than the sterile San Francisco apartment in which she'd dwelled for half of the past decade. Odd, she thought, that this homely box of a building with its faded clapboards and ugly flat roof could evoke such affection in such a short period of time.

She hurried up the steps on her side of the long porch, surprised to hear music floating from the open door of Ethan's apartment. Normally his duplex was silent, except for the occasional sports show on television, or the sound of him pacing the hardwood floors in the middle of the night.

She paused at his door, strangely compelled to knock and offer him some of the lovely cherry pie she'd baked last night.

His voice drifted through the screen, sharp with tension. "You know what I want. My demands are clear." He paused a moment. "That isn't my problem, nor is it negotiable.'' Another pause, and Deirdre realized he was on the telephone. ''You tell them,'' he snapped as if pushing the words through tightly clamped teeth. ''If they cross me again, things will get real ugly, real fast.'' The receiver jarred as if slammed down. Footsteps hit the hardwood floor, moving quickly toward the door.

Deirdre stepped into her own apartment a moment before Ethan strode onto the porch. She peeked out the window, saw him leaning over the peeling rail with an expression so forlorn it broke her heart, and oozing an undercurrent of anger that gave her pause. He shifted his stance, glanced toward the driveway where her car was parked, then stiffened and looked toward her apartment. Their eyes met, held. Her breath backed into her throat, along with a peculiar yearning she hadn't felt in a very long time. It took her by surprise.

A wisp of fur brushed her elbow as Dublin hopped to the windowsill. She glanced down at the purring kitten, and when she looked back out the window, the porch was empty.

Feeling oddly bereft by Ethan's disappearance, she turned her attention to the insistent creature using her sleeve as a scratching post. ''And a fine afternoon to you, my sweet. Have you had a good day for yourself?'' Dublin mewed. ''Well that makes one of us. My own day was rather unnerving, to say the least.'' She scooped the animal into her arms, and kissed its little head. The kitten issued a soft trill, burrowed its whiskered face against her throat. ''You needn't ask,'' she murmured. ''You know I love you, too.''

After changing from her business clothes into a pair of comfy corduroy pants and a deliciously floppy knit top, Deirdre whipped up a quick casserole for supper.

She'd just slipped the dish into the oven when Dublin's insistent meow at the front door drew her attention. She crossed the small living room in time to hear familiar footsteps on the porch. A peek out the front window revealed a freshly laundered tea towel folded on the sparkling clean scone platter, along with a single red rose and a cellophane pouch of kitty treats.

"Ooh, now isn't that sweet?"

Dublin meowed frantically, scratching at the closed door as if well aware that something delicious awaited him on the other side. Ignoring the kitten's pleas, Deirdre continued to watch the fascinating man who was heading toward the old car parked in his driveway. He lifted the hood, spread a few tools on the fender and bent into the engine compartment.

He never looked up when Deirdre opened the front door to retrieve the items he left. She hovered there a moment, then ducked inside, pausing to offer her excited kitten a few crunchy morsels from the package of treats before hurrying to the kitchen to place the rose in a vase of water, and whip the casserole out of the oven long enough to double the ingredients. "We might have a guest for supper," she told the kitten rubbing her ankles. "It's always best to be prepared."

A few minutes later, she slipped outside, foolishly smoothing her hair and wishing she'd thought to freshen her lipstick.

Hunkered beneath the yawning hood, Ethan appeared to be struggling. He clutched a ratchet in his left hand, while his right hand repeatedly slipped off something he was apparently trying to fasten inside the tangle of hose and wire. Frustration etched his face. His hand slipped, followed by a metallic clink as something dropped into the engine compartment. He swore, crawled under the car to retrieve the item, which appeared to be a small bolt, then returned to his task with his back still toward the porch where Deirdre was standing.

She descended the steps, quietly crossed the worn lawn and came up behind him. "Do you need any help?" To her horror, he reared upright and struck his head on the hood.

He spun around, cussing and clutching his skull. "Don't do that!"

"Do what?"

"Sneak up on a man."

"I'm sorry. I thought you saw me."

"How could I see you with my head in the engine?"

She shrugged, feeling stupid. "Men have a way of seeing everything that goes on around them, even when they're not looking." She bit her lip, noting that he'd hit himself hard enough to make his eyes water. As he probed the top of his skull as if assuring himself it was still there, she cleared her throat. "I truly am sorry. Shall I have a look at it? I'll not hurt you. I can be quite gentle when it suits my mood."

He eyed her suspiciously. "And when it doesn't suit your mood?"

"Oh, I can be fierce, as my brother Liam discovered when he beheaded my favorite doll."

"What did you do to him?"

"Ah, it was quite gruesome. Indelible ink, an angry sister and a chagrined lad who spent much of the third grade sporting a hand-drawn mustache and horns. Now, let us have a look."

Fighting a small smile, Ethan loosened his shoulders with a shake, didn't resist when she touched her fingers to his temples, tilted his head forward to inspect the damage. She gently parted his hair, which was softer than she'd imagined with an intriguing soapy scent. A gentle heat radiated into her fingers, crawling up her arms like an erotic caress. Her heart beat a little faster at his nearness, and she was exquisitely aware that his face was nearly touching her breasts.

"It doesn't look so bad," she murmured. "A bit of a lump, but the skin hasn't been broken."

He straightened slowly, with some reluctance. "So I'll live."

"Indeed."

He regarded her for a moment. "The scones were good."

It took a moment. "The scones? Oh. Of course." She giggled again, as she always seemed to do in front of this man. "I'm glad you enjoyed them."

A curt nod, a brusque grunt and he turned back to his work.

"The rose was lovely," she told him. "Thank you."

He rolled a bolt in his left palm, spoke without looking up. "No problem."

Although she'd been effectively dismissed, Deirdre made no move to leave. Instead she watched as he placed the bolt between two fingers of his right hand, and tried to hold it in place long enough to pick up the ratchet with his left. The bolt slipped free, clinked its way through the engine onto the driveway below. He sighed, crouched to retrieve it. That's when she saw the scars running up his forearm, terrible jagged welts still fresh and red.

As he straightened, she laid a hand on his wrist, startling him. She cupped his hand, turning it over to examine it more closely. At least she would have if he hadn't jerked away as though burned by her touch. "What happened?" she asked simply.

"An accident." He turned away, replaced the bolt between seemingly numb fingers and lowered it in place.

Without a word, she reached past him and steadied his hand. The press of his shoulder against her upper arms made her quiver. He didn't look at her, but she felt the intake of his breath, the telltale ripple of his flesh against hers.

He hesitated, then said, "Hold it steady against that opening."

She did so, and the bolt was ratcheted into place in less than two seconds.

He stepped away, averting his gaze as he retrieved a faded cotton rag from the fender and wiped his hand. "Thanks."

"It was my pleasure indeed," she replied with a smile. No wonder he'd been working on the car for so long. Even putting in a bolt was a major effort for a man with limited use of one hand. "I know nothing about what goes on under a hood, I'm afraid. My husband used to take car of the cars. I should learn how to do these things for myself. Perhaps you could teach me?" The ruse would allow her to assist him in a manner unobtrusive enough for his ego to allow.

Laying the rag aside, Ethan glanced pointedly at her bare ring finger. "Your husband...I take it that he's no longer part of your life?"

She followed his gaze, felt her heart jerk. "I'm a widow."

"Oh." He swallowed. "I'm sorry for your loss."

Deirdre was sorry, too. The memory was no longer raw, but the ache was still there. "Have you ever been married, Ethan?"

His jaw tightened. "Yes."

This was none of her business, none at all. She simply

couldn't help herself. "But you aren't together any-more?"

"We divorced."

Bitterly divorced, if the edge on his voice was any clue. There was so much she wanted to know about this man, so many questions she wanted to ask. Questions she would ask in due time. His uneasiness told her that this was not the moment, that he wasn't quite ready to allow her into his personal space. But instinct told her that he would be ready soon. Very soon.

She took a deep breath, flashed a bright smile. "So, how about my first lesson on car engines. What's that dooly-bob?"

He followed her gesture. "That holds washer fluid."

"Washer fluid? Oh, that foamy stuff that squirts the windshield when you pull the thingamagig on the steering column? How interesting!"

"Look, Deirdre—"

"And what is that peculiar object?"

A chuckle slipped out, apparently against his will. He shook his head, smiling. "It's the battery."

"The battery, is it?" Of course she knew a battery when she saw one. She also recognized a spark plug when she saw one, and knew what an air filter was, although the one for this engine had apparently been removed to access the inner workings. "Fascinating. Why, I've learned so much already!"

"What a crock." His grin conveyed no umbrage, and she took none.

"A crock of what?" she asked with feigned innocence.

He chuckled, shook his head. "Never mind."

She snatched up the closest tool, which happened to be a hinge-handled ratchet. "So what kind of repairs are we doing?"

"We?"

"Of course 'we.' I am going to assist you, and you are going to teach me everything you know about car engines." She glanced at the glare of the sun hanging over the eucalyptus grove. "And we have less than thirty minutes, so you'd better get cracking."

"What happens in thirty minutes?"

"I'll be taking our supper out of the oven…. You will join me, won't you? I'm afraid I've made much too much again."

Folding his muscular arms, he propped a lean hip against the fender and regarded her with a knowing gleam in his eye. "You do that a lot, don't you?"

"Make too much food? Ah, that I do, an old habit ingrained from so many years of cooking for a family the size of a small town."

"You come from a large family, do you?"

"Ten of us." She laughed as he flinched. "And you, Ethan?"

"One like me was enough."

"You've no brothers or sisters, then?" The thought was appalling. How lonely he must have been. Deirdre couldn't imagine what it was like to grow up in a home without the laughter, and the squabbles, and the constant chaos of a house full of happy children. Her own siblings had scattered throughout the country, and she missed them terribly. "Well, then, can you be helping me polish off dinner? Noodles and asparagus, with lots of juicy chicken chunks in a mushroom sauce to die for."

This time he didn't bother being coy. "Yeah, I can help you out."

"Then it's settled." Deirdre instinctively understood that a breakthrough of sorts had been achieved. She didn't know exactly what had changed between them, or precisely how that evolution had been accomplished, although the sparks leaping between them had little to do with the ceramic-tipped plugs inside the engine compartment.

Deirdre suspected the evening would be memorable. She had no idea that it would change the entire course of her life.

Chapter Four

"Hurry up! We don't want to miss the sunset." Deirdre bounded down a path scoured from vertical terrain by those who had gone before. Beyond a few planks strategically placed to serve as steps along the most precarious descent, the trail wound down a rocky hillside where brushy stubble clutched any patch of sparse soil that escaped erosion by a raging sea.

The ocean was calm now, spilling gently into tidal pools, with foam fingers lapping skimpy ribbons of sand. This was not the postcard-perfect shoreline of sparkling beach so prized by recreational surf lovers. It was a wilderness of sorts, a ragged seascape sharply carved in bedrock. Deirdre thought it glorious.

Pausing at the base of the path, she was struck by the enormity of the panorama, by the primitive beauty of this place where a continent ended. A heartbeat later, Ethan stood beside her.

She spun around, fried with excitement. "Isn't it magnificent?"

"Yes," he agreed, although he wasn't gazing at the rippling sea, where a fiery sun kissed the horizon with sparkling splinters of gold. He was staring straight into her eyes. "Magnificent."

She felt herself flush, and turned away, her pulse pounding wildly. She moistened her lips, reluctantly turned her back to him and gazed at the ocean. "Now aren't you glad I wouldn't let you sit on the sofa and groan about being stuffed from eating too much dinner?"

A chuckle brushed her hair, and she realized he'd stepped closer. Electric intensity permeated her thick sweater, tingling directly through her spine. "Take it as a compliment," he said affably. "I haven't eaten enough to groan about in quite a long time."

"I'm pleased you enjoyed it."

"I enjoyed it very much." He laid one hand on each of her shoulders, a gesture initially casual, but becoming more intimate as their body heat mingled. She felt him so acutely, it was as if there was no barrier between them, no thin layer of salty air, no bulky clothing, no skin, no muscle, no bone, simply the merging of two ethereal souls.

He spoke softly, his breath a whisper on her hair. "Have you ever seen a starfish up close?"

"Not a live one."

"Ah, then you haven't met Jasper."

"Jasper?" Feeling strangely bereft as he stepped away, she watched him maneuver the uneven terrain with practiced efficiency, and squat at a spot where seawater filled a gouge in the bedrock shore.

Ethan scrutinized the pool. "Great, he's home." Rolling up his shirtsleeves, he glanced up and seemed surprised that Deirdre hadn't moved. "Starfish are virtually harmless."

"Oh, I know." Inhaling deeply, she let the salty tang invigorate her lungs, freshen her mind. The power of his touch, of that brief, innocent contact had overwhelmed her, left her shaken to the core. It was normal, she supposed, for a woman so long alone to feel a certain yearning in the presence of an attractive man. What she felt toward Ethan, however, was unexpectedly visceral, frightening in its intensity.

Chiding herself for indulging such romanticized nonsense, she shook off the sensation, picked her way across the pitted landscape and crouched beside Ethan just as he lifted a peculiar creature from a watery crevice. "Oh my goodness, it's so tiny."

Ethan cradled the animal in cupped palms submerged below the water's surface. "I'm not sure if it's just a baby, or if this particular species doesn't grow any larger."

The little starfish was about four inches across, a creamy ivory color with a pitted, shell-like exterior that reminded Deirdre of sharply sprayed stucco. When she reached beneath the water to stroke it with her fingertip, its thin, triangular tentacles contracted slowly, closing itself into a protective ball. "I don't think he appreciates the attention."

"Probably not. This area is only exposed at low tide. The rest of the time it's underwater."

After returning the creature with the same gentleness he'd displayed to comfort a frightened kitten, Ethan sat back on his heels, shook the water off his arms. Deirdre's gaze was again drawn to the jagged scars extending upward from his inner wrist.

As he reached to roll down his shirtsleeve, she touched

his bare forearm. "Will you ever regain full use of your hand again?"

For a moment she thought he wouldn't answer. His gaze clouded, his lips turned tight. He studied her hand lying warm against his skin. "Yes," he said finally, and with a vehemence that startled her.

"How did it happen?" The question slipped out naturally, although she regretted asking it the moment she spotted pain in his eyes. "I'm sorry. It's none of my business, really."

He regarded her for a moment, as if contemplating whether or not to answer. He stood slowly, completed the task of pushing the knit sleeve down to conceal the ragged reminders. "It was a traffic accident, a moment of stupidity that never should have happened."

"Were you driving?"

"No, my partner was driving."

"Your partner?" A thought struck her. "You used to be a police officer?"

"I still am." His gaze hardened. "I had to take some time off to heal. That doesn't mean I'm relegated to the scrap heap."

"Of course not." She glanced away, annoyed with herself. "I didn't mean to be insensitive."

He sighed. "You aren't. It's my problem, not yours."

At the moment Deirdre felt as if his problems were indeed hers, although she couldn't fathom why that should be. She simply knew that it was, that everything that affected this man was of interest to her. There was a sorrow in his eyes that went beyond that of a man whose career had been interrupted by injury. Instinctively Deirdre realized that the emotional cost had been far greater than the physical one. She paused, touched his hand. "Was your partner also hurt?"

His eyes betrayed him, filling with a pain so deep that she felt it in her soul. The brisk ocean air ruffled his hair as he turned his face toward the sea. "He was killed."

Confirmation was a shock even though she'd suspected as much. "It wasn't your fault," she said, although she couldn't have possibly known whether or not that was true. She was compelled to say something—anything— to alleviate the suffering in his eyes.

Ethan scooped a smooth pebble, studied it as he turned it over in the palm of his left hand. "Maybe it was, maybe it wasn't."

"But you weren't even driving."

"I wasn't paying attention, either. We were in an unmarked cruiser heading back to the station to write up a robbery investigation report."

"You were—I mean you *are* a detective?"

He nodded. "I never cared much for patrol. It was just a means to an end. For as long as I can remember, I always wanted to be an investigator, to piece together puzzles and solve mysteries."

When Ethan made no further comment, she prodded him. "So you and your partner were driving back to the station?"

A muscle vibrated below his ear. He flipped the pebble aside, cooled his face with his hands. "I was reviewing witness interview notes. If I'd been watching the road, I might have seen the truck coming and realized it would run a red light."

"If you had seen it, what could you have done?"

"Shouted a warning, given my partner a few extra seconds to hit the brake." The speed of his reply indicated that he'd spent considerable time rolling that very question through his mind. "The pickup broadsided my side of the cruiser, then pushed it across the intersection to crush the driver's side against a telephone pole. A split second one way or the other—'' He clamped his jaw, stood and folded his arms like a shield.

Before Deirdre could question her own motive, she rose as well, and laid her hand on his arm. He appeared not to notice, but his muscles quivered beneath the knit sleeve of his shirt. She slid her fingers down to his wrist, eased the cuff up to expose a small area of crimson scar tissue.

Something cracked deep inside her. She didn't know what possessed her at that moment, but without conscious thought of consequence, she loosened his tucked hand and lifted it to her lips. She kissed each knuckle gently, reverently, then kissed the scars at the inner pulse of his wrist. A few drops of saltwater clung to his skin. She savored the taste, the tang, the tickle of fine hairs against her lips, and the moist smoothness on her cheek when she rubbed her face kittenlike into his palm.

Ethan took a sharp breath. When he spoke, his voice was broken, raw. ''Deirdre—''

She touched a finger to his lips, silencing him. ''I know,'' she whispered, her own heart so swollen, she felt it might burst. '''Tis the whisper of the waves, the romance of a glorious sunset, the need of two people to feel that for one shining moment, neither is truly alone.''

He gazed at her with wonder, caressed a knuckle along her brow, then smoothed a wind-ruffled strand of hair from her face before cupping her temples with his hands. Behind him, a tangerine glow smeared twilight clouds with an explosion of brilliance.

Deirdre barely noticed. Her fingers rested lightly on Ethan's chest, counting the beats of his racing heart. His mouth was near, so very near. His eyes were warm with question. She parted her lips in reply.

He accepted the offer with a kiss so poignant, so profound, so achingly sweet that the world as she'd known it ceased to exist. From that moment on, Deirdre's life would never be the same.

And she knew it.

"Wait a minute, let me adjust the fuel mix." Ducking under the hood, Ethan twisted the screwdriver a quarter turn, then stepped back, wiping his forehead with the back of his hand. "Okay, try it now."

In the driver's seat of his vintage sedan, Deirdre nodded, took a deep breath and reached toward the ignition. The pink tip of her tongue peeked from the corner of her mouth, as it always did when she was nervous. Ethan had noticed that about her. He noticed everything about her.

So focused was his attention on the beautiful woman who held such power over his thoughts that the roar of an engine startled him.

"It works!" Deirdre shouted over the din. "It actually works!"

As she grinned at him through the windshield, his heart skipped like a happy child. Ethan laughed. He couldn't help himself. Happiness just bubbled up unabated, an effervescent elation.

His world had changed last night. He'd tasted heaven, honeyed paradise in the sweetness of a single kiss.

But, oh what a kiss it had been. He'd never wanted the rapture to end, had wanted to spend the rest of his life wrapped in the mellow warmth of an embrace so simple and loving that he'd been dizzied by its power. She was a sweetness in his blood, genuine, sincere, utterly guileless in her honesty. "You're a fine man," she had whispered, her breath like fresh dew against his cheek. "I like you, Ethan. Perhaps more than I should."

Such simple words, spoken without coyness or subterfuge. Her honesty had affected him with a blow to the
heart. He'd been speechless, breathless. She'd stroked his
face then, the merest hint of silky fingertips tracing from
brow to jaw, while her gaze held his with the innocence
of a child, and the knowledge of a woman.

Ethan had never been so completely beguiled in his
life.

Even now, less than twenty-four hours later, he had no
clue how long they'd stood there gazing into each other's
eyes. He knew only that the fuchsia sky had faded into
darkness before their fingers entwined, and they'd carefully picked their way back up the hillside path.

I like you...more than I should.

Fresh goose bumps erupted at the memory.

And then she was there in front of him, eyes sparkling
with excitement, breath slipping rapidly through a dazzling smile. She grabbed his upper arms, then spun
around in a celebratory dance. "I knew you could do it!"

It took a moment for him to realize she was talking
about his mechanical prowess. "You helped."

Her laugh was like an angel's song. "I turned a key.
You did the work, clever man that you are." She tossed
her head the way a frisky mare might do to entice a mate.
Gleaming strands of midnight wrapped around her cheek,
caught in a patina of moisture. "Now you won't have to
be waiting for that belchy old bus every morning."

"You saw me at the bus stop?"

She flushed as if she'd been caught doing something
naughty. "I happened to look in my rearview mirror one
morning, and noticed that's where your journey up the
street had ended."

"Ah. Just as long as you haven't been stalking me."

"Stalking you, is it?" Another delightful laugh.

"Well, a handsome man like yourself must have had some experience with unwanted attention from the opposite sex."

Hardly. He hadn't even been on a date since his divorce. There hadn't been time for a social life even if he'd wanted one, which he hadn't. All of his time and attention had been focused on a single goal. Determination had propelled him from death's door back into a life not of his choosing, a life of pursuit for all that he'd lost, all that had been stolen from him. Courage had driven him forward, courage and the unwavering conviction of his cause.

Ethan had strived for satisfaction, for completion, for a sense of accomplishment. Happiness had never been his goal, because it had never occurred to him that it was achievable, that it was possible for him to experience what others took for granted.

Then again he'd never dreamed a woman like Deirdre O'Connor would enter his life. Now he couldn't imagine what life would be like without her.

He laid his palm against her cheek, and knew by the gleam in her eye that he was smiling stupidly. "Women throw themselves at me all the time. I have to beat them off."

"With your strong hand or your weak one?"

For some reason, her reference to his injury didn't bother him. "With my strong hand, and a big stick. They are quite persistent."

"I don't blame them," she said with a chuckle. "Men like you don't come around every day." She slipped her arms around his waist, lowered her voice to a throaty husk. "From now on, you tell them to come see me. I'll set them straight."

"How will you do that?" His own voice sounded

strangely soft, the intimate whisper a man used with a lover.

A suggestive gleam in her eye indicated that she'd noticed the change in tone, and approved. "I'll just tell them you're taken." A peek of pink drew his gaze to the corner of her mouth. "If that's all right with you, of course."

"It's very all right," he whispered. Then he kissed her, and felt the wonder all over again.

Horace's angry voice boomed through the closed office door, strengthening the throb working its way along Deirdre's forehead. She covered one ear, as was her habit now, but the excited buzz on the other end of the telephone receiver was drowned out by her boss's loud shouts. Still, she could guess what the whining investigator was asking. It was a conversation she'd repeated too many times over the past weeks. "No, we don't have a social security number for Mr. Rodriguez. No, we don't have a driver's license number, either. I know that makes it difficult to locate him, which is why we need assistance."

"I don't care what he wants," Horace hollered. "I don't care what the law says, and I don't care what's fair."

Deirdre turned away from the din, hunched forward as if a slight change in position could help. "Yes, yes, I understand it's a common name. Surely a professional investigator has other ways of locating—"

A shout from the corner office drowned out the rest of her words. "If that's what he wants, he can ask me personally. No lawyers, no damned subpoenas—" A swish, a crash, as if something had been thrown across the room. "When he can come to me like a man, admit he's been wrong, wrong about that damned woman he married, wrong about every rotten choice he ever made just to spite me, then I'll talk about what's fair. Until then, *I* make the decisions.''

Straining to hear, Deirdre recognized the apologetic tone filtering through the telephone line from the fifth private investigator she'd queried that week. ''I understand. Yes, of course, thank you for your time.''

She hung up, crossed yet another private investigator's name off the shrinking list of possibilities and stared down at the Rodriguez file in frustration. She'd never realized how difficult it was to give money away. Probate law, she'd discovered, was considerably more than codifying wills and doling out inheritance.

The newest temporary receptionist peeked around the partition, wide-eyed and clearly distressed. ''Umm, Mrs. Devlin is on the telephone.... What should I do?''

''Ask her to hold until Mr. Devlin is free—'' Deirdre flinched at the sound of a slammed receiver followed by the jangling crash of a phone being flung as far across the room as the cord would allow. She managed a smile, although the horrified receptionist looked as if she might faint. ''Mr. Devlin is free now. You can put the call through.''

Every trace of color drained from the woman's face. ''Yes, Ms. O'Connor.''

Deirdre took pity on her. ''Actually, I was just on my way into his office,'' she lied. ''I'll tell him about the call.''

''Oh yes, thank you, thank you.'' The woman looked so relieved, Deirdre feared she'd rush over to kiss her feet. ''Line one—no, two... Whichever one is blinking.'' She swallowed hard, tossed up her hands and disappeared.

Deirdre listened for the sound of a desk drawer being opened. She heard it, and knew the poor woman had retrieved her purse. Before she could count to five in her mind, the entry door gave a telltale squeak. Making a mental note to call the temp agency again, she headed into Horace's office and found him flinging papers from one side of his desk to another. The crystal bowl had been upended, strewing candy from one end of the office to the other. An exploding piñata couldn't have made a bigger mess.

"Where the hell is the Ames codicil?" Horace bellowed.

"On my desk."

"Bring it here!"

"The revisions haven't been completed."

"Why the hell not?"

"Because you haven't dictated them yet." She scooped the telephone off the floor, reassembled the dislocated face plate, a task at which she'd become quite proficient, and set it on the corner of his desk amidst a clutter of cellophane-wrapped candies. "Nettie is on line—" she glanced at the blinking button "—two."

His scowl softened. "Why didn't you say so?" He grabbed the receiver, punched the button. "My sweet, precious sugar cake," he crooned with buttery calm. "You know you're supposed to call on my private line, so these incompetents don't keep you waiting.... Hmm...? It was busy? Oh...that's right...."

He shifted, ignoring Deirdre as she picked papers from the office floor and stuffed them back into eviscerated files. "Yes, I was on the phone with Nielsen," he said, confirming the conversation with their lawyer.

Deirdre knew she should leave, that the conversation

was private, but for some odd reason was compelled to remain, and busied herself sweeping up scattered candy.

Horace's tone was soft, but unyielding. "He is demanding immediate unsupervised visitation, and full custody by the end of the year. Of course, I refused...." He rocked forward, swiveled his chair until his back was toward the desk, and Deirdre. "But honey pot, we've discussed this. It's the only leverage we have.... Yes, yes, I know he's our son..." A stony silence, the hint of a sigh. "Don't get soft on me, sugar bug. You know why we're doing this, why we must do this. He made the choice a long time ago."

A lump formed in Deirdre's throat, an exquisite sorrow that this family—that any family—could be so fractured by bitterness. She couldn't comprehend such strident fury between father and son, couldn't imagine the heartache of a mother caught in the middle, as Nettie undeniably was. It was clear to Deirdre that Nettie adored her son, just as she adored her husband and grandchildren. Although Deirdre had no clue as to what had caused the rift in the Devlin family, she was nonetheless saddened by it.

She tiptoed out of the office, closing the door behind her. Clearly Clementine had sent her here to help the Devlins through this time of crisis. At the moment Deirdre had no clue as to how that could be accomplished. She knew only that it must be accomplished. For the children.

Ethan leaned forward in the chair, propped his elbows on his thighs and watched the physician in charge of his entire future flip through his file as if skimming a boring novel. "So, Doc, what's the verdict?"

Glancing up, Dr. Benjamin Stein removed his glasses,

leaned back in his chair. "Your progress has been nothing short of miraculous. Motor function in the right hip is ninety percent of normal, and the artificial kneecap is functioning at a higher level than expected." He closed the file, laid it aside. "Few people with injuries as extensive as yours are able to retrain themselves to achieve the muscular regeneration that you've managed. Your effort and persistence this past year have definitely paid off."

Ethan allowed his breath to slide out on a relieved sigh. "When can I go back to work?"

Dr. Stein pursed his lips, gazed down at his desk. "For all intent and purpose, you can lead a perfectly normal life."

For Ethan, his career was his life. "Great. Sign the release, and let me get back to my job."

"The physical requirements for a police officer are considerably more stringent than most other professions. You realize that, of course."

"I've never been in better shape."

"Except for the nerve damage in your right hand."

"It's improving every day." That was a lie, of course, and Stein knew it. Ethan maintained eye contact even after the doctor glanced away. "Sign the release. By the time it gets through the bureaucratic mass of paperwork onto my lieutenant's desk, my hand will be as strong as it ever was."

"No, Ethan, it won't." He leaned forward, gave him the same paternal expression his middle-school principal used every time he'd gotten into a squabble with a playground bully. "There may be some slight improvement, but the nerve damage is irreparable."

Ethan shrugged as if panic wasn't swelling in his chest. "So what? I've been practicing at the range. I'll never

earn a sharpshooter medal with left-handed target practice, but I'm close enough to department standards to
know that I'll eventually pass."

"My job isn't to determine whether or not you're capable of performing the duties of a police officer, Ethan.
My only responsibility is to assess your conformance
with the department's physical requirements."

Even as Stein spoke, Ethan imagined himself struggling to handcuff a combative suspect, or even grappling
to retrieve the cuffs from his belt in the first place. He
was convinced he could manage, that he could work
around the inconvenience of numb fingers, a lack of
strength.

"Are you saying I'll never be released for duty?"

A pause. "If it was anyone but you I'd be saying that,
Ethan, but you have amazed us in the past. There's always a chance." Stein plucked a pen from his white coat,
tapped it on the file. "I can release you for light duty, if
you wish."

"A desk job?"

"It's the best I can do."

Panic surged like bitter bile, nearly choking him. Light
duty. A desk job. For most, that was simply an inter-
mediate step on their way back to the squad room. For
Ethan, it would be the end of the career that he loved,
and for which he'd sacrificed everything.

He'd have to give up the quest that had kept him alive
in those dark days immediately following the accident,
that had given him the strength to persevere throughout
the agonizing months of blood, sweat and tears. He'd
have to give up the one thing that meant more to him
than his career, more than life itself. He'd have to give
up that which he loved more than anything else in this
world.

And that was one thing he was not willing to do.

"Forget it." He stood so quickly, the chair tottered. "Give me a clean bill of health, or give me nothing."

"Ethan, I'm sorry—"

"Don't bother being sorry," he said quietly. "I'll be back next month, and the month after, and the month after that. You haven't seen the last of me. You haven't seen the last of the miracles."

Despite a grueling, emotionally draining day at the office, Deirdre sang all the way home. She had a marvelous supper planned, a repast that would tempt Ethan's appetite into mouthwatering passion. And afterward, perhaps another kind of passion, one that had haunted Deirdre's dreams since they'd shared that first, soul-shaking kiss beside an ocean bathed in twilight.

She was utterly enamored, dizzied by an infatuation and emotional intensity she'd thought she'd never experience again. This was a man she could care deeply about. This was a man she could love.

So anxious was she to see the object of her desire that disappointment struck with physical pain when she realized that his newly repaired vehicle was not parked in the driveway. After parking her own car, she grabbed the bag of groceries from the seat beside her and hurried up the porch to tap on his door. There was no answer, no sound from inside.

Feeling oddly dispossessed, she retreated to her own dwelling, greeted the exuberant Dublin and was unloading the groceries when alerted by the sound of a vehicle entering Ethan's driveway.

"It's about time!" she said to the kitten, who gazed up agreeably. Smoothing her hair, Deirdre hurried outside, only to come face-to-face with a uniformed courier poking Ethan's doorbell.

Disappointed, she inspected the driveway to assure herself that Ethan's vehicle wasn't parked behind the Express Company truck. It wasn't.

"I'm sorry," she told the courier. "He's not at home right now."

The fellow frowned, tucked a red-and-white document mailer under his arm. "This has a six o'clock deadline." A glance at his watch apparently confirmed that there was less than forty-five minutes to go.

"I'm sure he'll be home shortly. You could leave it on the doorstep."

"It needs a signature." He brightened, shoved a clipboard at her. "Yours will do."

"Oh, well..." She smiled, shrugged. After all, she would be seeing him later. "Where do I sign?"

Clearly relieved, he X'd the proper line, handed her the pen. She scrawled her name, accepting the courier's thanks and the document pack, gave him a cheery wave as he headed back to his truck.

Then and only then did she glance down at the package in her hands. Her heart nearly stopped.

Despite the closeness that had developed between her and Ethan, he'd never mentioned his last name. It hadn't seemed particularly deliberate or evasive. After their initial meeting, the subject simply hadn't come up again. Never in her wildest dreams could she have imagined that an omission she'd considered little more than a minor social mishap could carry such devastating consequence.

The man whose touch sent shivers down her spine and steamed the blood in her veins, who rescued kittens and got teary-eyed watching sad movies, the man who haunted her thoughts and touched a secret part of her soul was none other than Ethan Robert Devlin, notorious son of her bilious boss and eye of the current custody storm that had split the family apart.

At that moment Deirdre finally understood what was expected of her, and she wept.

Chapter Five

Ethan arrived home that evening shortly before dusk. Concealed by damask drapes, Deirdre watched through the window as he emerged from the car. He looked tired, emotionally undone. For the first time she understood the sadness in his eyes, the faraway look of loss and of sorrow. She understood, and it broke her heart.

A soft mew, a silky nuzzle at her ankle. She absently stooped to tickle the kitten's tiny ear. "I know," she murmured. "But it must be done." A throaty purr seemed assurance that her dilemma was understood. She straightened, filled her lungs for courage, then picked up the courier package and took it next door.

Ethan answered on the first ring, his bleak expression warming when he saw her. "I was just thinking about you."

"Were you?" Deirdre tried to smile; she really did. Judging by the cautious flicker in his eye, she suspected it bore more resemblance to a grimace. "This came for you."

"Thanks." Holding the screen door open, he accepted the package without enthusiasm, gave it a perfunctory glance and tossed it aside. From her position on the porch, she couldn't see where it landed. "Are you in the mood for a movie tonight?" he asked. "We could go to the video store and see what's in stock."

"Maybe later." Later wouldn't come, not after he learned that she'd been furtively tucked into his world to satisfy the agenda of others. "Actually, I was hoping we could talk. Do you have a few minutes?"

Caution clouded his gaze. "Sure." He regarded her for a moment, stepped back away from the doorway to allow her access.

She took a deep breath and stepped inside while he hastily gathered a rumpled newspaper from a nondescript sofa to tuck in an untidy roll under a table.

He shifted, eyes darting around his modest living quarters as if searching for other embarrassing clutter. "The place is kind of messy. I just got home."

"I know."

"Right." Seeming pleased that she'd been watching for him, he flashed a sheepish smile, moved the courier package from the sofa where it had landed to a lamp table beside a leather lounger, presumably his favorite chair because of the comfortable worn areas on the back and arms, and the supple indentations on the seat cushion. "Can I get you something? Coffee, soda, beer?"

"No, thank you."

Clearly unnerved by her first visit to his home, Ethan hovered in the small living area, which was the mirror image of her own although more sparsely furnished. There were no pictures on the walls, no photographs on display. Other than an empty soda can lying on its side next to the leather lounger, and the ruffled newspaper he'd shoved aside, the area was clean and well tended.

A dining table beside the kitchen door was piled with files and documents, an open telephone book and a legal pad covered by hurried scrawls.

"So what's going on?" he asked.

Deirdre moistened her lips, clasped her hands and grasped for a final straw. "I noticed from the address label that your last name is Devlin."

"It always has been."

"You never mentioned that."

"I didn't?" A quizzical expression melted into a shrug. "I've always been a bit lax with social details." Flashing that breathtaking smile that made her heart wiggle, he took her hand with exaggerated courtesy. "Deirdre O'Connor, meet Ethan Robert Devlin, who thinks you are just about the most beautiful woman on the face of the earth, and who has this incredibly powerful urge to pull you into his arms—" a slight slip of his palm at the small of her back nudged her closer "—and kiss you senseless."

That was exactly what she wanted him to do, needed him to do. Deirdre knew he could read the yearning in her eyes.

He read something else there, as well. His smile faded as she turned away, easing herself from temptation. "What's wrong, Deirdre?"

She touched the corner of her mouth with her tongue, forced a lighthearted tone. "You wouldn't happen to know a Horace Devlin, would you?" His sharp intake of breath dashed all vestige of hope of vain coincidence. She chanced a glance over her shoulder, saw the darkness in his eyes. "He practices probate law in—"

"I know what he does. He's my father." Ethan shifted his stance, biceps bulging as he folded his arms. "What's this all about, Deirdre?"

God, this was difficult. There was no easy way to tell him, so she simply blurted it out. "I work for him, Ethan."

His arms sprung apart. "You what?"

"I didn't know, Ethan. I swear I didn't know until that package came, and I saw your full name —"

"You work for my father?" He repeated the statement with a heart-wrenching combination of befuddlement and disbelief. Shaking his head, he wandered across the room, paused with one hand on his hip and the other tangled in his hair. When he glanced over his shoulder, the hurt in his eyes broke her heart. "You've been spying on me?"

"Of course not." The accusation wasn't entirely unexpected, but it hurt nonetheless.

Ethan shook his head again, looked so wounded and lost that it was all Deirdre could do to keep from weeping. "I don't understand."

"I know," she whispered. "I don't understand, either." It was the truth. She didn't fully understand why she'd been placed here, although she certainly had her suspicions. "When the attorney I work for in San Francisco went on sabbatical she asked me to come down here to assist one of her colleagues. Clementine handled everything, from hiring the movers to subletting my old place, and the rental agreement on this one. She handed me a map and a set of keys to the duplex, and—" she managed a limp shrug "—here I am."

"Quite a coincidence."

The bite in his tone didn't escape her notice. "Clearly it wasn't a coincidence."

"Clearly." He walked to the kitchen, retrieved a beer from the refrigerator.

Sensing he needed space and a moment to gather his thoughts, she didn't follow. She watched through the open doorway as he drank deeply, then leaned against the counter, staring at the blank wall. There was no window over his sink, as there was no window over hers. Initially that had bothered her. She'd always enjoyed an outside view from the kitchen.

Eventually, however, she'd come to treasure the sound of his movements on the other side of the wall, the gentle rush of water as he washed up, or made a pot of the strong, black coffee he favored. She relished his nearness, anticipated the subtle sounds of his life around which hers had become so dependent.

That would all change now. It had to. She studied Ethan's profile, tight and harsh, his jaw clamped, his complexion paler than it had been only moments before. Her chest constricted, ached with the need to comfort him. But she couldn't comfort him, because it was she who had caused his pain.

After taking another long drink of beer, Ethan returned to the living room without meeting her gaze. "My father is a lot of things," he said. "Stupid isn't one of them. He'd have never put you here unless it was to his advantage to do so. He must have believed you could, and would, give him information he wanted." He still wasn't looking at her. "Have you?"

"No, Ethan."

He twirled the moist can in his left hand, studied it as if fascinated by the movement. "But he's asked about me, hasn't he?"

Denial teetered on her tongue until she remembered the offhand questions Horace had posed about her "neighbor." Puffing her cheeks, she blew out a breath. "Yes."

"And you answered those questions?"

"There was nothing sinister, Ethan. He asked if I'd met my 'neighbor,' if there were any problems with my living arrangements, that sort of thing. He never mentioned your name."

"Do you honestly think he believed we go on blithely sharing a living unit without introducing ourselves?"

That bothered Deirdre, as well. "You're not a terribly communicative person, Ethan. He may have thought you and I would never speak beyond casual greetings when our paths crossed on the porch."

"Do you believe that?"

She sighed. "No, I don't."

"Neither do I. I can guarantee that he sized up your personality in the first five seconds, and knew perfectly well that you were someone who turned strangers into friends, and earned their trust." He drained the beer, set the empty can aside. "He's usually right about people. He was right about you."

Her skin heated. "I've already told you he hasn't asked me to spy on you, and I wouldn't have done so if he had."

"Of course you wouldn't. It's not in your nature." He shrugged, more in resignation than anger. "My father has a draconian way of manipulating people into doing his bidding through whatever means is necessary. If he hasn't already gotten what he needs from you, he will."

"That's not true, Ethan. All that has been asked of me is exactly what I initially agreed to do, which is assist in running the office and help Nettie care for the twins—"

"My kids?" His head snapped around. "You've seen my kids?"

The longing in his eyes affected her like a punch to the stomach. "Yes. They're beautiful children."

"How are they? Are they happy? Healthy?" He took a step forward, crouched as if preparing to spring. "What about Timmy's asthma? Is he getting treatment?"

"Yes," she whispered. "They're happy, they're healthy. Nettie showed me where Timmy's prescription inhaler is kept, but says he hasn't had an attack in months." The eyes, she realized, as moisture gathered in her own. She should have known the moment she saw those exquisite babies, had looked into those thick-lashed hazel eyes that Ethan had fathered them. "How could you, Ethan? How could you have abandoned your babies?"

His jaw dropped as if dislocated, snapped back with a vengeance. Fury smoldered in his gaze, dark and dangerous. "Is that what Horace told you?"

"He said you hadn't seen them since they were barely a year old."

"Did he tell you why?"

To her shock, Deirdre realized that he hadn't, although his inference had been clear. "No, not specifically."

"That figures." His laugh was bitter, unpleasant. "Ask him sometime."

"I'd rather ask you."

A flash of pain in his eyes was quickly blinked away. "The story is a bit too tawdry for an optimistic Pollyanna like yourself."

The words stung. "If you're implying that I've never suffered a moment's grief in my life, you'd be mistaken."

His anger faded into contrition. "Your husband, of course. I'm sorry."

She swallowed, feigned a casual shrug. "You might

as well tell me, Ethan. I've been put in the middle of this mess without my permission. Tawdry or not, I'll not be satisfied until I've uncovered all there is to know.''

A pause, a sigh, a glance across the room. ''All right.''

''Why did you leave your children?''

''Because I was dying.''

Whatever Deirdre had expected, that wasn't it. She steadied herself against the back of a chair, and must have looked as if she was about to faint because Ethan reached out to her, then stepped quickly away, as if burned by her touch.

Propping a lean hip against the sofa, he gazed into thin air and spoke with deceptive calm. ''After the accident, I was in a coma for several weeks. I'm told there were several surgeries to relieve pressure on my brain, and that it was touch-and-go on more than one occasion.'' He wiped his face with his hands, pushed away from the sofa to pace the small room. ''I don't remember anything, of course. One minute I was studying interview notes while my partner nattered on about some barbecue he was planning, then I woke up in a hospital bed with half my body in a cast and some fellow in a priestly collar grinning as if he'd personally intervened with the Big Guy on my behalf.''

Deirdre was stunned. ''I had no idea…. I mean, you never indicated how seriously you'd been injured. Your poor wife must have been beside herself.''

''Oh, yeah, she was heartbroken. Couldn't stand to see me all swollen and bruised, which is why she sent a guy in a gray suit to serve me with divorce papers the day after I came to.'' He hiked a brow at her horrified expression. ''Did I mention that my wife and I had, shall we say, a less-than-cordial relationship?''

She shook her head stupidly.

"Ah, well, timing never had been her strong suit. I wasn't terribly surprised that she'd sued for divorce, and was too sick to care. What I didn't know is that she'd dumped the kids with my parents, and taken off for parts unknown with her new boyfriend." His expression softened for a moment. "My mother wouldn't let anyone tell me. She was afraid the trauma would hinder my recovery, and—gentle soul that she is—was certain my wife would regain her senses and return for the children before I learned what she'd done."

At this point Deirdre's knees failed her, and she lowered herself into the chair. No wonder Nettie had been so venomous when the children's mother was mentioned. "Oh, Ethan. I'm so sorry."

"My wife—my ex-wife—died eight months later, shortly after the divorce was final. Some kind of skiing accident, I'm told."

"Were you still in the hospital?"

"I'd been moved to a rehabilitation facility by then." He straightened, shifted. "That's also when I learned that the boys had been with my parents all that time." A flash of pain, and his jaw twitched. "All that time I'd thought my ex had kept my sons away out of spite. Imagine my surprise when I discovered that the boys had been with my parents all along."

"And they didn't bring them to see you, not even once?"

"Nope, not even once." He rolled his head, massaging the back of his neck as if trying to knead out kinks. "My mother came to visit every month or so, but my father never did. I hadn't expected he would. Horace and I don't get along." He cast a rueful glance. "But you already know that."

She glanced away, her mind reeling. In the short time

she'd worked for Horace Devlin, she'd found him to be blustering and arrogant, with a brusqueness that most people would find distastefully rude. She'd also come to respect him as an excellent attorney and a decent man, with a strident sense of fairness in both his professional and personal dealings. She couldn't believe what Ethan was telling her.

She couldn't disbelieve it, either. "I can understand why they would mislead you about who was caring for the children. Under similar circumstance, I might have considered doing the same thing to protect you from emotional pain."

"You would have considered it, but you wouldn't have done it."

Startled by the firm pronouncement, she studied his eyes and saw grudging admiration. "How do you know that?"

"Because it would have meant lying to me. And you're not a liar, are you, Deirdre?"

"Not a very good one, I'm afraid." The concession was issued candidly, with neither pride nor embarrassment. "What I do not understand, what I cannot accept, is why your parents made a deliberate decision to keep your children away from you during all those months you were in the hospital."

"Their excuse was that they were too young." His reply was slow, issued with obvious caution. "They felt the boys would have been upset by seeing their father so battered and bruised. By the time I realized that they were actually trying to ease me out of my sons' lives, it was too late. They'd actually done it."

Appalled by the allegation, Deirdre shook her head. "That doesn't make any sense. I just don't understand how such a thing could have happened, and why you would have allowed it.''

Ethan regarded her for a moment, as if trying to gauge the legitimacy of her confusion. ''I underwent about twelve different surgeries, and never saw the light of day outside of one hospital room or another for nearly fourteen months. I've got steel pins in my thigh, metal plates bolted to my hipbone and a spiffy new kneecap to replace the one that was pulverized.'' He paused a beat as she flinched. ''Once I found out where the boys were, I called my parents' house a dozen times a week. All I wanted was to talk to them, to hear their voices and let them hear mine. There was always some excuse why they couldn't come to the phone. They were in bed, or they were outside playing, or they had the sniffles and were too cranky.'' He whirled on her, his voice rising more out of frustration than anger. ''Did I know something was wrong? Sure, I did, but there wasn't a heck of a lot I could do about it. As soon as I was released from rehab, I bundled up my canes, hobbled to the train station with my leg in a cast, hauled my sorry butt to my parents' doorstep and demanded my kids.''

''They wouldn't allow it?''

''They called the cops and slapped a restraining order on me.''

Feeling the blood drain from her face, Deirdre knew she must be pale as death. ''They can't keep you from seeing your own children.''

''They can, and they do.'' He turned away, but not before she saw the bleakness in his gaze, and the frustration. ''My error was that I hadn't fought the divorce, hadn't bothered to hire a lawyer, hadn't a clue that my ex-wife had been granted sole custody of the children, which she'd then signed over to my parents. After she died, the court awarded my parents full guardianship of the children because I was incapacitated and unable to care for them.''

"That could not have been done without your knowledge.''

His gaze skittered away. He raked his hair again, angrily this time. "I was given some legal papers.''

"And you signed them?''

"I couldn't even pee without help,'' he replied ruefully. "It's not like I had much of a choice.''

"No,'' she murmured. "I suppose not.''

"Besides, I thought it was temporary. The truth is that I was grateful to them for taking care of my sons.'' The despair in his eyes broke her heart. "It never occurred to me that they'd actually try to steal them away.'' He sighed, sagged against the side of the sofa. "I knew my father hated me. I just didn't realize how much.''

Deirdre stood shakily, extended her hand only to lower it when he turned away. "I won't pretend to understand what has gone on between you and your father, Ethan, but I can't believe that he hates you.''

Cold silence hung between them. When Ethan glanced over his shoulder, his eyes were frozen ponds, devoid of emotion. "What you believe is no longer of concern to me.''

Reflexively she clutched her stomach. "You don't mean that.''

A flicker of emotion was quickly blinked away. "I've made a lot of mistakes in my life, but I've never made any of them twice.'' He strode to the doorway, held the screen open for her. "I'll have to ask you to leave now. I have been advised not to discuss specifics of the custody case with my father's representatives unless my attorney is present.''

Astounded, Deirdre could barely find her voice. "I don't represent your father."

He regarded her mildly. "Yes, Deirdre, you do."

"What a lovely surprise, dear." Clearly startled by Deirdre's unexpected appearance, Nettie garnered a smile that seemed more wary than welcoming. "Do come in."

Deirdre marched into the modest foyer with blood in her eye. Her stomach churned, her brain buzzed, her skin was flushed with anger and the humiliation of having been deliberately used by people she'd trusted.

"Horace is just tucking the twins into bed. They're not asleep yet, if you'd like to go up and see them—"

"It's Horace I'd like to see, Nettie. I'll wait down here."

"Of course, dear." The pupils of Nettie's eyes contracted. She blinked, clasped her hands together. "You seem distressed. Is there something I can do?"

Deirdre regarded the woman, saw fear in her eyes and swallowed a surge of sympathy. "You can tell me why it is that you lied to me, Nettie. You can tell me why you've been lying to your son, and why you're trying to steal his children from him."

The color drained from her face, leaving only two garish splotches of cosmetic blush on her sallow cheeks. "I see you and Ethan have been comparing notes."

"Did you honestly think we wouldn't?"

Before Nettie could reply, a familiar rasp from the stairway drew Deirdre's attention. "So you and my son have put your heads together, have you?" Horace descended the stairs the way he did everything in life, in rushed jerks, a blur of momentum that resulted in more motion than movement. "Took you long enough. I was beginning to wonder if Clem was pulling my leg about how damned smart you were.''

Deirdre spun to face him. "Insults, is it? Fine. Carry on with your bluster. It's not a bit of concern to me since I'll not be putting up with it for one more day. Find another dupe for your dirty work, Mr. Devlin. I'll not work for a man I cannot trust.''

Horace displayed no surprise at the announcement, nor did he appear particularly disturbed by it. A sudden sheen of moisture along his hairline betrayed the bluff. "So you're quitting, are you?''

"I am.''

Nettie touched her arm. "Deirdre, please, hear us out before you make that decision.''

"What is it you'll say, that you didn't steal your son's children while he was busy fighting for his life? That you had nothing to do with me ending up living right next door to him at the same time your lawyers are trying to cut him out of their lives forever? That you haven't deceived me, misled me, deliberately tried to use me as…as…'' At a loss for words, she chose one of Ethan's. "As a spy?''

Chuckling, Horace ambled to a small wet bar by the dining room. "You've been reading too many detective novels, my dear. I presumed you understood the full nature of your assignment. Apparently you've been left in the dark, and have chosen to fill in the blanks with glamorized fiction. Brandy?'' He held up a cut-crystal decanter half filled with amber liquid. When she refused, he filled two small glasses, handing one to his wife. "Clementine indicated to me that you were a natural negotiator, a mediator with extraordinary insight and perception. Of course I'd hoped to take advantage of that. I'm not a fool.''

"You're not a particularly nice person, either." Deirdre was stunned by the harsh condemnation in her voice. It wasn't like her. "I'm disappointed in you, Mr. Devlin."

He eased himself into a leather lounge chair strikingly similar to the one in his son's home, and regarded her with peculiar blankness. "If you expect that to wound me, Deirdre, I should mention that I've never given much credence to the opinion of others."

A gentle touch on her shoulder turned her around. Nettie smiled at her, a sad smile reminiscent of her son's. "Sit down, dear. Please. We'll answer your questions."

After a moment's hesitation, Deirdre did as she asked, and posed her first question to Horace. "Why didn't you tell me that Ethan was your son?"

Horace took a sip of brandy, then twirled the glass between his palms. "Because you would have acted differently toward him if you'd known. You would have been cautious, unnerved. He would have seen deception in your eyes, and withdrawn. He wouldn't have trusted you."

"He doesn't trust me now."

"Yes, he does." Horace set the glass aside. "I knew you'd figure out who he was sooner or later. In fact, I was surprised it took as long as it did, even though I know my son has a habit of avoiding the use of his surname. It galls him, you know, sharing a name with a man he despises."

For the first time, a flash of something that could have been pain invaded the older man's eyes. He blinked it away, just as Ethan did. The similarities astounded Deirdre, mannerisms that were so obvious to her now, that she couldn't understand why she hadn't noticed them earlier.

Steepling his hands, Horace inspected his fingertips and spoke carefully. "The law firm of Devlin and Son has been in our family for three generations. I became the 'son' when I passed the bar, as did my father before me, and his father before him. Ethan broke that tradition just to spite me." He paused a beat. "He married that shallow tramp to spite me, too, a woman so mindless and self-absorbed that children were an inconvenience." A rasp in his voice visibly annoyed him. He coughed it away, numbed it with another sip of brandy. "She walked out on him, you know, him lying at death's door and all she worried about was that paychecks would stop." He glanced up. "Did he tell you?"

Emotion thickened her tongue. "Yes."

Horace nodded. "Good. At least he can face it now. There was a time he couldn't. Blamed himself for her insipid pettiness and greed, moaned that he shouldn't have worked such long hours, that he shouldn't have spent so much time away from home trying to earn enough money for a vengeful witch who saw him as nothing more than a meal ticket."

Deirdre swallowed. "He also said he was grateful to you for caring for the twins while he was recovering." That seemed to surprise Horace, but he covered it well. A provocative question edged into her mind. She took a deep breath and posed it aloud. "Refusing to return his children to him... Is that your way of punishing him for having made choices in his life that you didn't approve of?"

She expected Horace to deny it. He didn't. Instead he leaned back thoughtfully, spoke with more emotion in his voice than he'd probably intended. "Decisions create consequence."

The acknowledgment knocked the breath out of her.

Refilling her lungs slowly, she leaned forward, hoping she'd misheard. "So you've decided to pursue a vendetta against your own son because he chose to enforce law rather than practice it?"

"You're damned right," Horace snapped. "Instead of admitting he made a mistake, Ethan has done everything but cartwheels to get back onto the force, back to the job that damned near killed him in the first place. Now that he's got that rattletrap car running, nothing is stopping him from returning to Los Angeles. If he wants to commit suicide, I can't stop him, but I sure in hell can keep his children from watching him do it."

That was it, Deirdre realized, the hidden crux of the matter. Horace was terrified for Ethan's safety, and too stubborn to admit it. "It's a battle of wills, isn't it? You're using your grandchildren as leverage to force your son into following the path you have laid out for his life."

Horace didn't answer, but Nettie did. "The children have already been uprooted once. What will happen to them if they are returned to Los Angeles, cared for by strangers while their father is out putting his life on the line for a job that means more to him than his own children, a job that will eventually destroy him? Children need stability. They need to be nurtured by people they can count on."

"What they need," Deirdre said quietly, "is their father."

Nettie's face crumpled. "I know."

Across the room Horace drained the rest of the brandy in a single swallow, grimaced, set the empty glass aside with a resounding thunk. "If Ethan wants to destroy his own life, I can't stop him. But by God, I won't let him destroy those children, I won't let him take them away from us.'' His ragged expression revealed more than his words.

Deirdre chose her own response carefully. ''I know you love the boys, Horace. They love you, too. That's as it should be. But what you are doing is wrong. Someday Tommy and Timmy will understand the choices you've made for them. They'll understand that you've kept their father out of their lives, and they will resent you for it. You cannot erase mistakes made with your own son by trying to re-create the past through your grandchildren.''

A subtle vibration along Horace's shoulders revealed that her words had hit their mark, but he simply folded his arms and looked away.

Frustrated, Deirdre turned to Nettie. ''This custody suit is wrong. You must realize that.''

The woman held her chin high, but her eyes were red, and bright with moisture. ''Our attorney believes we can convince a judge that it's in the best interest of the children to remain in our care.''

From what Deirdre knew about family law, she realized that Nettie could be right. No one could dispute that the twins were healthy, happy and well cared for. No one could dispute that the Devlins loved their grandchildren deeply. A court might be sympathetic with Ethan's plight, but the best interest of the children was always the primary concern in these matters. If Ethan's ability to financially and emotionally care for the boys was challenged, he may indeed lose custody. In Deirdre's mind, that would be tragic.

''Don't tell me what your attorney believes, Nettie. Tell me what you believe.'' When the woman glanced away, Deirdre touched her hand. It was cold. ''Are you honestly convinced that the children will be better off without their father?''

Nettie shook her head.

"Then you must allow Ethan to see his children."

"I know," she whispered.

Deirdre leaned back, her mind spinning. In the space of a heartbeat she realized that everything—her move to Santa Barbara, her job, her living quarters—had been scrupulously arranged to create a human conduit between the Devlins and their estranged son. It was all part of the assignment, all intricate pieces of the plot hidden like tiny treasures to be discovered one fragment at a time.

And every detail bore Clementine's mark of distinction. Nothing was arbitrary, nothing left to chance. It was evident that the sly old woman had anticipated Deirdre's attachment to the babies. Emotional involvement would be crucial if she was to effectively mediate the warring factions of a family in crisis.

The plan was brilliant, of course. And it broke her heart.

Chapter Six

A sliver of moonlight peeped through a ghostly smear of clouds, the only hint of illumination in the bleakness of night. As Deirdre pulled into the driveway, the duplex windows glowed like watchful eyes. She'd left the light on in her own unit, since returning to a dark dwelling unnerved her. Ethan had proven himself more thrifty with electricity, only turning on lights when needed. A soft glow bled through his draperies, enticing her. He was home, and he was awake.

She mounted the porch steps, found herself hovering in front of his door rather than her own. Nervous moisture cooled her palms. She flexed her fingers, took a cleansing breath, directed a gentle tap on the screen door's aluminum frame.

They had to talk—if not now, then very soon. Deirdre hated how things had been left between them, hated the reproach she'd seen in his eyes. And the hurt.

Deirdre, too, was hurt—hurt and sick at heart. Her mission as she now understood it was to reunite all three generations of the splintered Devlin clan. Despite Clementine's apparent presumption of emotional involvement, Deirdre knew that if there was any hope of accomplishing that, she must detach herself from a man who had touched her more deeply than she dared admit.

Ethan was not available to her. He was a man in crisis, a man at a crossroads of his own destiny. Even if ethical considerations hadn't prohibited her from becoming emotionally involved, logic certainly would. He was, in effect, one of her clients, the emotional core of a tumultuous maelstrom that she was charged with mediating. If Deirdre's mission was successful, she would return to San Francisco while Ethan raised his children and repaired his relationship with his parents. That was—that must be—her sole focus. To accomplish it, she had to regain Ethan's trust on an entirely different, and wholly unemotional level.

Unfortunately she didn't have a clue how that could be done.

She knocked again, more forcefully this time. Crickets chirped from the cherry bush hedge lining the driveways. A distant rumble heralded the arrival of another train. Ethan's door remained stubbornly shut.

After the succession of clattering boxcars had passed, Deirdre pressed her thumb on the doorbell, and heard the responding chime. Finally she noted movement inside, the purposeful stride echoing across the hardwood floor. Her pulse raced in anticipation of seeing him, an involuntary reaction for which she chided herself. She wanted to personify calm professionalism, not a starry-eyed infatuation.

Rearranging her features, she waited for the door to

open. Instead, a blast of sound blared from inside the duplex. It took a dumfounded moment before she realized Ethan had turned on the television, effectively drowning out any further attempt to garner his attention.

The message was received and understood. Deirdre's job had just become a whole lot harder.

Despite the cheers of football fans emanating from the televised game, Ethan was attuned to the sound of Deirdre's footsteps on the porch, the rasping creak of her front door opening. He heard her moving beyond the wall, caught a tantalizing whisper of her voice as she spoke to her kitten.

There was a comfort in her nearness, a comfort he didn't want to acknowledge, but was helpless to control. That troubled him, because he couldn't allow himself to think about her, to be suckered by that guileless gaze, betrayed by yearnings he hadn't felt in a very long time. He'd let his guard down with Deirdre, allowed himself to care about her. To trust her.

He should have known better. Choosing women had never been Ethan's strong suit. His father had been right about that. It was a character flaw, one of many that Horace had been all too willing to point out over the years.

Failure had always been a dark shadow over his life. Failure as a husband, a father, a son. Even failure in the career he had loved. On the surface, Ethan wasn't ready to accept that he would never be a detective again, never fulfill that burning ambition that had driven him since he'd seen his first old *Dragnet* rerun on television. If a voice in a distant corner of his mind whispered that it was time to move on, time to take another direction in his professional life, Ethan ignored it. Relinquishing control was not something he relished. He wasn't very good at it.

Control was something a man kept firmly within his grasp—control of himself, his own emotions, control of his future. Horace had taught him that much. Never let others usurp your personal power. Ethan had tried to take that lesson to heart only to discover that he didn't have his father's ambition, that thirst for authority over others as well as oneself. He possessed neither the desire to manipulate those around him nor the ability to recognize that trait in others. An inner softness was his Achilles' heel, a compassion that made him vulnerable.

His feelings for Deirdre were proof that he hadn't overcome that weakness. He'd allowed himself to be distracted, to be taken in by her beauty, by her sweetness, by an indefinable something that still haunted his heart.

Now he faced a dilemma. Willing or not, Deirdre had become his father's pawn. Ethan couldn't trust her. Trouble was, when it came to Deirdre he couldn't trust himself, either.

She was a passion in his blood. He simply could not get his mind off her. Even now he strained to hear her movements beyond the thin wall, and fought an overwhelming urge to go to her, to see the gentle acceptance in her eyes, feel the soft nurture of her touch.

When a man is at war with himself, the victor inevitably becomes the vanquished. Ethan was doomed to defeat.

"Hi!" Deirdre's perky greeting belied the frantic race of her heart. Two days she'd been trying to get close to Ethan. Two days he'd been scrupulously avoiding her. Today they would talk, even if it killed her. And it just might. "Getting ready for a jog?"

It was a stupid question since Ethan, dressed in sweats and running shoes, was performing peculiar stretching exercises that even Deirdre, who maintained a strict exercise-free zone around her own personal space, recognized as warm-up.

"What a coincidence. I was just going out for a run myself." Trying to ignore his incredulous expression, Deirdre splayed her right leg as far as humanly possible, then rotated her stiff torso forward in a torturous effort to bump her nose on her knee as Ethan had done. The attempt was less than successful. A grunt of pain slipped out. She covered it with a sheepish smile. "A bit out of shape, I am."

Narrowing his gaze, Ethan eyed her own jogging ensemble, which consisted of a floppy sweater with frayed hem, cotton slacks and a pair of leather-soled loafers. They were the only exercise togs she could rummage up after she'd spied him heading out for a morning run, and recognized the opportunity to corner him before he got away. Clearly he wasn't pleased by her unexpected appearance, although he continued with his workout by raising bent arms to shoulder level and twisting his upper body with amazing agility. He angled a furtive glance. "Aren't you supposed to be at work?"

"My hours are flexible." Awkwardly raising her own arms until her elbows were as high as her ears, she emulated his movements. Something popped in her spine, loud enough for Ethan to do a double take. She froze in that ludicrous position, with her stupidly folded arms protruding like a pair of malformed wings. "The hours are flexible, not the body."

Ethan didn't smile, although he looked as if he might secretly want to. Nonetheless, he continued with his own warm-up without so much as a second glance in her direction. "Where's your car?"

"In the garage." Flinching, she lowered her arms, probed her lower back with her fingertips and decided the peculiar noise had not been indicative of any permanent damage. "I hid it so you'd think I was gone for the day."

"Why?"

"Would you have emerged from your cave otherwise?"

"No." He rolled his neck, shook his body with boneless fluidity, then slipped his right hand into his sweatshirt's pouch to retrieve a small rubber ball as he kicked off to jog down the driveway.

Deirdre sucked in a determined breath, and hurried after him.

She caught up at the corner. "Lovely morning for a run, isn't it?" Eyeing the rubber ball he was squeezing, she stumbled, righted herself, struggled for a rhythmic stride. "Is that to exercise your hand?" He didn't respond, just kept moving forward as if she wasn't puffing alongside like a jerky shadow. "Considering what you and your mother told me about the extent of your injuries, I'm really impressed by how physically fit you are." Her gaze was riveted to a gleaming row of perspiration settling along the base of his neck, moistening the hair at his nape into wet curls that were oddly enticing. "Nettie also told me that she is sad that you haven't kept in touch with her since this, er, legal unpleasantness began."

His jaw twitched, the only indication that he'd heard her. He veered left without warning, and crossed the street. Determined, Deirdre followed. Her breath came in short puffs, her mouth was dry as a desert but she had him in her sights, and she wasn't about to let him go until he'd heard her out.

"Nettie says she has tried to call you," she said when she'd caught up with him. "Why won't you speak with her, Ethan?" She paused for breath. "She's your mother."

Without breaking stride, Ethan finally replied. "I won't put her in the position of choosing between her husband and her son."

"There's no reason for her to choose. She loves you both." A salty drop slipped down to sting her eyes, blur her sight. She wiped frantically, and nearly ran into a tree. By the time she veered around it to catch up with Ethan, she was puffing madly. "Your father...loves you, too."

Ethan made a sound deep in his chest. A growl, perhaps, or a bark of jaded laughter. "My father wants to control me. There's a difference."

"Horace can be—" she gulped air "—difficult."

A smile jittered at the corner of his mouth before his lips clamped. He regarded her from the corner of his eye. "Horace and I have always clashed. He demands authority. I resist it."

"So you deliberately chose the path...furthest from the one...he wanted you to take?" Frustrated by the difficulty of trying to breathe and talk at the same time, Deirdre wiped her wet forehead, wishing she'd actually used the exercise video her brother Sean had given her as a joke. Her dislike of any exertion resulting in the unpleasantry of dripping sweat had always been a source of great amusement for her own extended family.

Ethan subtly shifted his rhythm. "It's my life, not his. I don't need his permission to live it as I see fit."

"Of course not." Her breathing came a bit easier now.

"You had every right to pursue the career you wanted." She inhaled with less effort, stole a yearning glance at the handsome man who had furtively slowed his pace so she could keep up. A small kindness, performed without fanfare. It was so like him, she thought, and the strength of character that had drawn her to him in the first place.

She wanted to touch him, to hold him, to caress away his pain, his loss. But she couldn't. Things between them had changed. Nothing would be the same. Nothing.

She reeled in her emotions, tucked them firmly in a dark corner of her mind. "Your father's protestations aside, you also had every right to marry a woman of your choice."

His stride faltered for a step, then smoothed back into a steady rhythm. "So he told you about that, did he?"

"He mentioned it." She noted a subtle pallor to his complexion, the deepening stress lines bracketing his mouth, grooving his forehead. "I understand that he has disagreed with certain...choices you've made in the past." Even at a slower pace, attempting to jog, talk and breathe took a toll. Words rushed out in short bursts, punctuated by gasps for air. "He also regrets that rift...in your relationship...those differences...have caused."

At the intersection Ethan stopped, maintaining motion by jogging in place. Deirdre collapsed against a light pole, panting.

"I refused to follow the career my father chose for me," he said. "And I married a woman he despised. If you're under the impression that Horace is willing to let bygones be bygones, if you believe this attempt to steal my children isn't his way of wreaking vengeance for having defied him in the past, you're seriously deluded."

"I don't think it's vengeance. I think from his perspective—" When the light turned green, she regretfully heaved her body forward and followed Ethan across the street. "I think Horace believes that his apprehension has proven correct."

That clearly hit a nerve. Ethan swung his head around to stare at her, stumbled out of rhythm and had some difficulty regaining his stride. "What do you want me to say, that my wife was shallow and self-absorbed, incapable of loving either me or our children?"

"I wouldn't presume to—"

"Okay, fine, Horace was right about her. I married the first woman I met who was as lonely as I was, and the marriage failed just like my father said it would. Is that what you want to hear?" Raw emotion roughened his voice, and touched her heart. His jaw clenched, his right hand pulsed angrily over the rubber ball. "What she did was lousy, but it wasn't entirely her fault."

Ethan's defense of a woman who'd clearly betrayed him was unexpected, and oddly unsettling. "She divorced you while you were in the hospital, Ethan, fighting for your life."

A flash of pain in his eyes was quickly concealed. "So her timing was crummy. The marriage shouldn't have survived the first year, and wouldn't have, except for an unplanned pregnancy."

That surprised her. "You realized so soon that you were incompatible?"

"I guess you could say that. During the first months of our marriage, I had a routine patrol shift. I left the same time every morning, came home the same time every night. She knew I was only biding time until I could make detective, but she didn't know what that actually meant until it happened."

"What did it mean?"

"A detective doesn't work by the clock." He

shrugged. "It wasn't unusual for me to leave before she woke up in the morning, and not return until she was asleep at night. She resented that. After the kids were born, she resented it even more."

"Oh." That explained Nettie's comment that the children didn't know their father. By his own admission he'd spent little time with them even before the accident. The puzzle pieces were falling into place. "It must have been difficult for her, caring for two babies on her own like that."

They ran for half a block before Ethan answered. "She asked for a divorce right after the boys were born. I wouldn't give her one."

"You still loved her," Deirdre murmured, mystified as to why that thought should pain her so.

Ethan didn't respond immediately. When he did, he spoke thoughtfully, and without the breathless pause for air that plagued Deirdre. "I'm not sure either of us ever truly loved the other. We married for all the wrong reasons, and by the grace of God still managed to produce two small miracles. I felt we had the responsibility to put our feelings aside, and make the best home we could for our children." He fell silent for a moment, frowning as if determining whether to say anything more. "I always wanted to be a good father. I'll concede I fell miserably short of that goal while the twins were infants. I thought establishing financial stability for them was more important than hovering over their cribs day and night. I was wrong."

Deirdre, feeling considerably less winded now that Ethan had slowed his pace again for her benefit, saw the opening, and took it. "So you'll agree that being a parent isn't easy, that mistakes are possible, even inevitable?"

A few strides later, he replied. "If you're attempting

to draw a comparison between mistakes I made with my sons, and the mistakes my father made with me, you're missing one important difference.''

That had been exactly what she'd been trying to do, hoping to soften his stance to get the two Devlins in the same room long enough to negotiate their conflicts. ''What difference is that, Ethan?''

''To correct mistakes, you have to admit having made them.'' He glanced over his shoulder without breaking rhythm. ''Don't forget to cool down.''

With that, Ethan lengthened his stride and sped away, leaving Deirdre to limp home silently cursing two extraordinarily stubborn men, one meddling, white-haired old woman and her own idiocy in trying to convince herself that her heart was racing only out of exertion.

She knew that it wasn't.

Horace slammed down the phone just as Deirdre hobbled into his office. ''What in hell happened to you?''

''Blisters, back spasms, leg cramps... Take your pick.'' Flinching, she lowered herself into a chair, barely stifled a groan. ''I guess 'cool down' doesn't mean crawl home and take a cold shower.''

Sympathy wasn't Horace's forte, particularly when offering it had no value to his personal agenda. ''Did you talk to Ethan?''

''Yes.''

Obviously pleased, Horace leaned back, steepled his fingers. ''I knew you'd use those feminine wiles to get through his line of defense, clever girl that you are.''

Deirdre hiked a brow. ''I haven't been a 'girl' for many years, Mr. Devlin, although if there was a compliment buried in your condescension, I thank you for it. As for feminine wiles, you obviously don't know your son very well if you think him so hormonally predictable.''

A flick of his fat wrist waved that suggestion aside. ''Ethan has always been a sucker for a pretty face and a sad tale. That's what makes him weak, what makes him a loser.''

Inexplicably angered, Deirdre flashed him a furious look. ''Your son is a fine and honorable man, Mr. Devlin, although he obviously inherited compassion and sensitivity from his mother since you hold those traits in such little regard. If you're wanting any more help from me, you'll stop referring to your son in derogatory terms, and treat him with the respect he deserves.''

A peculiar gleam flickered in Horace's eye, an odd combination of admiration and something Deirdre couldn't quite identify. ''Fair enough,'' he said affably, surprising her. It wasn't like Horace to take criticism, or even disagreement, without a fight. ''So, has he agreed to drop his lawsuit?''

Since Deirdre didn't relish confessing that the subject hadn't been broached, she offered a casual shrug and switched the topic. ''Have you agreed to drop yours?''

Horace narrowed his gaze. ''Whose side are you on anyway?''

''The children's.'' Sighing, Deirdre massaged the back of her neck, which was so stiff, she could barely turn her head. ''I made my position very clear the other night. I'll stay on only if you permit Ethan immediate visitation with his sons, which is all that his lawsuit requests, after all. Once he's given the opportunity to reacquaint himself with them, he'll be in a better position to negotiate what's best for their future.''

''I already know what's best.''

''Clearly you don't.''

Drawing himself up as stiff as his rotund body would allow, Horace glared at Deirdre as if she'd committed heresy. Although aware she was allowed a liberty to speak her mind far beyond boundaries others dared cross, Deirdre realized she'd stepped over the line.

Frankly she didn't care. Horace Devlin didn't frighten her, nor did he particularly annoy her. He was who he was—a man with strength and weakness she recognized and accepted as a part of his character. She didn't believe him a cruel man with a vendetta, although she could certainly understand why Ethan saw him that way. She did, however, believe him capable of attempting to shatter anything or anyone not pliable enough to bend to his will.

She spoke with more care. "The boys need to be loved and nurtured by both their father and their grandparents. Until you permit their father to establish a place in their lives, you are assigning more emphasis to your own interests than the needs of your grandchildren. I don't believe that's what you truly want."

Horace regarded her with an expression she couldn't define. "My son can see his children any time he wants." Before the smile in her heart could reach her face, the older man's next words dashed hope entirely. "All he has to do is come here to the office, and ask my permission."

A surge of anger swelled in her chest, settled into a cold lump in her stomach. "In other words, you want Ethan to grovel on your personal turf, where your authority cannot be challenged."

"Precisely."

"You know he won't agree to that."

"That's his prerogative."

Deirdre managed a nonchalant shrug that hurt her heart as much as her stiff shoulder. "Then you can explain that to the judge next week. I'm certain that any fair and impartial jurist will be most impressed by a man who uses his grandchildren as twin clubs with which to beat his own son into submission.'' She rose with as much dignity as the agonizing charley horse in her calf would allow, and hobbled toward the office door.

"Deirdre?"

Hoping Horace had come to his senses, she painfully turned her stiff torso. "Yes?"

"Have you found Rodriguez yet?"

Her stomach clenched with outrage, but she managed to maintain a modicum of poise. "I've located a private investigator who has agreed to take the case, but his fee is exorbitant. This matter has already cost you six times more than your executor's fee."

Horace shrugged. "Doesn't matter. Rodriguez has money coming, and it's our job to get it to him. Do whatever it takes, but get it done."

"Very well." Closing the door behind her, Deirdre returned to her desk wondering how a man so respectful of a stranger's rights could be so narrow-minded and cruel when it came to the feelings of his own flesh and blood.

There was more to this father-son chess game than met the eye, motives still unchallenged, secrets not yet exposed. It was time, Deirdre decided, to rattle a few family closets and see what fell out.

Tommy bounded downstairs, legs churning, face alight and so excited he could barely talk. "Dee-dwa, Dee-dwa, I—I—I—got, I got—" he filled his lungs "—a new car!"

"You did?" Instinctively she scooped him into her arms, then grunted in pain as she straightened. Her eyes blurred as a gleaming blue object was waved in front of her nose. "Gracious me, if that isn't the loveliest little car I've ever seen. And who bestowed this magnificent gift upon you?"

Tommy's eyes went blank. "Huh?"

"Who gave you the car, sweetheart?"

"Gwampa!" Swallowing air, Tommy's gaze widened until the hazel irises were surrounded by white, and Deirdre feared the excited child's eyes would pop right out of his head. "We got, we got, we-e-e-e got, umm—"

At that moment, a large plastic object descended the stairs above a pair of stubby, denim-clad legs. Timmy's muffled voice filtered from behind the colorful toy, which appeared to be a plastic parking garage, complete with tiny driving ramps, miniature vehicle hoists and storage places for their collection of diminutive little cars. "Look, Deeda, a car house!"

"So it is." Carefully lowering Tommy to the floor, Deirdre clutched the base of her spine, until the spasm passed. The remnants of yesterday's minor marathon continued to plague her aching body. When she straightened slowly, Tommy had snagged the precious car house away from his brother, who was regarding Deirdre with huge, solemn eyes.

"Owie?" Timmy asked, clearly concerned.

She smiled, kept her spine straight as she gingerly squatted down to the child's level. "Just a small 'owie,' sweetheart. Deirdre is not as young as she used to be, and should respect her aging old bones."

Timmy giggled. "Uh-uh, you p'etty."

"Pretty, am I? Now isn't that a precious thing to say? Give us a kiss." The child wrapped his little arms around her neck and planted a moist smack on her cheek before scampering off to join his brother, who sat cross-legged in the parlor, zooming his zippy new car through the colorful "car house."

A fluid warmth slipped through her veins as she watched the children play. Her time with them had become the highlight of her week, special hours that never ceased to refresh her spirit and renew her aching soul. At thirty she was hardly ancient, although there were times when she was alone in her duplex, cooking for one, that she wondered if life had completely passed her by.

Such unpleasant thoughts dissipated when she was with the twins. They delighted her, invigorated her, made her feel young and vibrant and completely alive. She saw Ethan in the children, felt his presence in their sweetness, saw his strength in the sturdiness of their little bodies, and the determination of their headstrong baby souls.

The reminder ached as much as her sore muscles. She missed Ethan. She missed the friendship they'd shared, the blossoming tenderness that had been closed down at the apex of its bloom.

Deirdre had believed she could turn off her emotions, to detach herself from the yearnings of her heart. That hadn't been easy. So far, it hadn't even been possible. She might be able to conceal her feelings, but she realized now that eliminating them was beyond her control.

The jagged jangle of a doorbell refocused her attention. She cast an instinctive smile toward the playing children, then answered the front door and stiffened in shock.

There stood Ethan, dressed as if for church, with a shocked expression on his face and a colorful plastic parking garage clutched in his hands identical to the one the twins had received from their grandfather.

Horace, it seemed, had struck again.

Chapter Seven

"What the...?" Ethan's gaze darted over Deirdre's shoulder then back again. His voice lowered to a harsh whisper. "Is this some kind of a joke?"

She glanced toward the living room, lowered her voice to a sharp whisper. "What on earth are you doing here?"

"My lawyer called last night. He said I'd be allowed to see the boys at 10:00 a.m."

This was all news to Deirdre. "I wasn't told."

"Then perhaps you should verify that with my mother."

"She left about twenty minutes ago. This is, ah, her bookkeeping day at the office." With a sinking heart, Deirdre shifted focus to the plastic toy in his hands. "A gift for the children?" she asked stupidly.

He managed a nervous nod. "Are they here?" An embarrassed flush crawled up his throat, along with a nervous twitch at his Adam's apple. "Of course they would be here, unless you've come all the way over to baby-sit the parakeet.''

''There isn't any parakeet.''

''Tweedy's gone?'' He seemed perturbed, but covered it with a manly shrug. ''I'm sorry to hear that. He was a good bird.''

Another brief glimpse of his soft heart. ''Was, er, Tweedy a childhood pet?''

''Yes.'' A sheepish shrug. ''I hadn't realized how long ago that was. By now he'd have been pretty ancient in bird years, I suppose.''

''I suppose.'' Moistening her lips, Deirdre angled a glance toward the living room, where the twins were playing. ''I wish I'd known you were coming today.''

Ethan regarded her thoughtfully. ''If you'd known, you'd have insisted that my parents participate in the big reunion.'' When she couldn't dispute that, he continued on as smoothly as if their deliberate evasion hadn't hurt him in the least. ''It doesn't matter. In fact, I'm glad neither of them are here. Less tension that way.''

Deirdre was tense enough as it was. Her attention was riveted on Ethan's anxious anticipation as he scanned the interior of the house. She swallowed, forced a smile. ''That's a lovely gift, Ethan. Quite unusual. How did you happen to select it?''

''A speciality store downtown.'' Beaming, he fondly stroked the plastic roof of the toy garage. ''My mother once mentioned the boys liked miniature cars. This seemed perfect.''

''Yes, perfect,'' she murmured, stealing another glance at the twins. She chewed her lip, decided that a warning was in order to diminish the inevitable disappointment. ''So perfect in fact...well—'' she gave a nervous laugh ''—you'll not believe this. It's such a coincidence.''

Ethan's smile flattened. "I don't believe in coincidence."

Before Deirdre could respond, Tommy skidded into the foyer babbling madly. "Dee-dwa, Dee-dwa, I—I—I—" he gulped air "—want juice. I'm firsty—" The child's attention jerked toward the man in the foyer. He tilted his head with a friendly grin, and not so much as a flicker of recognition. "Hi."

Ethan's face took on an almost ethereal glow. He smiled, licked his lips, smiled again. When he spoke, his voice was low, choked. "Hello there." He crouched down to the boy's level. "Do you remember me…?"

When he glanced up, Deirdre caught the panic in his eyes and mouthed the word, "Tommy." The twins were so physically identical that it was difficult even for those who knew them well to tell them apart, let alone someone who hadn't seen them since they were toddlers.

Ethan exhaled slowly, smiled at his curious son. "Do you remember me, Tommy?"

Tommy, whose rapt gaze was glued on the colorful toy, didn't seem to even hear the question. "We got that, too!" he announced with obvious glee.

Ethan's eyes went blank, then focused on Deirdre for clarification. "That's the coincidence I was mentioning," she said with forced cheer. "Horace brought home the same toy for the boys just last night."

The pain in Ethan's eyes hit like a body blow. He blinked it away, but even the strained smile he leveled on his son couldn't loosen his jaw. "Ah, but there are two of you, aren't there?" When Tommy issued a hopeful nod, Ethan held out the gift. "And now you each have a special place for your favorite cars."

Tommy's eyes lit like neon as he accepted the toy, then spun toward his brother, who'd sidled silently to the edge of the foyer and was peeking out from behind a fluffy potted palm. "Look, Timmy! We—we—we got *two!*"

Timmy shoved his finger in his mouth and ducked behind the palm.

Grinning madly, Tommy hurried into the living room to set the new play set next to its twin, while Timmy cast a final furtive glance at the strange man who had brought it before scuttling off to join his brother.

Ethan stood slowly, his expression rigid, his eyes dulled by pain. Deirdre wanted to weep for him. "It was so long ago," she whispered. "Give them time. They'll remember."

He nodded. "They've grown so much. They were barely walking last time I saw them."

She truly didn't know what to say. In her desperation to dispel the pall of tension, she blurted, "The gift was perfect, you know."

The moment the words had been uttered, her mistake was reflected in the flash of angry hazel eyes. "Yes, perfect."

"Oh, I know you're disappointed that they already had an identical toy, but think of it as a fortuitous serendipity, sort of a divine message that two really is better than one."

He leveled a cool gaze in her direction. "It was a message, all right, although the source was hardly divine."

"Excuse me?"

A cynical smile lifted one corner of his mouth, leaving the other side flat and bitter. "It was just Horace's charming way of letting me know there was nothing I could provide for my sons that he couldn't provide first."

Deirdre thought the accusation ridiculous. "There was no way Horace could possibly know what you'd purchased as a gift for the children unless he had you followed—'' She sucked in a breath, stared up in shock. "Oh, good grief, you wouldn't be suggesting such a tawdry thing, now would you?"

"It isn't a suggestion, it's a fact. Horace has had me tailed off and on since the day I hit town."

"I'll not believe such nonsense." Even as the words snapped off her tongue, the "Subject X" file popped into her mind, and Horace's comment about Ethan's newly repaired vehicle. She hadn't mentioned the car repairs to Horace, and certainly Ethan hadn't. How else could Horace have known about them? It was a sobering thought.

Ethan, however, merely shrugged. "I've been a cop for over ten years, Deirdre. I've spent more hours on surveillance than I can count. I'd be a pretty lousy investigator if I couldn't spot someone doing the same thing to me that I've done to dozens of others over the course of my career."

"That's…that's…" At a loss for words, she could only gaze up, dumbfounded that Horace could stoop to such deceptive subterfuge against his own son, and bewildered as to why Ethan wasn't more upset by it. "That's unethical."

"Not at all," Ethan replied with peculiar dispassion. "Investigative surveillance is routine in civil proceedings. Horace probably hoped to gather proof I was partying with folks of dubious repute, or committing felonious assault as a hobby, something he could lay out in front of the judge to bolster his case. It happens all the time."

Ethan's matter-of-fact demeanor was as surprising as the allegation itself. A closer look, however, revealed a tint of sadness in his eyes, nearly imperceptible to one who wasn't seeking it, clearly visible to one who was. "This is your father we're talking about, Ethan. I can't believe he'd attempt to deliberately discredit you. At heart, Horace is a fair man."

Tilting his head, he scrutinized her with a peculiar combination of empathy and jaded amusement. "He played you like a fiddle, didn't he?"

She stiffened. "I beg your pardon?"

His laugh was genuine, not unkind. "Don't be insulted. My father is a genius in a perverted sort of way. He's like a junkyard dog, snarling so loud that all you see is teeth without realizing the more deadly threat is being backed into an electric fence."

"I'm sure you're mistaken." She wasn't sure at all. "Charm is not one of Horace's strong suits, but I can't believe he's the cunning conniver you make him out to be." Actually she could believe it. She simply didn't want to. "A misunderstanding is all it is. We'll clear things up, get to the truth of the matter, and that will be that."

Ethan seemed to understand her reluctance to presume the worst, and oddly enough to appreciate it. "Your loyalty is admirable."

It didn't seem the proper moment to reveal that loyalty to Horace had less to do with her ambivalence than a desperate need to contradict Ethan's hurt, and offer some faint hope that his father hadn't betrayed him. "Right now," she said, grasping a firm hold on his hand, "we've more important matters to attend to."

His fingers laced through hers comfortably, warmly, with a gentle squeeze that made her pulse leap. "Like what?"

"Like a proper introduction to your sons." She felt his

palm cool against hers, a touch of nervous moisture. "Unless you'd rather wait a bit."

"I've already waited too long."

Taking a deep breath, Ethan allowed himself to be led into the living area where the twins were rolling miniature cars around and through the roadways of their identical plastic toys. Deirdre felt his rigidity, his uneasiness, saw fear in his eyes, and understood it. The twins were almost three now, old enough to accept or reject his attempt to reenter their lives.

Tommy was engrossed in play, making such loud zooming sounds as he ran his little car along the floor that he didn't notice their approach. Timmy did notice. Dropping his car, he scooted backward until partially concealed by a nearby end table.

"Boys," Deirdre said brightly. "There's someone I'd like you to meet."

Tommy flashed a grin over his shoulder. "I got a wed car."

Ethan moistened his lips, squatted down. "So you do. It looks like a red Corvette. Do you like Corvettes?"

The child's eyes went blank. "Wed car," he repeated.

A flash of distress puckered Ethan's forehead before he regrouped to focus on the shy boy kneeling behind the table. "Hello, Timmy."

Timmy scuttled back a few inches, stuffed one fist in his mouth while the other remained hidden behind his back.

"Do you have a favorite car, too?" Ethan asked.

Timmy nodded, still chewing his fingers.

"What color is it?"

After a moment's hesitation, the child withdrew the hand behind his back to display a tiny toy.

"Ah, blue. Is blue your favorite color?"

Timmy shook his head.

"What is your favorite?"

Blinking rapidly, Timmy glanced up at Deirdre for courage. She smiled, nodded to encourage him. The boy shuddered, carefully removed his wet hand from his mouth. "Red."

"So you both like red?"

Timmy nodded again, stuffed his fist back into his mouth. Silence descended as the three Devlins, one large, two small, eyed each other. Ethan seemed at a loss, as if he simply didn't know how to communicate with these children he so deeply loved, but didn't really know. "You've grown so much," he blurted. "I had no idea what big boys you'd become."

"I—I—I go potty by myself," Tommy announced proudly. "Timmy makes his bed all wet."

"Uh-uh!" Aghast at the revelation, Timmy bounced the blue car off his brother's skull. Tommy howled, grabbed his head while his furious twin leapt forth, flailing his tiny fists in mortified fury.

Although clearly stunned by the transformation from shy child to lethal weapon, Ethan instinctively held the struggling little boy while his brother hid behind Deirdre and sobbed. "Whoa, buddy, you can't go around hitting people just because you get mad."

Timmy suddenly dissolved into tears. "I big, too."

"Of course you are," Ethan said, gathering the distressed child into his arms. "You're such a big boy, it takes my breath away. The last time I saw you, Timmy, you were so little, you wouldn't even walk unless you could hold on to a table with both hands." Timmy sniffed, eyed Ethan with renewed curiosity. "And you had this habit of carrying a bottle around in your mouth. You'd bite the nipple between your teeth so the plastic bottle dangled down like a baby elephant's trunk. I used to call you Jumbo.''

A small smile quivered at the edge of Timmy's wet little mouth. He sniffed again, wiped his wet face, regarded Ethan with a flicker of something Deirdre hoped was a memory. Meanwhile Tommy had become uncomfortably aware that he was no longer the center of attention. Wriggling out of Deirdre's embrace, Tommy pushed his way onto Ethan's lap, elbowing his twin out of the way.

Dislodged from his place of honor, Timmy scowled, folded his fat little arms into an angry shield that made him look so much like his father that Deirdre nearly laughed out loud.

Not one to be ignored, Tommy yanked on Ethan's shirt. ''I—I—I Jumbo, too!''

Grinning now, Ethan focused on his more exuberant child. ''Actually, I called you Mumbo, because you babbled in baby talk all the time, but no one could ever figure out what you were trying to say.''

Tommy seemed tickled by the notion. ''Me Mumbo, him Jumbo.''

Ethan laughed, Timmy scowled, Deirdre nearly wept with relief. The ice had been broken. One revelation remained, however. It was a big one.

''Ethan, perhaps you could remind the boys of that special name they had for you.''

A flash of fear, a hiss of breath as he filled his lungs. He angled a wary glance at Deirdre, then swallowed hard before returning his attention to the rapt youngsters jockeying for position in his lap. ''Do you remember what you used to call me when you were little?'' he asked.

The boys quieted, gazed up, and shook their heads in unison.

Deirdre held her breath. She'd never spoken to the twins about their father, had never even thought to ask Horace or Nettie what the children had been told about him. She had no idea what their reaction might be.

Judging from Ethan's tense expression, he had no idea either. He finally exhaled all at once, forced a poignant smile. "Daddy," he said quietly. "You called me Daddy."

A hush settled over the room, thick enough to slice. Timmy cocked his head, eyed Ethan as if seeing him for the first time. Tommy squirmed, pursed his lips as if in concentration. Neither child spoke. Neither adult breathed.

After a small eternity of silence, Ethan cleared his throat. "You can call me Daddy now, too. I'd really like that."

Timmy stuffed his fist in his mouth, angled a questioning glance at his twin, upon whom he clearly relied to decide such matters. For a moment Deirdre feared the boys would reject Ethan's request...reject Ethan.

Just when she thought her pent-up breath might explode from her chest, Tommy suddenly heaved an exaggerated shrug that lifted his small shoulders up to his ears. "Okay. Want juice now."

Ethan angled a glance upward, his eyes moist with joy. Deirdre couldn't have spoken if she'd wanted to. Her throat was blocked by a lump of emotion. Ethan had been accepted by his children.

A crucial first step. But the journey had just begun.

"Hold still, buddy."

"Not tight, Daddy."

"Okay, son, not tight."

Standing on the grassy lawn, Timmy squirmed, shifted

an anxious glance toward his brother, who was inspecting bushes on the far side of the yard while a frustrated Ethan struggled to tie shoelaces on sneakers so tiny, he could have concealed the pair in his palm. He felt awkward, tentative, embarrassed by the difficulty in forcing his numb fingers to perform the delicate task. A dad was supposed to teach his sons how to grow into men. How could he do that when he couldn't even handle a simple skill like tying a shoelace?

The entire day had been frightening, exhilarating, poignant and sobering. Ethan didn't know how to be a father. He just didn't. If not for Deirdre swooping in to redirect focus, or handle awkward moments, Ethan honestly didn't know what he'd have done.

For months he'd dreamed of being reunited with his sons. In his mind's eye, he'd envisioned two babies toddling into his arms with welcoming grins, and the image had made his heart ache. He'd never followed through in his imagination, never gone beyond that first fatherly hug.

He'd never considered the daily details, like de-crusting one peanut butter sandwich, and cutting the other into precise triangles. Improper preparation, he'd discovered, led to angry tears. Just about every frustration in the twins' young lives led to angry tears. Anything from unacceptable slicing to chipped cookies, to a glass of juice containing a millimeter less liquid than deemed appropriate, all fodder for a tiny tantrum and vocal protestation liberally sprinkled with the boys' favorite word—*No!*

There was more to this father business than Ethan had dared imagine. He was awed by the responsibility, unnerved by the instinctive understanding Deirdre displayed of behavior that left him befuddled, bewildered and downright scared.

"Too tight, Daddy, too tight!" Clearly anxious to be released from tedious personal housekeeping, Timmy yanked his foot away, leaving the shoelace untied and dangling over the side of the sneaker.

Embarrassed, frustrated, Ethan heaved a sigh. He'd just spent two minutes on a five-second chore, and still hadn't gotten it right. "I know, buddy. Let Dad try again, okay?"

Timmy backed up, shaking his head, just as Tommy came dashing over with his hands cupped together and a mischievous gleam in his eye.

"Look!" Tommy chortled, opening his palms an inch from his brother's startled face to expose the fattest, ugliest potato beetle Ethan had ever seen. "He's gonna eat you all up!"

With a shriek that could shatter glass, Timmy knocked Ethan flat on his back, used his stomach as a springboard and bolted across the yard screaming wildly. Tommy let out a gleeful whoop and took off after him, threatening to stuff the hideous bug in his terrified brother's ear.

Timmy shrieked.

Tommy taunted.

Ethan wheezed.

Barely able to breathe, he struggled to refill his lungs, vaguely aware that the patio door had opened. Deirdre's voice filtered from what seemed a great distance, barely distinguishable through the ringing in his ears.

"Tommy, stop teasing your brother. What the— Oh, what a vile creature! Put it down this instant."

Ethan rolled onto his stomach, and managed to lift his face out of the grass just as Deirdre flung the bug into the bushes. She shuddered adorably, gathered the sobbing Timmy into her arms. "There, there, darling, 'twas homely to be sure, but one of God's creatures all the same.''

Mesmerized, Ethan watched Deirdre wipe one moist face, shine an angelic smile at the other and miraculously create contentment out of chaos. She was incredible, he decided. Probably the most perfect human being on the face of the earth.

Too bad she'd sworn allegiance to the enemy.

"Go on with you," she said, giving one denim-clad bottom an affectionate pat. "If you two can't play nice, I'll assume you're needing an early nap."

"No!" came the simultaneous reply. Before she could do more than issue a light laugh that did peculiar things to Ethan's heart, the twins scampered off to play on a swing set on the far side of the yard.

Eyes twinkling with amusement, Deirdre sauntered toward Ethan, who was still sprawled prostrate on the grass like a monk at prayers. "Is it a doormat, or is it a daddy?"

"It's both." Ethan rolled over, levered into a sitting position. "Or perhaps it's neither." He groaned, raked his hair. "Maybe I'm not cut out to be a parent."

"Having second thoughts, are we?" Clucking her tongue, she knelt beside him with a sweet smile on her lips and compassion in her eyes. "Too late for that, big guy. You are officially a dad, and a fine one indeed."

"How can you say that? I panic when they start squabbling, I don't know how to cut a decent sandwich and I can't even tie a shoelace. I don't know the first thing about being a father."

"Ah, but you do."

Her hand was warm against his cheek. It was a natural gesture for her, he knew. He tried not to read too much into it, but his heart jittered in his chest, and his breathing shallowed at her touch and he could no longer feel his limbs because every fiber of his being was focused on this exquisite woman whose nearness never ceased to overwhelm him.

"The first thing about being a father is the love," she said. "And yours, Ethan, is bright as a beacon. Your children see it, feel it, know it. That's all that matters. The rest will come soon enough. Parenthood takes practice, like everything else."

She said it with such strength, such conviction that for that moment all doubts dissipated. "I know." He covered her hand with his, pressing her palm more closely against his face. Her cheeks pinked, as if she'd suddenly realized the intimacy of her touch. She made no move to retrieve her hand, but gazed into his eyes with a question he wasn't ready to answer.

Ethan didn't trust himself, didn't trust his instincts, his ability to discern reality from the fantasy of his heart. No matter how deeply this woman affected him, he couldn't lose sight of the fact that she worked for a man who'd sworn to destroy him.

As if reading his thoughts, the tip of a deliciously pink tongue peeked from the corner of her mouth, betraying anxiety. "Ethan, you must believe that I'm on your side. I—" She yanked her hand away as her gaze flitted over his shoulder.

At the same moment, the twins scampered across the yard, squealing in delight.

"Gamma!"

"Gwamma!"

Ethan swiveled around in time to see his sons charge into his mother's waiting arms.

"Gamma, Gamma, Daddy is here!"

"Yeah, Gwamma, our—our—our *real Daddy!*"

As the twins scuttled into the house, Nettie glanced up with moist eyes. ''Yes,'' she murmured, ''he certainly is.''

Emotion surged into Ethan's throat. He was vaguely aware that Deirdre was on her feet, briskly brushing grass from the knee of her slacks. He also stood, his attention riveted on the woman who had borne him, nurtured him, loved him all his life.

He'd missed his mother, missed her smile, missed the rock of support she'd always offered him. Warmth seeped through his veins, a sense of peace and well-being that he hadn't experienced in a very long time. Everyone he loved was here now. His children, his beloved mother and a woman who had touched him more deeply than any other.

A touch of trust hovered around his heart, trust in Deirdre, whom he never doubted had created these moments with his children, trust in the mother who had never truly failed him, trust in life itself. For the first time he honestly believed that everything would be all right, that the future would turn out as it should.

Those eyes, those magnificent eyes, windows to a valiant soul he couldn't conceal, not from her. Deirdre knew this man, knew him better than she knew her own mind, better than she'd known the husband who had been so dear to her.

This was the man of her heart. She knew it, felt it, was dizzy with the thrill of it. He knew it, too. She could see it in his eyes. And she could see the trust resurfacing, little by little, that spark of faith that had drained away when he'd learned she worked for his father.

Now Deirdre watched Ethan's reunion with his mother, hoping that trust wouldn't be shaken.

Nettie gazed at her son with a poignant smile. "You're looking well, dear. It's so good to see you."

Ethan took Nettie's hands, placed a warm kiss on her cheek. They were nearly the same height, Deirdre noted, this stately woman and the magnificent man who was her son.

"You look pretty good yourself," Ethan told her. "How have you been?"

"Wonderful, dear." She took a step back without releasing his hands, scrutinized him as mothers tend to do. "You've lost too much weight. Aren't you eating well?"

His cheerful laugh rumbled straight into Deirdre's heart. He was truly happy, she realized, and she could have wept with joy for him. "What is it with women always trying to stuff food into a man's mouth?" He laughed again, angled a warm glance in Deirdre's direction. "Don't worry, Mom. Deirdre is a wonderful cook. She's been taking very good care of me."

Nettie lit up. "Has she now? Isn't that delightful!"

Ethan's smile spoke volumes. "Yes," he murmured. "Delightful."

"Oh, my, that reminds me," she murmured. "Deirdre, dear, Horace would like to see you back at the office right away."

Since Deirdre wasn't scheduled to return to the office until tomorrow morning, the request was unexpected. "Is anything wrong?"

"Not that I'm aware of. He does seem anxious to see you, though. Something about the investigator you hired—" Nettie pursed her lips, offered a befuddled shrug. "Horace was rather tight-lipped about details, but he did seem quite eager to hear your report. I presumed you'd understand what it was all about."

Deirdre sighed. That danged Rodriguez case would be the death of her. "Yes, I—"

The words clogged in her throat as Ethan's cold gaze sliced like a blade. "Of course she does, Mother." Harsh, raw, rough with anger. There was no trust in his eyes now, no hope, no faith, only the silent fury of betrayal. "Deirdre and Horace understand each other perfectly."

Deirdre felt as if she'd swallowed a brick. "Ethan, no, it's not what you think."

"You'd better hurry." His jaw twitched. "My father doesn't like to be kept waiting."

"Ethan, please—"

"Close the gate on your way out." With that, he ushered his mother into the house and slid the patio door shut.

Deirdre stormed into Horace's office with murder in her eye, slammed his door behind her even though he was on the telephone. His eyes widened, then narrowed quickly. "I'll call you back" was all he managed before Deirdre snatched the receiver out of his hand and hung up the phone.

She flung the "Subject X" file on his desk. "This is Ethan, isn't it? You sicced a private investigator on your own son."

"I did no such thing, my dear." Horace regarded her for a moment, the hint of a smile tugging one corner of his mouth. "You did."

At that moment, Deirdre saw the Machiavellian gleam in his eye, and realized that Ethan wasn't the only one who'd been set up.

Chapter Eight

Nettie had always worn disapproval like the latest fashion, with immense dignity and thinly veiled pride. Ethan had barely clicked the sliding glass door shut when he felt the power of his mother's reproach singe the back of his neck.

"That was unkind, dear. Deirdre is a fine young woman. She doesn't deserve to be so disdainfully dismissed."

"I know." Ethan rarely argued with his mother even when she was wrong. He certainly wouldn't dispute her when she was right. "She's caught in the middle of this mess—" he cast a fond glance over his shoulder "—as are you."

Nettie smiled, held out her arms. Stepping forward, Ethan embraced her, comforted by her familiar fragrance, the welcoming warmth of maternal love that he'd never questioned throughout the dark days of estrangement.

A fierce hug, a motherly pat on the shoulder, and she took a single step back, maintaining a firm grasp on his upper arms as if fearing the loss of physical contact. "It warmed me to see you playing with your sons. They are so like you, Ethan. Such a precious gift, the opportunity of reliving those joyous years of childhood all over again."

"A gift is given, not stolen." Regret pricked him as the light drained from her eyes. She turned away, clasping her hands together as was her habit when faced with unpleasantry. It was a silent request for curtailment, for the courteous avoidance his mother had always favored in lieu of direct confrontation.

In the past Ethan would have respected the mute appeal. His pain was too deep now. It roughened his tone. "I understand Horace's motivation. Two more chances to re-create himself, to mold his own image from the soft clay of a child's mind. Hurting me was just an added bonus."

Nettie spun around, eyes wide in protest. "That's not—"

"But you went along with it, Mother. More than that, you encouraged it."

"Ethan—"

"Why? Why are you trying to take my children away?"

A flash of white, a glimpse of tooth scraped her lower lip before she turned her face away. "We were trying to protect you, Ethan, you and the children. You were so terribly injured, so terribly alone. You needed all your strength just to survive. When that woman abandoned you and your babies, we had no choice but to step in, to care for them while you recovered."

"Look at me, Mother." He paused until her reluctant

gaze met his. "I am well, I am whole and I want my children back."

"It's too soon."

"That's not for you to say."

"Yes, it is." Nettie's trademark strength squared her shoulders, hardened in her eyes. "Physically you have recovered. Emotionally you are still wounded, still struggling to come to terms with how your life has changed. You can't go back, Ethan. The past isn't available to you. It's time to go forward."

"I am going forward."

"No, you're trying to recapture what was, ignoring your limitations and trying to re-create a career that's no longer available to you." The force of her words knocked him back a step. She continued on as if his struggle for breath was of no concern to her. "When we brought the children here, they were babies, but they knew their world had been torn apart. Timmy began to withdraw, to exhibit fear of being abandoned. He feared strangers, would cling to my skirt every time I tried to leave the house and would sob uncontrollably until I returned. Tommy handled his fears with bravado, by becoming more and more aggressive. He stopped speaking for months, not even uttering the few words of baby talk he'd learned. All he did was grunt and howl like an angry animal. Both boys were prone to temper tantrums, but Tommy was the worst. He'd throw anything he could get his hands on, and when there was nothing more at hand he'd throw himself. He'd kick and shriek and pound the floor with his little fists, and with his head. We feared for his safety, we feared for his brother's safety. Most of all we feared for his mind, his emotional stability. And as Tommy vented his fury, Timmy withdrew further and further into the sanctity of his own world."

There was more, much more. Each word struck like a bullet, a burning pain in the soul. Ethan flinched, cringing as his mother continued to describe the twins' agonized adjustment to a world not of their choosing, a world they couldn't understand.

In excruciating detail Nettie related the patient months of recovery and growth as the tiny boys came to terms with the profundity of their loss with the protective adaptability of a child's mind. "It took time for them to feel safe with us, Ethan. You can't simply snatch them away from that safety without regard to what they've been through."

He shook his head, not so much to refute what his mother was saying, but to throw off the impact of her words. "I'm not trying to do that."

She moistened her lips, steadied her gaze. "If you were to regain custody of the children tomorrow, what would you do?"

"Do?" The question shouldn't have been unexpected, but it was. "I'd take them home."

"Your home or theirs?" When he simply stared at her, she went on. "You'd take them back to Los Angeles, wouldn't you?" He conceded that by averting his gaze. "You'd separate them from the only family they know, then you'd go back to work, leaving them in the care of strangers."

"Strangers like Deirdre?" Having exposed the paradox of her argument, he expected her to flinch.

Instead, her eyes softened and glowed. "Deirdre is wonderful, isn't she? So loving and intuitive. The children adore her." A sly gleam flashed so quickly, he barely saw it. "From what I observed a few moments ago, you seem rather impressed by her yourself."

"That isn't the point." He squirmed in place, as aggravated by having exposed feelings he wasn't even ready to acknowledge as he was by having those emotions used against him. "You've already placed the children in the care of a stranger—"

"Deirdre is not a stranger, dear."

"Not to mention the fact I was in day care when I was the twins' age. It didn't warp me."

"You hadn't been repeatedly yanked from place to place, from world to world, abandoned by everyone you loved." She extended a pleading hand. "Think about it, Ethan, think of how alone you feel right now, how betrayed and abandoned you feel, and imagine how a child would react to what you are going through. You are driven by recapturing your past, by returning to a job that nearly killed you once, a job you are no longer capable of performing."

"That's not true." Blood rushed to his head, made him dizzy. "I'm a good cop. I've always been able to do the job, and I always will. A weak hand doesn't change that."

Nettie exhaled in that slow, familiar way that indicated she was not being understood. The fight drained from her eyes, replaced by sad resignation, and a determination he recognized as impenetrable. "The children deserve stability, security, the love of a parent who puts their needs above all else. You can't give them that, Ethan, not now, not while you're obsessed by a reality that no longer exists."

A peculiar wheezing sound rushed by. He realized it was coming from him. His father's investigators hadn't missed anything. "So it all goes back to that. Give up my career, capitulate to Horace's blackmail or suffer the consequences. Same dance, different tune."

Her sigh was soft, sad. "I have not always approved

of Horace's tactics in the past, and believed it was wrong of him to try and force you into a career not of your own choosing. But this isn't about you and your father, it's about your children.''

"That's right, Mother. *My* children. Not yours, not his. *Mine.*''

Her lips whitened, the flesh on her chin crumpled like a wadded bag. "Children are not possessions, nor are they prized pets. They are human beings who deserve to be nurtured, cherished and loved. You can't give them that, Ethan. You don't know how." Her eyes softened. "It's not your fault, dear. Your heart has been hardened by betrayal, and you've protected yourself by learning to turn your emotions on and off like a spigot."

The accusation was not meant to wound, but it did. As much as Ethan wanted to deny his mother's hurtful allegation, he couldn't. Nor could he face it as truth. Instead, he teetered in emotional limbo, neither accepting nor rejecting the observation of a woman who knew him better than he knew himself.

A cold fog of silence shrouded the kitchen, muted his heart. He turned to gaze through the glass door to watch his children playing in the yard, and felt a smile settle comfortably in place. He did love them, loved them with every breath in his body. "Are they really better off without me?"

"No, never." Nettie came up behind him, laid a loving hand on his arm. "You are their father, Ethan. They need you in their lives." She paused as he turned back to face her. "But they still need us, too. Go slowly, dear. Give them time, give yourself time. You all have so much to learn about each other."

"I don't even know where to start."

She hugged him then and whispered against his cheek, "Just open your heart, Ethan, let yourself love again."

It would have been easier to step out of his skin.

Deirdre stared at the carbon copy of the contract she'd approved her first day on the job. "This means nothing. You gave me a stack of invoices and agreements to process, and I processed them. I had no idea who this anonymous subject was, and certainly had no conscious intent to approve covert espionage on your son."

"What you intended is irrelevant. You hired the investigator, approved the parameters of the surveillance and authorized payment." Chuckling, Horace leaned back in his chair. "You see, Deirdre, fact is irrefutable. Your signature is a fact. In a court of law, intent is frequently surmised from action. But is every action a purposeful result of intent? Apparently not."

The move was brilliant, effectively offering anecdotal evidence that what appeared obvious became nebulous when the question of intent was examined by a talented litigator. Deirdre backed off emotionally, allowing herself a moment to slip into a more objective frame of mind. She laid the contract copy on his desk, chose her words carefully. "So you concede that you've had your son followed, but would have me believe that your intention, which you've not yet explained to my liking, was pure."

Horace shrugged. "Define *pure*." Frustrated by the verbal joust, Deirdre would have left had Horace not spoken with a weariness that gave her pause. "Sit down, Deirdre. Please."

When she hesitated, he retrieved a key from his pocket, unlocked a desk drawer and pulled out a fat folder. She knew without seeing the label that it was the "Subject X" file.

A twitch at the corner of Horace's mouth betrayed emotion. Deirdre noticed because Ethan had the same habit, a delicate clench of jaw that was nearly imperceptible but for the tiny quiver at the edge of his lips. It was, she'd noted, the only visible hint of inner turmoil by both men who'd otherwise perfected the art of concealing emotion from casual observers. "This is my son's file." He laid it on the desk, pushed it toward her. "Read it. Then we'll talk."

The file both beckoned and repulsed her. "Whatever is in that file, it is none of my business."

"Really?" He narrowed his gaze, scrutinizing her as if every thought in her mind was scrolled across her forehead in Gothic script. "That wasn't the impression I got when you burst in here demanding to know why I'd had Ethan investigated." Her cheeks warmed at his knowing gleam. "Make up your mind, Deirdre. Is my son your business, or is he not? The choice is yours."

Flushing furiously, she snatched the file, sat down and began to read.

An hour later, Deirdre laid the file on the edge of the desk. A tear slipped down her face. She wiped it away, struggled to maintain a modicum of dignity. "Does Ethan know?"

"That his wife had been cheating on him since the day he met her?" Horace shook his head, retrieved a tissue box from his drawer. "The marriage was a mistake from the beginning. I suspect Ethan understood that, and was struggling with his own conscience as to whether he should stay or go. It was his choice."

She plucked a tissue from the proffered box, dabbed at her wet eyes. "His choice, yet you had her followed. Why?"

"To prove I was right, I suppose." There was a wistful quality to his reply that took her by surprise. "I'm a man who wants to be right, you see. I never liked that girl, never trusted her. If I'd kept my mouth shut, Ethan would have eventually seen her for what she was, and dumped her like a hot rock." Horace heaved a resigned sigh. "He only married her to prove me wrong."

"But you weren't wrong."

"No, I wasn't wrong."

"You could have shown him this report, could have rubbed his nose in it, made yourself feel pompous and superior." She saw the glint in his eye, noted the subtle shift of his shoulder, but didn't care. A ache in her heart fueled the relentless attack, a throb of exquisite pain for Ethan, for all that he'd endured and for all he was destined to suffer if he ever discovered the depth of his former wife's betrayal. "After all, that was what you wanted, was it not? Proof of your righteousness, a shatterproof heel to grind your own son's ego into dust. It was the weapon you sought, yet you never turned it on your enemy. Why?"

Startled, Horace shifted in his chair, seemed wounded by her words. "My son is not my enemy."

"Isn't he?" A peculiar tingle lifted the hairs on her nape. The older man's bafflement seemed genuine, as did his sadness at the accusation Deirdre had laid out with cunning care. Horace's response would be crucial. If Ethan was correct, if his father truly was out to destroy him, then reconciliation would be impossible, and Deirdre's mission was at an end. But deep down, Deirdre didn't believe that. She'd seen another side of Horace Devlin, a compassion and sense of justice frequently overshadowed by vanity and bluster. Was she right about him?

Or was Ethan right?

"My son is a fool," Horace said finally. Deirdre's heart sank. "Ethan is a good man in a bad world, trying to squeeze a place for himself without elbowing anyone else aside. He has his mother's heart—too soft, too trusting, too easily bruised. Success is the measure of a man, not sacrifice and self-immolation." Horace raised his voice to drown out a quiver. "I've tried to toughen him up, teach him the skills he needed to survive. If he hates me for that, so be it. I've done my job as a father, and by God, I've done it well. He's already survived what would have killed a lesser man. That's proof enough for me."

He was nearly shouting by now, punctuating his fervor by slamming his fist on the desk to emphasize each point. It was a telling display, one Deirdre recognized as a concealment technique both Devlin males frequently used, displaying an emotion in direct opposition to the one actually experienced.

"You admire him," she said quietly. "And you're afraid for him." Horace's eyes jittered, his Adam's apple bobbed. He didn't confirm her assessment, nor did he dispute it. "So why is it, I'm wondering, that you didn't tell him about his wife's infidelity?"

"What good would it have done? He'd have stayed with her just to spite me."

Deirdre studied him for a moment, saw the faraway look in his eyes. A thought struck her. "You didn't want to hurt him, did you?" Horace blinked rapidly, as if chagrined to have been caught in an act of compassion. "That's it, isn't it? You had your proof, could have lorded it over him that you'd been right, and he'd been wrong, could have destroyed his ego, his self-esteem, and broken his heart. But when it came right down to it, you couldn't do it, could you? You couldn't do it because you loved him too much to see him suffer.''

Clearly taken aback, Horace blustered, wheezed and finally pushed his chair back with a puff of indignance. ''The woman was pregnant,'' he said finally.

Deirdre digested the timing of that occurrence, and was chilled by it. ''You must have wondered if Ethan was the father.''

''Yes.''

''Do you still wonder?''

''No.'' A smile softened his eyes without extending to his lips. ''The boys are his. They are the image of him.''

''And if they hadn't been, would you have told Ethan?''

''Ethan would have known.''

That may or may not have been true; however, Deirdre doubted Horace would have revealed his information in either case. Family was too important to him, and to Nettie. Instinctively she realized that both grandparents would have loved and accepted the children no matter who had fathered them. She also realized that if Horace had doubted the twins' parentage, he would have gone to the end of the earth to keep Ethan from learning the truth.

She shook her head, bemused by the complexity of this father-son relationship, and bewildered by the paradox of a man who clearly adored his son, yet had repeatedly violated his trust. ''You had no right to interfere with his marriage,'' she said. ''You had no right to have his wife followed.''

''Is that what you'll tell Ethan?''

The question startled her. ''I'll be telling him nothing.''

''Why not? You're always harping about honesty. It

would be dishonest for you to withhold the information now that you have it.''

"Is that why you showed me the file, to make me complicit in your dirty dealings?''

"Partly, I suppose.'' He returned the file to his drawer, and locked it. "A parent has rights over his children, even grown children, that the rest of society doesn't have.''

"That's not what the law says.''

"The law, my dear, is an ass.'' He smiled. "Someone famous said that. I don't recall who. At any rate, my son and I don't communicate. I can't simply pick up the phone and ask how his therapy is progressing, how his life is going. Anything I want to know has to be reported to me by others.''

"You had him followed to the toy store.''

"Yes.''

"You found out what he bought for his children, and you deliberately bought the same thing for them.''

"Yes.''

The matter-of-fact answers infuriated her. "So Ethan was right. You were sending him a message.''

"Yes.'' Horace smiled. "One I knew he'd understand.''

"He understood, all right. Anything he can do, you can do better.''

For the first time, Deirdre saw uncertainty in the older man's eyes. "Is that what Ethan believes?''

"It is.''

"I see.'' A chilling bleakness darkened his eyes. He reached into the candy bowl, comforting himself with the familiar routine of unwrapping the colorful confection. "Have you completed your report on the Rodriguez matter?''

Deirdre realized that she'd gone too far. The door to honest emotion had cracked open, only to slam in her face. "Mr. Devlin, I am truly sorry if you're offended—"

"Five o'clock," he growled, snatching the telephone. "On my desk." His finger hovered over the touchpad, although he didn't punch in a number. Deirdre doubted he intended to. "Didn't you hear me?"

"I did indeed, Mr. Devlin." Crossing her legs, she settled into the chair.

A withering stare pinned her in place. "No one is irreplaceable, Ms. O'Connor. Not even you."

"Indeed, I am quite replaceable. Your family is not." She offered her sweetest smile, to which he responded with the expression of a puppy caught doing a naughty on the living room rug. "But of course, you already know that, so let's stop the blarney jig and get down to business."

His bluff called, Horace cradled the receiver. *Defeat* was not a word he recognized, of course, but his body language indicated a willingness to negotiate.

Which was exactly what Deirdre had been waiting for.

"A waste of water," she mumbled as Dublin happily lapped a drink from the running faucet. "You've a perfectly good bowl of liquid refreshment beside your supper dish. I can't believe it tastes any better in vertical mode."

The kitten issued a sad mew when she turned off the water.

"Don't give me that look." She sighed as her pet pawed the knob, tilting a curious head as if wondering how to create the miracle of running water from such a peculiar plastic orb. She couldn't help but laugh. "So you've figured out the delivery system, have you? Clever little devil.'' If cats had fingers, she decided, there was little doubt that they'd take over the world.

She scooped the animal into a snuggly hug, then set him on the floor. ''Be off with you now. Go hunt a bug or chase that wad of aluminum foil you're so fond of.''

Dublin wiggled his tail and attacked her ankle instead. The sting of needle-sharp little claws was softened by delight at his playful antics. Giggling madly, she shook off the determined creature, squealing in mock horror as he chased her around the kitchen. Just as she dodged Dublin's pirouetted pounce, the rattle of pipes caught her attention.

Water was running in Ethan's apartment.

Deirdre froze, gazing at the tile beyond the sink with such intensity that she could actually envision the outline of him standing there.

She wasn't the only one intrigued by the sound. Dublin leapt to the counter, meowing frantically. He rubbed the tile, purring loudly. Beyond the wall, the water turned off. Dublin meowed again.

A masculine whisper raised goose bumps on Deirdre's arms. ''Hey, Dubby.'' The animal responded with a yowl of greeting, then hoisted on his haunches like a whiskered prairie dog and scratched at the tiles.

Leaning across the counter, Deirdre heard Ethan chuckle. ''Are you being a good cat?'' he asked. ''No more sneaking out to play on the railroad tracks, eh, boy?'' On cue, the animal issued a soft trill. ''Good for you.''

Deirdre's mouth was suddenly dry. For a moment she hesitated to speak, fearing he'd leave if he realized she was here. Then she realized that he already knew she was listening, because he'd doubtless heard her own conversation with the kitten as clearly as she was hearing his voice now. It was an opening, an opportunity. Ethan was offering it. Deirdre accepted. "Hello, Ethan."

He paused a beat. "Hi."

She hoisted up on the counter, pulled her knees up under her chin and leaned against the cool tile. "Did you and your mother have a chance to talk this afternoon?"

"Yes." A scuffling sound indicated that he, too, had moved closer to the wall. "Deirdre...?" He sighed. "I'm sorry."

"Sorry about what?"

"Sorry about being such a jerk."

"Ah, 'tis that, is it?" She smiled, absently stroked the kitten scrambling over her knees. "Having spent the afternoon with your father, I've concluded that jerkiness is an inherited trait with which you've been genetically cursed." She nibbled her lip, exhaled slowly. "You were right about Horace. Indeed he is a manipulative man." She could almost feel Ethan stiffen through the wall. "He's stubborn, and pompous and downright infuriating...but he loves you, Ethan. That has to count for something."

For a moment, she feared he wouldn't answer. When he did, his voice had tightened. "Performance art is a lawyer's stock and trade. Horace has always been good at it."

Time for a different tactic, she decided. "When you went to the toy store, Ethan, you intended to buy a gift for each of the boys, didn't you?" His startled hiss was muffled, but audible. She spoke in a rush, hoping that she wouldn't compound the mistake his father had already made. "But when you found what you wanted, you couldn't afford two of them."

The only reply was the unmistakable thud of footsteps leaving the room.

Hopping down from the counter, Deirdre followed the sound of his movements into the living room. "No one is faulting you, Ethan. Out of work for nearly two years, with a mountain of medical expenses draining your savings." She'd learned that insurance had refused to cover his therapy for the past year because his physicians refused to acknowledge the possibility of further improvement. He'd proven them wrong, of course, but the cost had been dear. "It's not a shame, but a tribute that you've managed as well as you have."

She pressed her face to the wall, heard the angry footsteps move closer. His voice was even angrier. "Is that my father's strategy, to show the court I'm too broke to care for my kids?"

"Oh, you are such a stubborn sod!" Heaving a sigh, she pushed her hair behind her ears and wished she had a magic potion that would allow her to understand these irksome Devlin men. "Horace bought that gift for you, Ethan. Don't you understand? He knew you wanted each of the boys to have one, and he provided it as a peace offering. It was his way of letting you know that he was there for you, that he was willing to help." She waited, pressed her cheek to the wall. "Ethan? Did you hear what I said?"

A muffled thud quivered the Sheetrock, as if he'd leaned heavily against it. "I heard."

She swallowed, moistened her lips. "It was not the way I would have offered help, mind you, but Horace doesn't seem to view the world in the same way as most folks. To him, it made perfect sense."

A peculiar sound filtered through, like a deep sigh, or perhaps a groan coming from halfway up the wall. Deirdre sat on the floor, just as she suspected he was. A moment later, his voice vibrated through the thin barrier as if he was whispering directly into her ear. "When I was a kid, one of the neighbors was laid off his job. I heard my mother and father talking about it. Mom wanted to offer them money. My father refused, said a real man never took charity, that it would be kinder to slit the guy's throat than to offer it. I remember the incident because my parents argued that night. They so rarely argued." He was silent a moment. "The next day, my father came home with a beat-up lawn mower that probably hadn't worked in a decade. He'd paid the neighbor five hundred dollars for that lousy piece of junk. When I asked him why, he said the guy had been a shrewd negotiator."

Unable to think of an appropriate response, Deirdre remained silent. The story of helping a friend without causing him to lose face was both moving and disturbing because it revealed the compassion Horace kept hidden from the world, mingled with presumptive manipulation that was such an innate part of his personality.

"The moral is," Ethan continued, "that calling tails on a two-faced coin is a sucker bet."

"What on earth does that mean?"

"I have no idea, but it sounded profound enough that I hoped you'd be impressed."

She smiled, sighed, leaned against the wall until she could swear she felt his body heat emanating through the thin barrier. "Go on with you. 'Tis fishing for compliments, you are."

"Am I?" His voice took on a husky sensuality that thrilled her to the marrow. "And if I was, could you find one to wrap around my hook?"

"Oh, if I studied the matter, I might be able to dredge

up a wee one." She traced her fingertip along the wall, envisioning the strong jaw just beyond her reach. Closing her eyes, she imagined the rasp of whiskered stubble, the moist dip at the corner of his mouth, the delicate scar below his ear, reminder of his strength, and of his courage. "For example," she crooned softly. "I might mention the soft glow of your eyes when you gaze upon the faces of your children. Or I might comment upon that rascal twist of hair that teases a woman into smoothing it back into place. And with some serious contemplation—" she smiled at the image in her mind's eye "—I might even confess to having a sinful thought now and again."

"Sinful?" A rustle against the wall. "Tell me more."

"Hmm, it would puff up your ego, I'm sure."

"My ego is flatter than roadkill. It could use puffing."

"Ah, well in that case…" Her fingers flexed against the wall. She could practically feel the muscles of his magnificent shoulders ripple like waves over a hot sea. "They say a woman's hair is her crowning glory," she whispered. "For a man, 'tis his strength. Not just the flesh and bone, the twist of corded muscle, but the power of tenderness, a lust for gentle sensuality that sweeps a woman to passion."

She heard his breath catch…or perhaps it was hers. A wave of wet warmth enveloped her, a sexual arousal that shook her to the core. She wanted him. She wanted him so intimately, with such incredible force that her body shook with the power of it, with the need to hold him, to have him, to feel him deep inside until their bodies, their souls, and their spirits were so tightly entwined that neither knew where one ended and the other began.

"Deirdre…?"

A spasm physically rocked her, a painful paroxysm of

regret. She didn't answer him, couldn't answer him. At that moment, she wanted him more than she wanted her next breath.

And she was determined to have him.

Chapter Nine

Ethan rested his head against the cool plaster, eyes closed, mind ablaze with images of the woman whose vivid essence seeped through the walled barrier to permeate his very soul. He'd followed the sound of her movements for hours, mentally absorbing the nuances of her life as if his own meant nothing without it. His voice was a whisper, a sigh slipped out unbidden. "Are you wet?"

A stifled hiss of breath vibrated from beyond the wall, jolting him forward.

"I meant from the shower," he blurted. "Wet from the shower. I heard it running a while back. Not that I was listening—" He was making it worse, but couldn't seem to stop himself. "I mean, I was listening of course, but I wasn't...wasn't..."

Wasn't imagining her naked?

Wasn't imagining rivulets of water sluicing over her

voluptuous breasts, streaming down her soft belly into the moistness between her lush thighs?

Wasn't imagining himself stepping into that shower with her, pressing himself against her slick, soapy skin? Wasn't imagining the rising steam, the racing blood, the hiss of breath pulsing with passion?

A bead of sweat stung his eyes. He blinked it away, struggled for breath. "I wasn't paying attention," he lied.

"Oh." She almost sounded disappointed. "The walls are thin. It's difficult not to hear."

"Yes." A lump in his throat damn near choked him. "Difficult."

A soft rustle, as if she'd nuzzled against the plaster on her side of the wall. He responded automatically, pressing himself closer, thrilled by the delicate lift of hairs along his forearms when her aura reached out to him. Her voice floated like sweet music. "I am, you know."

"You are what?"

"Wet."

Goose bumps erupted from nape to spine. He moistened his lips. He could hear her moving, instinctively knew she was finger-combing her hair, which was doubtless still damp since he hadn't heard the telltale whine of the hair dryer.

It was the wet hair she was referring to. Intellectually he knew that. Emotionally he recognized the husk of her voice, the raw sensuality of her chosen words. Was she deliberately enticing him? Or was he so obsessed with this woman that he read sexual motive into the most casual conversation? "Are you?"

"Yes." She hesitated. "My gown is damp."

The image made him dizzy. "You should take it off."

"Excuse me?"

"I mean, ah…" He slapped his forehead, called himself six kinds of fool. "You could catch a chill."

A hint of amusement twinkled through her reply. "Right you are. It would be much warmer, me sitting here bare as a plucked hen."

Ethan could picture that in living color. His groin tightened. "Not if it's as hot on your side of the wall as it is over here."

She paused a beat. "It is indeed."

Puffing his cheeks, he blew out a breath, shifting his weight to alleviate the pressure building between his legs. Sweat beaded across his upper lip, trickled down his bare chest to dampen the fleece waistband of his tattered gray sweatpants. "My furnace seems to be stuck on high."

"Mine, too." Her voice was tiny, thin, unaccustomed to the double entendre of a seductress. "Perhaps we could—" a muted rubbing sound, rather like a fingertip stroking the plaster "—do something about that."

"Do something?"

"Yes." She lowered her voice. "Something to…cool the heat."

Ethan swallowed hard. A downward glance wasn't necessary to realize his arousal had stretched the floppy fleece, not to mention his nerves, to the breaking point. It was a peculiar sensation, so alien to his world the past few years that he'd almost forgotten what it felt like to be a pulsating, sensual being.

"Ethan?"

He rested his cheek against the plaster, laid his fingertips over the wall to join the rubbing motion from the other side. A prickle spread to his palms. He could almost feel her touch, could almost smell the sweet fragrance of her damp hair so very close to him, yet so very far away. "I'm here."

A breath rushed from beyond the barrier. "I miss you, Ethan. I miss our...friendship."

It was more than friendship. Or at least, it could have been. Would have been, had reality not intruded. "I miss it, too."

"Do you?"

The memory of her kiss taunted him, the lingering flavor of her lips, the paradox of chilling heat seeping down his spine when she'd melted into his arms. A Technicolor splash of twilight sky had paled in comparison to the burst of brilliance in his mind, the vivid explosion of light and color evoked by a kiss so intense that reminiscence made his heart race and his blood steam.

"I still care about you, Ethan."

He didn't answer right away. "I care about you, too." He paused to cherish the softness of her sigh. "I've never met anyone like you, Deirdre. There's a gentleness to your soul that envelops all you touch. Every time I gaze into your smiling eyes, every time I hear that lilting Irish voice, a sense of peace wraps around me like a blanket of sheer heaven." Closing his eyes, he let his head fall back against the wall. An ache of regret tightened his chest, roughened his words. "You make me feel whole again. You make me feel like a man."

A swish, a subtle vibration as if she'd laid her head against the wall. "It is a man that you are, Ethan, strong and vibrant, with a warrior's heart and a saintly soul."

He angled a rueful glance downward. "If you were on this side of the wall, you'd realize I'm no saint."

"It would be the manly part I'd notice first?"

"I should be so lucky."

A peal of delighted laughter warmed him to the marrow. "The luck, I suspect, would be mine as well." Her tone sobered. "Never doubt yourself, Ethan. Never doubt your worth or your value as a man, for a man you are, stalwart and true. Any woman, any real woman, would fall on her knees and thank God above for the blessing of one so fine and honorable as yourself.''

Words intended to offer reassurance had the opposite effect. Ethan tensed as the image of his petulant wife rolled into his mind, a woman who had not recognized his worth as a husband, because he hadn't exhibited any. Ethan had let her down, had put his career above his marriage, had basically abandoned her in every way imaginable short of actually walking out the door.

''Ethan?''

''Yes.''

''The wall between us, it's a bit of a nuisance.''

Her words were timid, hesitant, but nonetheless potent. Ethan knew what she was suggesting, what she was asking. He knew, and he wanted desperately to give the answer she sought.

A murmur enveloped him with promise, a gentle breeze of sound trembling with nervous anticipation. ''Here we are, two adults fully grown, sitting on the floor whispering like adolescents through a flimsy piece of plaster when there is a perfectly fine door not six steps away.''

He gazed longingly at the exit in question, knew he could reach it in a matter of moments and be in the warmth of Deirdre's arms a moment after that. It was what he wanted, what he desperately wanted.

But at what cost?

The words clogged in his throat, nearly choking him before he finally spit them out. ''It's late,'' he said miserably. ''It's too late.''

Since it was nearly midnight, he could easily have been

referring to the time. He suspected Deirdre knew that he wasn't.

The tremor of her voice confirmed that. "Of course. It...it was thoughtless of me to suggest such a thing." A swishing sound crawled the wall above him, as if she'd suddenly stood. "I don't know what I was thinking. Such a foolishness. Fumes from the brandy cake I just baked must have muddled my brain." Her humiliation was palpable through the thin wall, resonating from a laugh so tight, so audibly forced it broke his heart. "Forget I mentioned it."

"Deirdre—" Ethan scrambled to his feet, pressed his ear to the wall just as hurried footsteps echoed toward her hallway. A moment later, he heard her bedroom door close.

Groaning, Ethan thunked his forehead on the wall twice, then slid back to the floor in a puddle of pure misery. She believed that he didn't want her. Nothing could have been further from the truth.

In reality Ethan was protecting Deirdre, protecting her from a past that haunted him, tormented him, revealed a truth he'd never wanted to face. He, too, was a user, a manipulator, just like his father. Perhaps even worse than his father. At least Horace knew how to love a woman, how to cherish her, how to dedicate his life to her happiness.

Only once had Ethan promised a woman all those things. False promises, lethal lies. Failure had been predestined. Truth was shattering. Ethan had never been in love with his wife. He couldn't forgive himself for that, couldn't forgive himself for lying to her. For lying to himself.

He'd been emotionally attached to his wife, had empathized with her loneliness, with the strident pretense of apathy toward a family that had rejected her, and the world of strangers she secretly feared. He'd felt protective of her weaknesses, had admired her strengths, not the least of which was a natural defiance comfortably complimenting a particularly rebellious point in his own life.

Deep down, Ethan couldn't really blame his wife for cheating on him, although he was deeply wounded that she had. Of the gamut of emotions he'd felt for the woman he'd married, the most powerful had been lust. Once his sexual appetite had been sated, he'd begun to realize how little was left, how hormonal urges had blinded him to the shallow narcissism of a woman to whom he was inexorably linked, a woman who by then had been carrying his children. He had wanted her; he had used her. In the end, he had destroyed her.

Now he wanted Deirdre. He wouldn't allow himself to destroy her, too.

"Don't run so fast, Tommy, or you'll fall on your keister." Shading her eyes, Deirdre gazed across the grassy park to watch the child fling a colorful foam ball the size of a man's fist toward his father, who made a neat, left-handed catch.

Ethan bounced the ball on his palm while the boy anxiously danced from foot to foot, waiting for the return like a frisky pup. "Are you ready?" Ethan asked.

Tommy was about to burst. "I—I—I weady!" Splaying his sneakered feet so far apart that Deirdre feared he might topple over, the child held out his arms, hands stiff and oddly angled. Several yards away, partially obscured by the park bench beside which he crouched, Timmy chewed his fingers and watched, intrigued by the game but too timid to join it.

"Okay, here it comes." Ethan lobbed a soft toss that arched between the boy's outstretched arms, and bounced off his little chest.

Frustrated, Tommy ran forward to retrieve the ball, only to inadvertently kick it into a group of passing youngsters. A boy who appeared to be five or six picked the ball up, and might have returned it if given a chance. Tommy, however, let out an indignant screech and propelled himself into the startled child with fists flailing.

Ethan reacted quickly, scooping up his angry son while the attacked child dropped the ball in the grass and ran crying to his mother. "That's not nice, Tommy. You could hurt somebody."

"My ball, mine!" Arching and bucking, Tommy wriggled out of his father's grasp long enough to snatch up the ball while continuing to howl at the top of his lungs. Clearly befuddled by the unexpected explosion, an obviously appalled and mystified Ethan struggled to calm his furious son.

By the time Deirdre reached them, Tommy had worked himself into a full-fledged tantrum. Ethan was clearly panic-stricken. "What do I do?" he blurted, ducking his head as a flailing foot whizzed past his ear. "He's gone berserk."

"Ah, but that implies he can't control himself, doesn't it?" Deirdre crouched onto the grass where the howling child kicked and flailed violently. "I suppose if Tommy truly cannot control his anger, a wee time-out might be in order—perhaps even a nap until he's feeling better."

Still clutching his precious ball, Tommy instantly jolted upright, eyes wide and surprisingly dry. "No!"

Ethan blinked, obviously startled by the child's abrupt change in demeanor. Deirdre questioned Ethan with a look, received a curt nod indicating acquiescence to her authority in the matter. She turned her attention to Tommy, whose face had scrunched into a fearsome frown that was laughable. "Being angry is okay, but hurting other people is wrong." Her voice was pleasant, her tone definitive without being accusatory. "You'll not be allowed to play with others if you can't play nice. We've talked about this before, haven't we, Tommy?"

A mischievous gleam danced in the child's eye. "I—I—I Timmy!"

Clearly taken aback, Ethan blinked from the grinning, but now angelic child in front of him to the finger-chewing youngster still hovering by a tree several yards away. He started to speak, thought better of it, then cast a woeful glance at Deirdre.

She gave Ethan a conspiratorial wink before returning her attention to the matter at hand. "Timmy, is it? Well, gracious me. You fooled us again, didn't you?"

The grinning boy nodded so vigorously that his sable hair seemed in danger of vibrating off his head. "Timmy is a bad boy."

"No, Timmy is not a bad boy. Timmy is just a tired boy who needs a nap." She tried not to smile at the child's crestfallen expression. "Also, Timmy is playing with his brother's ball, so I'd best take this—" she plucked the object in question out of the boy's grasp "—and give it back to Tommy."

"No!" Horrified, Tommy thrust out his hands, jumping in place. "My ball, my ball!"

"I truly am sorry, Timmy," Deirdre replied with exaggerated regret. "But this ball belongs to Tommy."

A huff, a frown, then the child heaved a resigned sigh and angled a sheepish grin. "Okay, I—I—I Tommy."

"Are you now?" She feigned shock, slipped a peripheral glance at Ethan as a smile twitched to spring free.

"Ah, but that can't be so, for if you were Tommy, you'd be marching right over to apologize to the young man who was hurt." She punctuated that suggestion with a pointed gaze at the boy in question who was still being comforted by his mother.

Tommy eyed the boy, eyed the ball, heaved a sigh, then scurried over to mutter an audible, if not particularly sincere "Sorry."

Moments later, Tommy had retrieved his beloved toy and wandered over to play with his brother while Ethan followed Deirdre to the shade of a nearby oak. "You're incredible," he said. "You always know the right thing to say."

"A matter of practice," she murmured. "A child's job is to test life, to test parents, to find his own place in what seems a very big, very frightening world."

She kept her back toward him, watched the twins playing without allowing herself to meet his gaze. His nearness never failed to undo her, even more so in the two weeks following her own embarrassing lapse of judgment, when she'd lost sight of her own determination to maintain a purely professional relationship with a man toward whom her emotions were decidedly, and undeniably personal.

Instead of focusing on her mission, on the reunification of a family in crisis, she'd succumbed to a part of herself she'd never experienced before, that of brazen seductress whispering sensual suggestions through a flimsy plaster wall.

Since that humiliating night, she hadn't been able to meet Ethan's eyes, not once. She couldn't meet them now.

But she felt his gaze, felt the heat of it, the question he was much too gallant to pose. They hadn't discussed that night, not in words. They'd avoided the subject so judiciously, with such pained care that it loomed between them like the proverbial elephant in the living room that everyone is too polite to mention.

Acutely aware of him, she focused her gaze toward the bench some twenty yards away, where the twins played beyond earshot of their private conversation. She also noticed others in the vicinity—children scampering past on their way to a sand-carpeted play yard, a few couples walking nearby, some holding hands, others simply sauntering together in the warm sunshine and one couple that seemed to be engaged in a less-than-cordial discussion.

Signs of normalcy all around them, chirping birds, dappled shadows cast by fluttering leaves. There was also a peculiar edge to the scene, one Deirdre might have noted more adequately had she not been distracted by the pounding of her own besotted heart.

Beside her Ethan shifted to lean against a jutting branch of the massive white oak. "Being a parent is more than practice," he said. "It's instinct, a gut-level understanding of how a child thinks, what a child feels. How can I give my sons what they need without it?"

She squirmed under his scrutiny, but stubbornly refused to look at him. An angry shout from a distance made her flinch. She glanced at the couple still embroiled in argument, but otherwise paid them no heed. "You're a fine father to the boys, Ethan. Two weeks ago, you were but a vague memory from a long-ago time. Now you've become an intrinsic part of their lives."

"I'm a nice man who shows up twice a week to play with them. I still don't understand my children, Deirdre. I have no clue what makes them tick."

"You will."

"How can you be so sure?" A rasp of desperation

caught her attention. She looked at him. It was a mistake. Despair gazed back at her, despair and the fear of failure so blatant, it took her breath away. "What if I'm doing the wrong thing?"

"You're not."

"I don't know that."

"I do."

"How, Deirdre? How can you know that forcing myself into their lives won't jeopardize their happiness, their well-being, their emotional stability?" The ragged rasp of his fear was a living thing, corporeal and terrifying.

Unable to stop herself she touched him, simply laid her hand on his wrist as if it were the most normal thing in the world. The expected result was far from normal. Heat rose from his skin to hers, pulsed through her blood to melt the fabric of a heart she could no longer control. Her voice quavered, was barely a whisper. "You are their father, Ethan. Those children need you. They need you desperately. No one else can take your place in their lives. Not now, not ever."

He lifted her hand, tenderly cupping it between his palms as if he was cradling a small, fragile bird. He studied each finger, each smoothly polished nail, caressed each of her knuckles with his thumb. "My parents don't believe I can provide the financial support my sons need."

"Is that what you believe?"

"No." The word was not issued as firmly as she would have liked. "I'm a good cop."

"Of course you are."

"I'll be back on the job by Christmas."

That was a surprise. "Will you indeed?"

He issued a modest shrug, but allowed a hint of pride to reveal itself in his smile. "The weapons range master

signed me off yesterday. I'll never win any marksman-
ship pins left-handed, but I'm officially certified."

It took a moment for the importance of that to sink in.
"So that means you're one step closer to being returned
to active duty?"

"More like a hurdle than a step. All I need now is the
medical release."

"And you'll be receiving that soon?"

"Yes." He deflated his lungs, a subtle show of un-
derstated relief. "I meet the physical qualifications as laid
out in departmental policy. They can't refuse to issue the
release."

"Why would they want to refuse?"

The light in his eyes dimmed as he slipped an unobtrusive gaze to his scarred right hand. He blinked,
glanced away, seemed oddly perturbed by her question.
"No reason."

She saw it then, the flicker of evasion, the subtle hint
of contrite chagrin. Instinctively she knew. "You've
found a loophole, haven't you?"

A red stain brightened his earlobes and crawled beneath his jawline. "I didn't create the policy. Manage-
ment did. If they believed equal strength in both hands
was crucial to job performance, I'm sure they would have
included such a requirement."

"You can pass the test as it currently stands?"

"I can."

"Well, then." She shouldn't have been surprised, and
wasn't actually. If anyone on earth could overcome apparently insurmountable odds, it was this man. He'd
proven that time and time again. For some reason, however, her pride in him, her pleasure for his success was
tempered by ambivalence, and a prick of instinct that all

was not what it seemed. He was clearly relieved, clearly confident, yet he seemed oddly unsettled.

Deirdre sensed he needed encouragement. "It looks as if you were right all along. You'll soon be back on the job, doing what you love and taking care of your sons just like any proper dad would do."

He continued to study the hand cradled in his palms, then raised it to his lips. His breath was warm against her skin, the moist promise of his mouth elicited a quiver in her blood. He kissed each knuckle with exquisite sweetness. "You make me feel powerful, as if there's nothing beyond the realm of possibility."

"You've already proven that true," she whispered. "Look at all you've accomplished against odds that would have conquered a lesser man."

"A man." His smile was slightly wry, slightly rakish. "Do you know how long it's been since I felt as if that term actually applied to me?" No answer was expected, and none was given. Instead, he gazed at her as if contemplating something precious, something to be cherished and revered. "There's just something about you, Deirdre. You make me feel things I've never felt before."

The warmth in his eyes made her dizzy. Her mind swirled, her body melted with an all-too-familiar pulsing need. It was the same aching desire that enveloped her every time she remembered the thrill of his touch, the passion of his kiss. She was drowning in a surging sea of emotion, a passion of the soul that she hadn't experienced in years, yet recognized as if it had been only yesterday.

She recognized it, and was terrified. There was no denying it from herself, no concealing the power of her own heart. She was in love.

The realization struck with enough force to back the

breath into her lungs. She loved Ethan—truly, deeply loved him.

That changed everything.

Before she could digest the monumental implication of that revelation, Ethan shifted beside her. As he gazed across the park, his countenance tensed, his expression hardened. He released her hand, shifted his weight to the balls of his feet, more out of habit, she suspected than deliberate intent.

She followed his gaze, saw the arguing couple she'd noticed earlier. Angry words filtered through the idyllic scene, a shout of fury that sent both twins scampering across the grass into the safety of Deirdre's arms. As she crouched down to comfort the frightened boys, a woman's cry of pain jolted Deirdre to the bone. The man had struck her, she realized numbly. And was still striking her, over and over again.

All around the park, people stopped, stared, then hurried away from the unpleasantry. The moment the man had raised his hand, however, Ethan had sprinted forward.

Deirdre's heart leapt into her throat, nearly choking her. Ethan shouted a warning. The man spun, his face contorted. He released the struggling woman and lunged at Ethan. Everything happened so fast—grappling bodies, a blur of movement, a woman's shrill shriek of terror.

Only after Ethan slumped to the ground did Deirdre recognize the glint of a blade, and realize that she was the one who was screaming.

Chapter Ten

The hospital hallway was crowded with hustling personnel and milling visitors for whom the small waiting room was too confining. On a wooden bench across from the nurses' station, Deirdre comforted the worried twins with recited nursery rhymes and creative fables.

Tommy emitted a sudden squeak. "Gwamma, Gwampa!"

Deirdre's heart sank as the elder Devlins hurried down the corridor. Nettie was tense, pale, clearly distraught. Deirdre had expected that. What she hadn't expected was stark panic in Horace's eyes, the twisted slash of tight lips in a face so taut with terror that he appeared to have aged a decade since she'd last seen him that morning. His white knuckles were wrapped around his wife's elbow in a death grip as he propelled her forward with wrenching desperation.

Tommy darted to greet them, skidding along the slick

linoleum, and nearly upending a supply cart pushed by a startled orderly. "Gwampa, Gwampa, a man hit a lady and—and—and—" he sucked in a breath "—and Daddy got hurted!"

Nettie's lips puckered in upon themselves. Her spine straightened, her shoulders snapped to attention. In contrast, her husband's round torso folded like a deflated balloon. His lower lip loosened, quivered. Saliva gleamed from the corner of his mouth. "My son?"

"The doctor is with him," Deirdre said.

"Will he...live?" As Horace swayed forward as if on the verge of collapse, Nettie shifted her torso slightly to prop him up.

"Of course." Deirdre questioned Nettie with a look, saw dread in the older woman's eyes. "A couple of nasty cuts to be sure, but nothing a few stitches won't fix." Deirdre tried to stand, only to be dragged down by Timmy, who threw himself into her lap and clung to her with pitiful desperation. The boy hadn't spoken since the incident occurred, but had clearly been terrified. She stroked his hair, soothing him. "There, there, my brave little man, you don't want your daddy to see you all upset now, do you?"

Timmy sniffed, gripped a fistful of her sweater and burrowed his face against her breast like a frightened kitten.

Horace took a step forward, spoke in a voice so ragged she barely recognized it. "What...happened?"

The poor man was sick with worry, she realized, so stressed and frantic that she feared he might keel over. This was not the reaction she'd expected from the man apparently so unconcerned about his son's previous brush with death that he'd never bothered to visit him.

Deirdre found the paradox bothersome, but was too

emotionally drained to give it more than a passing thought. "There was an altercation in the park that escalated into violence. When it appeared a woman was being injured, Ethan intervened." The memory was painful enough to crack her own voice. She cleared her throat, scooped the trembling Timmy into her arms and stood. "It all happened so fast."

"Where—" Horace coughed, kept a firm grip on his wife's elbow with one hand and grasped her wrist with the other. Deirdre presumed it was to keep himself upright. Nettie was his rock, she realized, his strength. Beneath the blustering surface was a frightened man struggling to cope with a situation he could not control. "Where was he injured?"

"His arm, here—" she shifted Timmy, freeing one hand to trace a six-inch diagonal line from the back of her right wrist, around the forearm "—and here." Repeating the process, she gestured from biceps to elbow, noting that Horace flinched with every motion as if feeling the pain himself. "It sounds worse than it is," she assured him. "There was no nerve or muscle damage. He'll be right as rain in a couple of weeks."

Any solace Horace received wasn't reflected in his bleak gaze. "Have they caught the thug who did this?"

"Yes."

"Good." Horace's nostrils flared with his next breath, eyes focused on a point beyond Deirdre's shoulder. His entire demeanor changed from helpless to stoic. He tightened his shoulders, lifted his chin, released his grip on his wife so suddenly that the poor woman tottered forward a step to keep her balance.

Deirdre knew without looking that Ethan had entered the hallway. A glance over her shoulder confirmed it. Several yards away, Ethan had emerged from the examining room looking ragged and wan. His right arm was bandaged, tucked into a navy blue canvas sling. After exchanging a few words with the doctor, he nodded and turned wearily toward the tense group at the end of the hallway. Timmy shifted in her arms, eyes huge.

Tommy leapt forward with a yelp, dashed toward Ethan, hollering. "Daddy all better?"

"Hey, buddy." Ethan squatted down with a tired smile. "Yep, good as new." His smile faded as he glanced up and saw his parents. He tensed, stood, took his son's hand and led him forward. At the same time, he issued a lukewarm greeting. "I'm sorry your evening was disturbed, Mother." He kissed her proffered cheek before turning a narrowed gaze on his father.

Deirdre held her breath, and suspected Nettie was doing the same. This was the first time in years that Horace and Ethan had seen each other. The tension was thick enough to slice.

They sized each other up for an excruciating moment. Horace studied his son's bloodstained shirt without so much as a flinch, then refocused on Ethan's face without saying a word.

It was Ethan who broke the strained silence. "Since you're here, I presume that tail-sniffing hound you hired is still earning his kibble."

Horace didn't blink. "Unlike you, some people still work for a living."

Deirdre and Nettie gasped at the same moment, stared in disbelief that Horace would use his son's extended recuperation as a weapon against him.

"That's quite unfair," Nettie said. "Ethan's physical recovery has been a long, arduous process. It's most unkind of you to imply otherwise."

Deirdre had spent enough time with the Devlins to

realize that under ordinary circumstance even a mild rebuke from his wife would be enough to evoke instant apology. This time, however, there wasn't a flicker, not a hint or a blink to indicate that Horace had even heard her words.

Deirdre tried to intervene before full-scale hostilities broke out. "There was no investigator, Ethan. Horace canceled the contract after the, ah, last incident." Both men maintained the visual stalemate with identically shuttered gazes. "I called your parents," she blurted. "I left a message on their machine."

Ethan's head snapped around. He skewered her with a look, and she wasn't fooled by the pleasant tone he used for the children's benefit. "I specifically recall asking you not to bother them."

"That you did." She neither blinked nor averted her gaze, as cognizant as was Ethan that the twins were listening, absorbing every nuance of expression, every subtlety of tone. "I decided that they had a right to know."

"You decided?" He angled a glance at his wide-eyed sons, spoke through a smile so tight that his lips barely moved. "That was rather peremptory, don't you think?"

Before Deirdre could reply, Nettie stepped forward. "Are you all right, Ethan, dear? Are you in pain?"

A flash of despair flickered once, then disappeared into that reflective veil behind which Devlin men were so adept at hiding emotion. "I'm fine, Mother."

"You could have been—" She bit off the words, clasping her hands as she slipped a glance toward her grandsons. "I mean, it could have been much more serious."

Beyond a curt shrug, Ethan gave no indication that the comment either unnerved or concerned him. He simply shifted his stance, continuing to stroke Tommy's hair as the child clung to his belt. "I'm fine, Mother. Let's just leave it at that."

Clamping her lips together, Nettie acquiesced with a nod just as Timmy shifted in Deirdre's arms. The child reached out to touch his father's face. "Daddy hurt?"

Ethan's eyes softened, grew moist. "Daddy's okay, son. And look at the cool sling I get to wear."

Timmy regarded the object with renewed interest while Tommy jumped up and down, tugging his father's belt with enough force to jerk him sideways. "I—I—I want a s'ing, too! Can I have one, Daddy, can I, can I, can I...?"

Chuckling, Ethan used his free hand to unfurl the tiny, grasping fingers. "I think that can be arranged."

"Yay!" Tommy hopped in place, hooting happily while his shy brother shoved his fingers in his mouth and grinned.

Horace's sharp gaze skipped from one child to the other, then settled on his own son's face, although it was his wife to whom he spoke. "Take the children to the car."

Deirdre tensed, angled a glance at Ethan and saw the warning clamp of his jaw. To his credit, he forced a pleasant expression and spoke warmly to his sons. "Hey, guys, you go with Grandma now. I'll see you in a couple of days, okay?"

"Okay," Tommy said cheerfully. He gave his crouching father a huge hug, then scampered over to grasp his grandmother's hand.

Timmy hesitated, unwilling to release his grip on Deirdre's sweater even after she'd lowered him to the floor. Only when Ethan sat back on his heels and held out his arm did the boy move away from the safety of her embrace directly into his father's.

"You be a good boy for Dad, okay?"

"Okay," Timmy mumbled. The child turned away, paused, then scrambled back to plant a moist kiss on Ethan's cheek before allowing himself to be led away.

The moment Nettie had guided the children out of hearing range, Horace turned on his son. "You couldn't let it go, could you? You just had to be the hero."

"Mr. Devlin, please, this isn't the time—"

"Let him talk," Ethan said. "He'll pop a vein if he can't get it out. So go for it, Horace. Tell me again what a failure I am, how unworthy of the esteemed family name."

"This isn't about you." The words were harshly spewed, meant to wound. "It's about those children."

Ethan's gaze hardened. "Leave my sons out of this."

"Don't pretend to care about your sons. You've proven that you don't give a damn about them."

"Be careful," Ethan warned.

Horace was beyond caution. His face was purple, a menacing vein pulsed at his temple, spittle gleamed at the corner of his contorted mouth. "Did you give a thought about those boys, Ethan? Did you spark a single brain cell to consider the psychological trauma of seeing their father injured, possibly killed in front of their very eyes? Are you so obsessed by self-importance, by that pathological passion of destroying yourself to spite me that you couldn't spare a moment's consideration for your own children?"

Ethan paled with each hammered word until his complexion was ashen, and his bleak eyes seemed to sink into his skull.

Muted by shock, Deirdre simply stared in disbelief, unable to comprehend Horace's transformation from ter-

rified father to venomous bully in the space of a heartbeat.

"What if Deirdre hadn't been there?" Horace was
shouting now, creating a scene in the hospital hallway
where staff members stared and worried visitors slipped
farther away from the viciousness of his words. "What
if you'd been killed, and those poor babies were left to
wander the park alone, helpless prey for some passing
pervert? Did you think of that? Did you even care?"

Ethan swayed slightly, but never averted his gaze,
never uttered a word in his own defense.

"That doesn't matter, does it? You've got to play the
game, got to be the big, brave cop. Risking your life is
what you do, isn't it? To hell with family, to hell with
your children, to hell with anyone who dares give a damn
about what happens to you. You've got to prove your
manhood." Horace spit out the final word like a bad
taste. "Dying is easy. It's living that's hard. A real man
would know that."

With a hiss of expelled breath, Ethan jerked forward
as if he'd been punched in the stomach. Horace simply
spun on his heel and marched away without a backward
glance at his shattered son. All Deirdre could do was
touch Ethan's shoulder, struggling for something, anything, to ease the sting from the vicious verbal pummel-
ing.

"He didn't mean that," she finally said.

"He meant it." Ethan was white as a corpse. "And
he was right."

"No, he wasn't right." She snatched her purse off the
bench, hurried after Ethan as he strode down the hallway.
"I won't pretend to understand what it is that goes on
between you two, but I will say that I know a frightened

man when I see one. He's afraid for you, Ethan, so deathly afraid.''

"Go home, Deirdre."

"I'll not be going without you." A slap of cold night air stung her cheeks. She followed him into the parking lot, puffing to keep up with his lengthy strides. "The car is that way," she said as he veered toward the street.

"The bar is this way."

"Planning to drown your troubles, are you?"

"No." He stopped at the intersection, waiting for the light. "I'm planning to get drunk."

"Ah. Well, under the circumstances, I'd say you were entitled." She fell into step beside him. "Mind if I join you? I could use a wee taste myself."

He angled a glance. "It's a free country."

"That it is," she murmured. "That it is."

"O-o-oklahoma-a-a!" Lurching forward, Ethan tripped on the porch steps, grabbed a post with his left hand, spun around like a tipsy top. "Where the green stuff grows as high—" he paused, staggered a step forward and flung out his unfettered arm "—as a fat giraffe's eye-e-e…''

"Elephant," Deirdre corrected, grabbing him around the waist lest he tumble over the porch rail. "'Tis an elephant's eye."

He scrunched his face, hiked a brow and struggled to focus. "Giraffes are taller."

"That they are," she agreed, fumbling in the dark for her duplex key.

"I like giraffes." He burped, muttered a fuzzy apology, then flung a chummy arm around her shoulders. "I like you, too."

"That's lovely to hear." Smiling, Deirdre struggled

not only to find the keyhole in the darkness, but to hold the screen door open with her shoulder and maintain an upright position as Ethan sagged against her.

He suddenly dipped his face into her hair, inhaled deeply and noisily. "You smell good."

"That makes one of us," she murmured. "You smell like a brewery." A slip, a twist and the front door swung open. "Ah, here we go."

She reached inside to flip on the light, slid an arm around his waist and hauled him inside, where he once again broke into slurred song.

"Ain't nothing that's the sa-ame—" He stumbled, tripped, rolled over and onto the sofa, landing with his face in a cushion. The muffled warbling continued. "As a huggable, snuggable—" Hoisting his head up, he sucked in a breath, expelled it all in a rousing finale. *"Dame-e-e-e!"* His face flopped back into the cushion.

Deirdre sighed, closed the door and bent to stroke the purring kitten rubbing her ankle. "I know, I know, but we can't be leaving him alone tonight. He'd probably pass out in the shower and drown himself." Dublin blinked as if alarmed by the prospect. "So you can see the dilemma."

The kitten meowed, then leapt onto the sofa to examine the rumpled human sprawled there. Ethan suddenly rolled onto his back, snatched the startled animal with his free hand. "Dubby, my man!" He kissed the wriggling feline head, held the perturbed animal up and gazed into a pair of skeptical amber eyes. "Raced any trains lately?"

Issuing a sloppy chuckle, Ethan placed the cat on his chest and shook a finger in its face. "You must uphold the family honor. Never put yourself at risk. Shame on you." Ethan's crooked smile faded into an expression of pure misery a moment before his eyelids fluttered closed and his left hand flopped across the canvas sling in which his right arm was encased.

Dublin sniffed the sling, sniffed the man, then yanked his head away as if offended by the reek of whiskey and stale ale. He glanced up, issued a soft trill to Deirdre, who was unlacing Ethan's shoes.

"He's very sad tonight," Deirdre murmured, yanking off one sneaker and setting it beside the sofa. "And who can blame him? It was a cruel thing his father did—very cruel and very wrong." She placed the second sneaker beside the first. "Men are peculiar creatures. Not meaning any offense," she added when the male kitten stared up at her. "It is a puzzlement, though, why they feel the only way to show strength is to hide compassion, as is this peculiar notion that wounding those we love will somehow make them stronger."

She sighed, went to retrieve a blanket and a pillow from the linen closet. When she returned to the living room, Ethan was sitting up, stroking the kitten in his lap. She noted his pensive expression, the tiny flinch of his brow. "Are you in pain?" she asked.

His head wobbled up a notch, his eyes rolled into focus. "Pain?"

"Your arm," she said, piling the linens on the floor beside the sofa. "Is it bothering you?"

He blinked, held his uninjured arm out for scrutiny. "No, it just hangs on my shoulder until I need it."

Smiling, she perched on a nearby chair. "I was referring to the other arm."

Frowning, he looked around, clearly perplexed. "I seem to have misplaced that one."

"Look in the sling. That blue thing hanging around your neck," she added when he stared in befuddlement.

"Never mind. I'd be surprised if you're feeling much of anything at the moment, let alone pain."

"So I can stop looking for it?"

"Indeed."

He sighed. "I hope it turns up. It's been useful."

"I'm sure it will."

His head rolled loosely to the side. He regarded her, offered a sloppy grin. "You're pretty."

"Thank you."

"No, I mean it. You're more than pretty, you're beautiful."

"Thank you again."

Closing his eyes, he allowed his head to loll back. His breathing deepened. Thinking he'd fallen asleep, Deirdre rose from her chair, slipped an arm around his shoulders and eased his upper torso into a reclining position. She'd just lifted his legs from floor to cushion when his eyes snapped open.

"What does love feel like?"

The question took her by surprise. "Love?"

"Yes, love." He shifted on his left side, propped his head up with his hand. "How does a person know if he's in love or in lust?"

"Lust, is it?" Her laugh was thin, nervous. "I honestly don't know how to answer. I've not given such things much thought."

He regarded her with oddly sober eyes. "Have you never been in lust?"

Feeling the heat crawl along her cheekbones, she avoided his gaze. "Of course I have."

"What does it feel like?"

"I'm sure you already know," she murmured, certain she must be glowing like a neon tomato.

"I know what it feels like to want sex." He puffed his

cheeks, inspected her with a paradoxical blend of dispassion and drunken desire that completely unnerved her. "But how do you know when you want more than sex, when that ache in your gut is signaling something deeper, something that might last a lifetime?"

"I, ah—" She shifted, fanned her face with her hand. "I can't say for certain. I imagine it's different for everyone."

His gaze probed her. "What is it like for you?"

"It's…it's…" She bit her lip a moment, planning to avoid the question, and was startled by the sound of her own voice—clear, strong and resonant. "It's a warmth in one's heart that never cools, a sweetness in the blood that colors every day with joy simply to be alive, and to share that life with a person so dear that one can no longer imagine the sun rising if it couldn't shine on such a beloved face. It is a completion of the soul, a joining of spirit, a trust beyond measure, that a person, a very precious person enhances and enriches us. Love glorifies our goodness, forgives our failings. Love," she said finally, "makes us better than we are."

Ethan's eyes softened, almost glowed. For several long seconds he remained motionless, stretched sideways on the sofa propped up on his elbow with his chin nested in the palm of his left hand. The intense scrutiny heated her skin, quivered inside her chest.

When he finally spoke, her insides wiggled like warm gelatin. "Has anyone ever told you how special you are?"

She flushed at the praise. "Not in a very long time."

"Perhaps you haven't been listening." Whiskey still slurred his words, but he seemed otherwise coherent.

Averting her gaze, she concentrated on rolling a patch of cat hair from the upholstered arm of her chair. "A woman cherishes words of kindness,'' she said finally. ''Especially from an attractive man.''

''You find me attractive?''

A nervous titter slipped out before she could stop it. ''You know that I do.''

A lazy smile, a hooded gaze. ''Why?''

''Why?''

''Why do you find me attractive?''

''Well...'' How did she get herself into these predicaments? ''You're quite handsome, of course.''

''Am I?''

''Indeed.''

Grinning now, he wriggled for a more comfortable position on a sofa too short to stretch out his legs. ''No one has ever said I was handsome before.''

''Go on with you.''

''It's true.'' His eyelids drooped, then snapped open. She could tell he was struggling to focus. ''What else do you like about me?''

''Still fishing for compliments, are you?''

The question was poised with a teasing twinkle, so she was surprised when his grin melted into a morose frown. ''You're right, I'm being a jerk. A drunk jerk.'' He hiccuped, turned over onto his back, flopped his arm across his face and began to hum ''The Impossible Dream,'' a tune from *Man of La Mancha.*

The melody touched her, as did the lyrics evoked in her mind. This was not just a cocky bachelor swaggering his sex appeal like a flag of conquest. This was a deeply wounded man who desperately needed reassurance that someone in this world valued him, found him worthy.

If anyone on earth valued Ethan, it was the woman who could no longer deny that she loved him. ''Ethan—?'' He stopped humming. She took a stabilizing breath and plunged forward. "I'll not argue that you're a wee bit intoxicated at the moment, but you are a fine and decent man, and I'll not have you calling yourself names. You asked what I like about you. A fair question it is. It deserves an answer, and an answer it shall have."

One curious eye peered from beneath the elbow bent across his face.

Clasping her hands in her lap, she studied her own pale knuckles and spoke in a voice she hoped wasn't as quavering as it seemed. "I like you because you are a man of honor and courage, a man who doesn't regard kindness as weakness, nor compassion as a fault. You've a noble heart, Ethan, and a caring for others that is a rare gift indeed. I like you because you are strong and true and honest as the day is long. I like you because there's not a cruel bone nor a fiber of deceit in your entire body." She took a ragged breath. "I like you, Ethan, quite simply because you are who you are, and that is God's truth."

Exhaling all at once, she continued to stare at her tangled fingers, waiting for his reply. A moment ticked by, then another. Finally she heard a peculiar rasp, a thin rattle. When she dared glance toward the sofa, the eye that had been peeking out from beneath his arm was closed, and his chest rose and fell in the deep, even rhythm of sleep.

A soft mew drew her attention. "Thank you for listening," she told the kitten. "It's glad I am that someone was."

Dublin yawned.

"Your commentary is appreciated. Next time I'll try to liven up my presentation."

Suddenly exhausted, Deirdre retrieved the linens she'd placed beside the sofa. After covering Ethan with the blanket, she knelt to tuck the pillow gently beneath his head.

His eyes snapped open. Before she could blink twice, he'd reached up to tangle his fingers in her hair. His lips were inches from her own, his gaze clear, lucid, penetrating. "You do that for me."

Her knees turned to butter, her voice no more than a faint whisper. "Do what?"

"You make me better than I am."

She shivered, her gaze riveted, her heart pounding wildly. "Do I?"

His chest vibrated, his nostrils flared. Those incredible eyes probed into the very heart of her. He knew. He knew she wanted him. She could see it in his eyes.

His gaze shifted slightly as he slipped his fingers into her hair, then watched the dark strands flutter through his grasp. "I need to know what it feels like to be loved," he whispered. "Can you show me?"

Deirdre swayed. Heat coursed through her veins, rushed past her ears in a roar, drowning out the soft whisper of conscience in her mind. She knew this was wrong, knew that she would be taking advantage of a man who was emotionally wounded and drunk as a pickled boar. She knew she'd regret this in the morning. Worse, he would regret it. It would be difficult to live with her own guilt; it would be impossible to live with his.

She had to step back from the rage of emotions, from the pulsing need in her body and in her soul. They were poised on a precipice from which there could be no return. One step over the edge would change their lives forever. Ethan would become an intrinsic part of her. He would carry a piece of her with him always, an unrequited slice of her heart that she would offer gladly, as a gift not a barter. Reciprocation was neither anticipated nor expected. Ethan was a man for whom love was an elusive butterfly, an invisible wing-beat that he could hear but not see, touch but not feel.

Now he asked to feel it, to taste that sweetness of the heart if only for a moment. Deirdre could offer him that. Deep down, she realized that she was the only one who could.

There were a thousand reasons why that was unwise. In the space of a heartbeat, she counted them all in her mind. She knew that she was in command of the situation. The responsibility was hers, the heavy burden of discretion, of constraint, of ultimate control. A gentle smile, a subtle retreat would be accepted with chivalry and honor. The choice was hers.

She made it.

Chapter Eleven

Moist heat clouded her mind, blurred reality, engulfed her with liquid lightning. Deirdre melted into the steam, let the blanket of warmth envelop every inch of her body. It was what she needed, what she craved. A cleansing. An awakening. A restoration of spirit, a sunrise of soul. Hot, burning hot, stinging hot.

His moan rose above her own groan of pleasure, a masculine rumble barely audible beyond the deafening liquid rush. Again the sound beckoned, elbowing her consciousness from the warm cocoon into which she had retreated.

She turned off the shower.

A chill swept skin still prickling from the heat, from the stinging force of the water. She toweled dry hurriedly, without regret at the interruption. He needed her. That was all that mattered.

Slipping into a cobalt robe trimmed with ivory lace,

Deirdre finger-combed her damp hair and tied her robe sash on her way out of the bathroom. She found Ethan sitting on the edge of the sofa, feet on the floor, hunched forward with his head propped on his left hand. His bandaged right arm rested on his knee; a patch of gray-and-white fur peeked from a deflated rumple of blue canvas on the floor.

She smiled at the kitten, spoke to the man. "How are you feeling this morning?"

Flinching at the effort, he opened one bloodshot eye. "My hair is too tight."

"Is it now?"

With some effort, he refocused on the frisky feline emerging from the discarded sling to attack his ankle. "Your cat slept in my mouth."

"Oh, I rather doubt that."

"Then why does my tongue need a shave?"

She smiled, moved behind the sofa and begin to massage his taut shoulders. "Personally, I always wondered why whiskey is claimed to grow hair on one's chest when it's always the mouth that ends up furry." He groaned when she dug her thumbs into the knotted muscles between his shoulder blades. "My father always called it hair of the dog that bit you, and proclaimed the only cure was another dose of the stuff. In your case, I think a spot of black coffee is a better choice."

He rolled his head slowly around, flinching at the movement. "Do you have any?"

"Coffee? Indeed." She'd purchased a jar of instant especially for him. "First, let's loosen you up a bit. Lean back now.... There's a good lad." She dug her fingers along his scalp, ignoring his yelp as she rotated handfuls of hair with increasing outward pressure.

Recoiling, he ducked sideways, rotated his torso to

stare over his shoulder with the same expression one might focus upon a hooded executioner. "Are you trying to snatch me bald?"

"Now, now, no sniveling. Be brave and you'll soon be feeling better."

"How will ripping my hair out by the roots make me feel better?"

"Just loosening the scalp a bit." Wrapping a thick strand at the crown around her fingers, she applied steady pressure outward. "I know it's not comfortable—"

"My eyes are watering." He flinched, gritted his teeth.

"Almost done." After repeating the process from temple to nape, she massaged his entire scalp with her knuckles, then stepped back. "There. How does it feel?" Ethan probed his skull with his fingertips, eyed her suspiciously as she sat beside him. "It feels better, doesn't it?"

"Of course it feels better," he grumbled. "Now that you've stopped trying to rip off the top of my head."

"Stubborn man." It was an endearment, spoken softly, and with a love she hadn't meant to reveal. She glanced away as he looked at her. Her tongue nervously poked the corner of her mouth.

He shifted, cleared his throat. "Deirdre…about last night—"

"How about some breakfast?"

He laid his hand on her thigh as she started to rise. "We have to talk."

Her throat was dry as a desert. "About what?"

"About what happened." A chill replaced the warmth of his hand as he raked his hair, then used it as a prop against his own knee as he slumped forward. "Do I—" he hesitated, angled a sideways glance as if to gauge her reaction "—owe you an apology?"

The confusion in his eyes touched her. "Indeed you

do," she replied softly. "For having mangled some of my favorite Broadway show tunes in a most unforgivable manner."

His chagrined cringe flattened unto befuddlement. "Is that all?"

"It was quite enough. Even poor Dublin was appalled by your tone-deaf warbling."

"But I... That is, we..." He puckered his lips, absently scratched his head. "I remember, ah, more than that."

"Do you?"

"Perhaps I dreamed it."

"Dreamed what?"

"I recall having made an unusual and inappropriate request of you." He swallowed, frowned, concentrated on plucking a strand of sweater lint from his slacks. "Did that happen?"

"The request?" A frisson of electricity skittered down her spine at the memory. "Indeed it did."

He winced, muttered to himself. Squaring his shoulders, he straightened as if facing a firing squad. "And...?"

"And nothing, Ethan. You passed out cold as a mackerel on ice. I pulled a blanket up around your very green gills, and let you sleep it off."

"That's it?"

"That's it. Although I must say that the relief I'm seeing in your eyes is a wee bit of an insult."

The smile in her voice coaxed one from him. "The relief is that I wasn't so far gone as to have forgotten a moment that would have been the highlight of my existence." With a sensual softening of gaze, he touched her damp hair, rolling the moist ends around his fingertip.

"It's just as I imagined," he whispered. "Sleek, shiny, like wet ebony in moonlight."

The warmth in his eyes enveloped her like a balmy mist. It filled her lungs, steamed her skin, clouded her mind. He curled a moist strand around his index finger, caressed her cheek with the side of his hand. Gentle, so very gentle. Tears gathered in her eyes—tears of exquisite emotion, of joy, of profundity and passion.

It had been so long since anyone had gazed at her with such reverence, had displayed such tenderness, such wonder.

"You are so beautiful," he whispered. "You take my breath away." As if mesmerized, he allowed the moist strands of hair to flutter from his finger, then traced the curve of her throat, edging his fingertip along the lace trimming the V-shaped neckline of her robe. "Beautiful," he repeated. "Beautiful."

When he hooked his finger where the fabric joined between her breasts, a small gasp caught in her throat. It was a gasp of pleasure, of exquisite anticipation, but to her dismay, Ethan started, blinked and snatched his hand away as if burned.

Confused, chagrined, clearly contrite, he shook his head, wiped his face and mumbled an apology. Deirdre immediately refuted it. "Please don't," she whispered, stroking his shoulder. "It's been so very long since anyone has found me pleasing that it would break my heart if you truly regretted uttering such precious words."

His gaze clouded, his mouth moved. No sound emerged. He closed his eyes for a moment, and when he opened them, the depth of sadness she saw stunned her. "I don't understand a world like this, a world where a woman as perfect as you are isn't revered, and cherished. You should be nurtured, and loved, and protected, and told every day, every moment, how beautiful you are, how extraordinary.'' With some effort he turned away from her. His gaze settled on the bandaged arm he rested upon his knee. "You deserve all of that, and more. You deserve the moon and the stars, and everything good the world has to offer laid at your feet every day. You deserve these things from someone who is worthy of offering them.''

She saw his uncertainty, the flash of grief in his eyes, and it tore at her. "Ethan, please, if this is because your father said such terrible things last night—''

"No.'' He smiled at her, the kind of smile one wears to bid farewell to a cherished friend. "It's because the terrible things he said were right.'' Touching a fingertip to her lips, he silenced her protest. "I reacted yesterday out of instinct, without the slightest thought of how my actions would affect my children. A real father would never have put his kids at risk to play hero.''

"You were trying to save a life.''

"I was trying to prove a point.'' Heaving a sigh, he rested his head against the back of the sofa. He displayed his bandaged arm. "Do you know why this happened?''

The question took her aback. "Because he had a knife.''

Ethan shook his head. "No, it was because he was left-handed.'' That made no sense to her, and she said so. "He was facing me. He lunged with his left hand. I had to counter with my right. I tried to grab his wrist. I couldn't.''

The realizations slipped over her slowly, like an icy shroud.

"Police officers depend on each other,'' he said with frightening calm. "They put their lives in the hands of their partners. Strong hands, capable hands, hands that can do the job, and protect those in need. I can't do that anymore, can't subdue a drugged-out maniac, can't wrestle the gun from an enraged drunk, can't even knock the knife away from a scrawny, woman-beating coward. So you see, my father was right.''

It took a moment for Deirdre to find her voice. When she did, it shook with desperation, unconvincing even to herself. "Horace was not right, not right at all. You're a detective. Your job is to investigate crime, not chase after thugs. A weak hand doesn't affect your mind."

He shook his head. "A detective is a cop in a sport coat. A big part of the job is to chase, cuff and incarcerate scum that preys on the weak—muggers, protection thugs, pimps, drug runners…" He sighed, pinched the bridge of his nose. "The force has been offering me a disability retirement for months. I'm going to take it." The heaviness in his voice foreshadowed an even deeper pain. He took a deep breath before revealing it. "I'm going to withdraw my countersuit and let my parents have custody of the boys."

"You can't!"

"I have to. As of now, I'm just a broken-down ex-cop heading to the unemployment line. I can't support my sons, can't give them the stable life they deserve."

"They deserve their father. Do you think those babies care how much money you have in the bank? All they want is their daddy, Ethan. All they want is your love."

"I will always love them.''

"How will they know that if you're not a part of their lives?"

Startled, he snapped his head around to stare at her. "I'll be with them every week, every day if that's possible. I'm not leaving Santa Barbara. I'm not giving up my right to see them, to love them, to be there for them, to be as much of a real father to them as I'm able to be. But I can't give them everything they need, Deirdre, and I can't replace what they already have.''

''And what is that?''

''A family,'' he whispered.

She took a breath, lifted his hand, sandwiching it between her palms. ''They do have a family, Ethan, and you're the most important part of it. The children love their grandparents, as well they should, but you are their father. No one can replace your place in their lives, or in their hearts.''

Anguish reflected from deep within him, along with pain, confusion, a desperation Deirdre recognized, and understood. ''How can I support them, how can I provide all the things growing boys need? Law enforcement is all I've ever wanted, all that I know. I'll have to start all over again. I don't even know how to start.''

''With a single step,'' Deirdre said softly. ''Every journey begins that way.''

Opening the carton to expose dual rows of neatly nested eggs, Deirdre reached for a frying pan, distracted by the sound of running water from the hall bath. Ethan's torment still haunted her, a pain that couldn't have been more tangible if it had been her own heart being ripped into shreds rather than his.

In a very real sense, it was her pain, her heart. Whatever hurt Ethan hurt her, too.

With some effort, Deirdre had dissuaded him from leaving until he'd had a hot meal. He was washing up now. After breakfast, she'd have to think of another reason to keep him close. He shouldn't be alone, not now, not when the entire purpose to which he'd devoted himself for the past two years had come crashing down around his shoulders, yet another shattered reality for a man who had suffered so much.

The creak of a door startled her. She realized the water sounds had ceased as Ethan's footsteps echoed in the hall. Turning, she pretended to busy herself with food preparation, speaking as she felt his presence enter the room. "Bacon, ham or sausage?"

"Really, you don't have to bother."

"Bacon it is." She arranged several limp strips in the pan, and scooped two eggs out of the carton. "Boiled, fried or—" She glanced over her shoulder. It was a mistake. "Scrambled," she murmured as the eggs slid from her palm.

She barely heard the splat of shattered shells on linoleum. Her gaze was riveted on the man standing in her kitchen like a bare-chested mythical god, his wet hair tousled as if he'd just rolled out of a heavenly bed. Loose chinos rode low on his slim hips while his discarded shirt draped around his neck, accentuating a muscular torso sculpted by months of grueling exercise to increase upper body strength. Judging by the flex of finely honed biceps, the therapy program had been more than successful.

Ethan's body was lean, exquisitely molded. Deirdre had never seen anything so enticing, so erotic, so sensually, sexually male in her entire life. Air wheezed into her starving lungs, reminding her that she'd forgotten to breathe.

Ethan seemed blithely unaware of the effect he had on her. Flexing his fingers on the wooden back of the chair he'd pulled out, he studied the slimy mess on the floor. "You've decided on scrambled. Most people use a pan."

She found a voice—not her voice, but the thin, quivering rasp of a stranger. "Now where's the challenge in that?"

That's when he looked up and saw the hunger in her eyes. He caught his breath. "I'll, ah, just run next door and get a clean shirt."

The heat from his gaze was intense enough to cook the spilled eggs at her feet. She was vaguely aware that the curious kitten had emerged to investigate the interesting puddle of goo, and playfully bat a few scattered shell remnants. Ignoring all but the man who was the center of her focus, she managed a croaked reply. "Don't bother."

His gaze never left her face. "When it came to meals, my mother always enforced the no shirt, no shoes, no service rule."

"So do I." Deirdre had lost control of herself. She knew she'd stepped forward, was moving toward Ethan with slow, precise steps. She even imagined what she would do when she reached him, but the image was fluid, out of focus, as if she was watching herself from a distant corner of the room. "But what I plan to serve for breakfast, your mother never imagined."

She trickled her fingertips along his upper arm, saw the flesh quiver beneath her touch. Cloth brushed her knuckle as her exploration moved to his collarbone. A light tug on the fabric, and the shirt fluttered to the floor. "I hope you're hungry."

Ethan took a ragged breath. "Starving."

"So am I." Before she could consider the consequence of her brashness, she untied her sash, felt a cool breeze as the robe fell open. A shrug, a subtle shift of her shoulders, and the garment pooled at her feet beside the cotton shirt.

She stood before him, naked and unashamed.

Ethan swayed slightly, a nuance of movement barely noticeable below the glow of wonder in his exquisite eyes. A whispered prayer slipped from his lips, a hushed reference to a deity of love, and of beauty. "Incredible," he murmured. "You're exquisite. You...you take my breath away."

Again she traced the contours of his chest with her fingertips, marveling at the sleek warmth of his skin, the gleaming sheen of sculpted muscle over hard bone. "Magnificent." Her voice was as hushed as his, and trembled in awe. "Such strength. I had no idea..." Words dissipated, inadequate to describe the depth of her emotion, the power of her need. She bit her lower lip, allowing her touch to hover at the gauze enveloping his right forearm.

He responded to the question in her eyes. "It's all right."

"I don't want to hurt you."

"That isn't possible." Reaching out, he laid a timid palm on her shoulder, caressed upward to the curve of her throat. "I want to touch you," he whispered. "I want to touch you everywhere."

She shivered at the warmth, a peculiar reaction but one that shuddered the length of her body. "Yes."

Folding his hand, he brushed his knuckle along her collarbone, then downward, trailing his index finger between her breasts. As self-conscious as she was about most of her body, believing herself too broad of hip and with thighs too heavy to be pleasing, she was proud of her breasts. Lush and round as melons, they were perfectly formed, with nipples that reacted to his gaze by squeezing in upon themselves like tiny pink fists.

"So soft," Ethan murmured, caressing her belly. "I can't believe how beautiful you are."

"You make me feel beautiful." She closed her eyes, lost in the thrill of his firm fingers slipping along her skin, the gentle rasp of knuckles caressing the outside curve of her hips. "You make me feel as if that extra twenty pounds doesn't matter."

The shock in his eyes was genuine. "Your body is magnificent, perfect in every way."

She could have kissed him. And did.

Framing his face between palms that shook only a little, she touched her lips to his gently, reverently, tasting the minty remnants of mouthwash, inhaling the soapy freshness of his skin. She teased, touched and nipped until he groaned once, wrapped his left arm around her and crushed her against his chest with amazing strength.

Deirdre had read romance novels in which the hero plundered the heroine's mouth, dazing her with such electric passion that her knees buckled with desire. It had made wonderful reading, but she'd never believed that carnal yearning could strike with that kind of power.

But strike it did. Deirdre had never experienced a plundering kiss before, couldn't have defined it if she'd tried. Ethan's kiss was a ravishment, so intense, so deep, so desperate with desire that her knees turned to water and her soul turned to steam.

It wasn't enough. She wanted more, much more. Her fingers tangled in his damp hair, pressing him closer. Their mouths grappled, tongues darting, swallowing tiny whimpers and rumbling moans with equal aplomb. Every touch, every taste was so natural, so instinctively intimate that she was lost in a swirl of kaleidoscopic color and bursts of blinding light.

Stars. She was seeing stars. They weren't just a fictional flight of fancy. They were gleaming, sparkling explosions tingling from her dizzied mind to every nerve in a body so bursting with pleasure that she feared she might collapse from the sheer weight of such joy.

It was Ethan who broke the kiss with a ragged gasp, an incredulous stare. Deirdre knew then that he'd felt it, too, experienced the same blaze of color and light.

She sagged against him, breathing hard, waiting until her legs regained strength. When she stepped back, the power of his body struck her again, as intensely as if seeing it for the very first time. Her fingers followed her gaze, slipping over the taut muscles of his abdomen to the silky hairs encircling his navel. They tickled her fingertips, made her palms itch with need. Her knuckles rested on the sagging waistband of his slacks.

"These must go," she murmured. Before he could respond, her busy fingers had unsnapped, unzipped and unleashed the restraining fasteners. "Ah, the burning question is answered at last."

He stepped out of the rumpled pants, pushed them aside with a foot. "What burning question?"

She danced a fingertip along the elastic band. "I knew you'd be a boxer-shorts man."

A low rumble vibrated deep in his chest, emerged as a chuckle. "Briefs are too snug. My guys like room to move."

"And well they should." Hooking her thumbs at the waistband, she eased the shorts down until the garment slipped to his ankles, and his arousal sprang free. Every drop of moisture evaporated from her mouth. "'Tis a fine salute you have there."

"A sign of respect." His palm slipped from its resting place at her waist upward until his fingers brushed the fullness below her breast.

She sucked air through her teeth at the electric frisson of his touch. "Respect, is it? So that's what they call it nowadays."

He turned his hand slightly, allowing her breast to fill

his palm while his thumb caressed the rock-hard nipple. Jolts of carnal lightning slashed straight to the heart of her womanhood, a shock of white heat so intense that she cried out with the joy of it. She clutched his bare shoulders, knew her mouth was moving even as no sound emerged beyond a hushed whimper that seemed to arouse him even more.

His breath shallowed, became more rapid. Dipping his head forward, he pressed his lips to her exposed throat, tracing a moist trail of sheer heaven downward until his mouth brushed her unattended breast, and she thought she might die of delight.

"Yes." It was a gasp, a plea, a frantic cry of hope as his mouth moved closer to the quivering tip. When the heat of his lips touched it, her fingers went into a spasm, digging into the flesh of his shoulders. He took her nipple into his mouth, sending her into a frenzy. Sweet, so incredibly sweet, shards of unbelievable pleasure beyond anything she'd ever known.

He suckled her softly at first, then with increasing fervor. She arched her back, moaning, eyes closed, mind bursting with colors and lights and explosions of ecstasy. So intent was she on the delicious movement of his mouth on her breast that she barely noticed the furtive travel of his hand down her belly to caress her inner thighs.

A tense warmth radiated from his touch, spreading outward, upward into the most intimate recess of her body. Liquid fire—hot, moist, inviting. His fingertip ventured forth to test his welcome. She moaned again, shifted to allow him access, was startled when he lifted her thigh, swung her leg around and placed her foot on the chair.

She swayed, widened her eyes, and would have protested the peculiar storklike stance except that his hand immediately cupped her exposed womanhood, sending a shockwave of unbelievable sensation through every nerve of her body. Instinctively she rotated against his palm, massaging the sensitive nub over the heel of his hand until she was so frantic with desire that her body created its own brazen rhythm, and her mind surged with need.

When he slipped two fingers inside, she cried out in ecstasy. Her silky warmth instantly contracted, quaking with rhythmic spasms. Wave after wave of pleasure left her boneless, breathless, limp with relief.

She sagged against him, barely able to breathe. He kissed her face, her forehead, whispered against her hair, "It's been a while, hasn't it?"

Resting her head against his shoulder, she smiled. "A long, long while."

"For me, too."

With some effort, she lowered her foot from chair to floor, stepped back to study his smiling face. He looked pleased with himself, no doubt about it. She laughed. "Ah, but we haven't gotten to you yet, have we now?"

An endearing combination of hope and uncertainty widened his eyes. "Your pleasure is enough for me."

"Then you wouldn't deny me more pleasure, would you?" One of her hands slipped down to stroke his arousal.

He sucked in a sharp breath. "I aim to please."

She teased him with her fingertips, massaging the length of him until his chest quavered, and a groan rolled from his slack lips. Extending one leg, she shifted the chair with her foot. A deft nudge urged him backward. Before he could blink twice, he was seated. She straddled his lap, balancing on the balls of her feet.

His shock melted into an appreciative smile. "You surprise me. I had no idea how inventive the Irish were."

"Oh, you've more surprises in store." Placing a palm over each of his shoulders, she lowered herself until the silken tip of his erection was intimately positioned.

He shuddered, cupped her buttocks with his unfettered hand, and squeezed gently. "I presume this signifies the end of our platonic friendship?"

"That it does." Her breath caught as she sheathed the length of him inside her. "But it's also the beginning of something wonderful."

"Something wonderful." He dipped his head forward, nibbling the lush breast in front of his face. "I like the sound of that."

"As do I," she murmured, shivering as he mouthed her nipples into glistening pink stones. "As do I."

With that, her body dipped and swayed in a sensual dance of love, skin against skin, slicker, faster, their heartbeats synchronized and quickened, pulses pounded in rhythmic sync, until their glimmering bodies burst forth in the ultimate joining. United in body, bonded in soul.

Something changed deep within, an inexorable altering that each experienced, yet neither could explain. Life as they'd known it would never be the same.

Humming to himself, Ethan shook the frying pan, used a wooden paddle to cream the scrambled eggs as they cooked slowly. He felt Deirdre's presence before she slipped her arms around his chest.

"Hmm." She kissed his nape, released him and swung around to prop her hip against the counter. A sated smile touched her lips, pleasing him. "And he cooks, too. Surely a piece of heaven itself has wrapped around me this glorious morn."

Ethan laughed, feeling happier and more alive than ever before. "I have a few talents that are still useful."

"Oh, you have many talents indeed." She plucked the paddle from his grasp. "I'll finish up here, you sit yourself down and let me serve you."

"You've already served me, and several delicious helpings. It's a wonder we can still walk." He laughed as her cheeks pinked. "One minute you're a lusty, insatiable spitfire, the next you're blushing like a virgin bride. You never cease to surprise me."

Flushing furiously, she poked the spatula into the steaming scramble. "Keep teasing me, sir, and you'll have a real surprise when I shovel these eggs down those cute little boxer shorts."

"I can't control myself, you're so adorably teasable." He nibbled her ear until she went limp, then slipped the wooden utensil out of her hand. "Now let me finish my specialty, eggs à la Ethan."

Smiling, she glanced into the pan. "I see the eggs. Where's the à la Ethan part?"

"They're broken and beaten, aren't they?"

He'd tried for a jovial tone, but she caught the underlying tension, and frowned at him.

"You're not broken, Ethan, and you're certainly not beaten."

"It was a joke."

"Was it now?" She eyed him keenly, not fooled by the limp effort at concealment.

"Sure." Grabbing the handle, he swung the pan over two plates waiting to be filled, scooping out equal portions on each. He was annoyed with himself for allowing his uncertainty to seep through, giving her a glimpse of something he didn't even want to acknowledge in himself. This incredible woman had given him the most precious gift on earth, and he had nothing to offer in return. He was a man without purpose, without a future. Deirdre deserved so much more.

Stifling a sigh, Ethan squared his shoulders, lifted one plate and turned toward the table, expecting Deirdre to be seated there. She wasn't. "Deirdre? Breakfast is ready."

She called back from the bedroom. "I'll be right there."

Relieved that she hadn't run screaming into the street, Ethan arranged the table, sat down and waited for her. She appeared in less than a minute, eyes gleaming, face flushed. He instantly stood and pulled back the chair for her.

Smiling her thanks, she waited until he'd settled into his own chair, then laid a fat manila file beside his plate. Ethan blinked at it, tilted his head to read the vertical index tab. "Who's Manuel Rodriguez?"

"Someone I'd like you to find." She forked some eggs into her mouth. "Mmm. Wonderful."

He frowned, studied a peculiar glint in her eye. "Why?"

"Because they're creamy, not dry, and seasoned to perfection."

"I mean why do you want me to find this guy?"

"He has a wee bit of money coming." She took another bite, chewed slowly as he opened the file, perused the first few pages.

"It looks like he doesn't want to be found."

"He doesn't know we're looking."

Ethan closed the file, shoved it toward her. "Tell my father thanks but no thanks."

Her eyes widened. "Your father has nothing to do with this."

"It's his case."

"It's my case now." Sighing, she laid down her fork, dabbed her mouth with a napkin. "Of course, if it's too difficult for you, I'll have to tell Horace I've failed."

"Don't do this to me."

"Do what?"

"You know what." Ethan pushed back his chair, tapped his fingers on the table. "You think if I can find this character, my father will see what a brilliant detective I am and fall on his knees begging forgiveness for having doubted me."

"Why, Ethan, the thought never crossed my mind."

Her expression of wide-eyed innocence would have been amusing, even appealing under normal circumstances. "I'm not a fool, Deirdre."

"Of course not. Do you think I'd put my professional reputation in the hands of a fool?" Heaving a sigh that seemed a bit forced to him, she reached across the table and retrieved the file. "It's just that you've always told me what a good investigator you are, and— Oh, well, never mind." She flipped the file closed, placed it on the edge of the table. "I'm sure you've better ways to spend your time than doing favors for me. I'll find another way."

He scowled at her. "Fine."

She smiled at him. "Fine."

After breakfast, Deirdre kissed him goodbye and headed off to work, leaving the Rodriguez file on her kitchen table. Ethan cleaned up the kitchen, fed the cat and tidied the living room. When he finally headed to his own half of the duplex, the Rodriguez file was tucked under his arm.

Ethan had never been able to resist a challenge. He suspected Deirdre knew that.

Chapter Twelve

"Another work order?" Frowning, Horace studied the document Deirdre had laid in front of him. "ERD Investigations? Never heard of it."

"It's a new service," Deirdre said. "Quite highly recommended."

"Recommended by whom?"

"By me." She plucked a pen from a coffee mug packed with writing implements, and laid it atop the contract. "If you'll put your esteemed signature on the bottom line, I'll make the necessary arrangements."

Horace eyeballed her for a moment. She doubted he was fooled by the company name she'd pulled out of thin air, and quite frankly didn't care. If she'd truly wanted to disguise Ethan Robert Devlin's newly formed investigation firm, she would have created a more inventive title for it.

"Is this another assignment to the Rodriguez case?"

"Yes."

"You don't need my signature. I turned that over to you."

"According to generally accepted policy procedures, use of a new vendor or service provider must be approved at the highest level." She tapped the signature line. "Sign here, please."

Horace's bushy brows crumpled in a fierce frown. "This business address looks familiar."

"Does it now?"

To her consternation, he laid down the pen, leaned back in the swivel chair. "You must be pretty desperate, hiring a broken-down ex-cop to get you out of a bind."

"I'm neither desperate nor in a bind, Mr. Devlin. You're the one who, for reasons known only to yourself, are insistent upon unearthing the elusive Mr. Rodriguez to bestow such a paltry inheritance that you've already spent the executor's fee twice over hiring incompetent boobs who couldn't find their own mums with a compass and a field map."

His frown deepened. "May I remind you that this has been your case for several weeks now, and you've no results to show for my confidence in you."

"Which is why I've taken the liberty of locating an investigator with a talent for something beyond pocketing a paycheck and making excuses."

"You think Ethan can do better?"

"I know he can."

Horace regarded her for a moment, then signed the work order with a flourish and shoved it forward. Retrieving the contract, Deirdre had just reached the doorway when Horace muttered, "It took you long enough."

She glanced over her shoulder, saw the sly gleam in

Horace's eye. "It would have been easier if you'd simply told me what you had in mind."

Horace steepled his fingers and smiled.

"Has anyone told you what gorgeous eyes you have?" Deirdre circled a fingertip along Ethan's earlobe, satisfied by his sharp intake of breath, his sensual shiver. She stretched as far as the confining seat belt would allow, which was close enough for her breath to ruffle the fine hairs along his temple. "Hmm, I don't suppose I could convince you to pull the car over and park for a few minutes."

He swallowed hard, slanted a glance. "This morning wasn't enough for you?"

"That was hours ago." With a sensual stretch, she curled sideways in the passenger seat like a lazy cat, smiling as erotic images of their earlier lovemaking danced in her mind. It had been three days since their first intimate encounter in her kitchen, three glorious days of sharing every free moment locked in each other's arms. She'd lost count of how many times, and how many ways they'd made love.

Deirdre simply couldn't get enough of this man, wanted him more now than ever. A vixen dance of fingertips along his thigh rewarded her with a delicious quiver beneath his smooth khaki pants and an amusing clench of his jaw. She issued a throaty purr. "Umm, do you like that?"

"You know I do." Ethan moistened his lips, cleared his throat and struggled to look dignified despite the telling crimson flush crawling up his neck.

"And do you like this, as well?" Deliberately rotating the tip of her index finger from his inner thigh upward, she scraped her fingernail along the length of his zipper.

He bolted upright and hit his head on the car roof.

Deirdre chuckled. "Ah, then, it seems as if you do like it. Shall I continue?"

Puffing his cheeks, he curled his fingers around the steering wheel, eyes darting from the road ahead to the smiling woman beside him. "You're insatiable."

"I know."

"We're on duty."

"You're on duty. I'm just the navigator."

She glanced around the lush fields of the central valley northwest of Bakersfield, nothing but miles and miles of farmland. "Which is rather disconcerting, since I haven't the vaguest notion where we are."

"Maybe you should check the map." He angled an amused glance. "Appealing as your other offer is, I'll have to take a rain check, or we'll end up in the same ditch as poor old Nels did four years ago."

"Ah, yes, we're in the vicinity, aren't we? The place where Mr. Svenson and Mr. Rodriguez shared the historic meeting that started this entire crusade." Shading her eyes, she pulled a dog-eared roadmap from between the bucket seats, comparing their current location with data from the highway patrol report detailing the original accident. "According to accident investigators, Nels Svenson's vehicle swerved into a roadside irrigation canal—" she glanced out the window "—not unlike this one."

"It *was* this one," Ethan said. "The car landed on its side, trapping the driver underwater."

"That's when one Manuel Rodriguez inexplicably appeared to release Mr. Svenson's seat belt, and hold the poor man's head out of water until help arrived." She smiled, gave Ethan's shoulder a teasing smack with the folded map. "Which proves that both of us have read the accident report. What I want to know is how you've managed to locate a hot lead on the elusive Mr. Rodriguez in three days, when nobody else has been able to do so in months.''

''That's because nobody else did anything beyond checking Social Security and driver's license records, which don't exist for the fellow we're looking for, then calling every Rodriguez in the phone book without considering that our guy may be in the country only seasonally, using a temporary work permit to follow the harvest. When the season ends, he and his family probably head back home to Mexico.''

''How do you know that?''

''I don't for certain, but it makes sense. According to information in Svenson's will, Rodriguez mentioned that his wife and children were nearby. A lot of families routinely move north, following the harvest from Imperial County in the south to San Joaquin County in the north, then return home for the winter months.''

''Sounds like a difficult life.''

''It is, but it provides a fair living and keeps the family together.'' Ethan touched the brake, turned onto a paved road that cut through miles of ripening tomato vines. ''There are dozens of migrant worker camps along the harvest route. We'll check them all out, interview anyone who crosses our path, and maybe we'll get lucky.''

''That could take days.''

He shrugged. ''It'll take as long as it takes.''

Deirdre smiled at the glow of anticipation in his eyes. ''You love this, don't you? The challenge, the thrill of the chase.''

''I like puzzles,'' he confessed. ''There's a sense of accomplishment in having solved them.''

''By the time all is said and done, you could end up earning less than a dime an hour on this case. No wonder the other investigators gave up after a couple of phone calls.''

''They'd have spent more time if enough money was at stake. Frankly, I can't figure out why my father didn't stuff the fifteen hundred bucks in an inheritance trust and forget about it.''

''Because it belongs to someone,'' Deirdre said. ''Your father has his faults, but he also has an ingrained sense of decency and determination to do the right thing by his clients, no matter what the cost.''

She knew the moment Ethan's shoulders stiffened that she'd said exactly the wrong thing.

Bitterness roughened his tone. ''Yeah, my father, patron saint of the economically challenged.'' The knuckles of his left hand whitened as he gripped the wheel, his right hand flexed below the bandaged forearm. ''Let's get something straight, Deirdre. I took this job as a favor to you, not for my father. No matter how pure you believe Horace's motives are, I'm here to tell you that he never does anything that won't benefit him in the long run.''

A protest bunched on her tongue, was quickly swallowed. She remembered the gleam in Horace's eye when he'd signed Ethan's work order, the satisfaction displayed by that cocky half grin of his. The entire Rodriguez matter had been a brilliant strategy to guide Ethan away from a career door that had slammed shut, toward one opening in welcome.

Deirdre had been a big part of that strategy. She knew she'd been manipulated, although for the life of her she couldn't quite figure out how, nor could she regret her part in the process, not when she could see the results, the bloom of confidence as Ethan slipped into a role for which he was so perfectly suited.

No, Deirdre didn't regret opening the door for Ethan,

even if Horace had been the one who'd given her the key. What she did regret was the gnawing sense that there was yet another doorway hidden in this maze of good intentions, a furtive path toward which both she and Ethan were being inexorably propelled. She didn't know where that secret corridor was located, or what they'd find at the end of the trail. But she suspected that Horace knew.

That's what worried her.

Hour after hour, camp after camp, they crisscrossed the byways of central California's agricultural heartland, questioning dozens of people, following dozens of leads. By midafternoon, yellow school buses rumbled up the dusty roads, depositing gaggles of children, who transformed the encampments of tents, trailers and small cottages into lively playgrounds abundant with laughter.

Hours later the sun drooped low over the horizon, and the tantalizing kitchen scents wafted on the warm valley breeze. Clothing flapped from rope lines strung between massive oaks shading a cluster of tiny, one-room cottages. Voices floated on the wind, conversational tones emanating from one open door, childish giggles from another. A pickup truck rumbled into camp, packed with tired workers spilling from the open bed to sniff their way toward the delicious aromas emanating from various cottages.

Mingling with the returning men, Ethan and Deirdre received a few curious looks, a few pleasant nods and the break they'd been looking for when one of the workers pointed toward a slightly built man ambling toward a cottage at the edge of the encampment. Two school-aged children dashed down the cottage steps and were swept into his arms. A woman appeared in the doorway, balancing her toddler on a belly again swollen with child. Her smile of welcome was returned by her husband, who gazed up as if the sun rose and set upon her fragile shoulders.

As Ethan sprang forward, Deirdre remained rooted in place, watching the poignant scene with a sense of wonder. Love surrounded the family like a shroud of pure light. It touched her soul, warmed her heart. It was, she realized, the embodiment of that which she missed most in her life, that which she still craved with all her heart. A loving family, a cherished life.

As the woman noticed Ethan's approach, her serenity chilled. Worry lines touched her face, tightening to mirror her husband's concern at the appearance of a determined stranger.

The two men spoke briefly. Ethan opened the file he carried and held up the legal documents to which a certified check had been clipped. Clearly this was indeed the elusive Manuel Rodriguez. With the beguiled gaze of one beholding a religious icon he stared at the check Ethan offered. Moisture gathered in his proud eyes, alarming his wife to the point that she shifted the toddler in her arms and awkwardly descended the steps. When she reached her husband's side, he spoke to her in Spanish. Her eyes widened, her hand flew to her lips. Tears slipped down her cheeks. Tears of joy.

Ethan glanced over his shoulder, his own eyes bright with moisture. He understood. He finally understood.

''Where's my underwear?''

Groggy with sleep, Deirdre rolled over, blinking. ''Umm, I can't remember. On the living room floor?''

''We're in a motel. There's only one room, remember?''

She sighed, smiled, stretched like a satisfied cat. ''Oh, yes, I remember.'' Shifting, she propped up on one elbow, watching the shadowy form crawl through darkness intermittently broken by a blinking neon glow from the Vacancy sign on the parking lot. He scooted on his knees, patting the floor as if trying to burp it.

Yawning, Deirdre propped up on one arm. ''What's that lump on the chair?''

Rising on his knees, Ethan shifted through the objects in question. ''Your sweater, your bra and a cookie bag.''

''Cookies?'' She bolted upright, salivating at the thought.

Cellophane crinkled. ''No, just the empty bag.''

''Ah, that's a shame. I'm starving.''

''So am I, which is why I need my damned underwear.''

She wrinkled her nose. ''I'm not hungry enough to chew boxer shorts yet. However, that does bring to mind something much more appealingly edible.''

''I'm shocked,'' he muttered, crouching to search under the chair. ''You truly are a wild, wild woman.''

''I'm Irish, don't you know?''

''I've noticed. If I ever find my blasted clothes, I'll bring you flapjacks with shamrocks from the coffee shop. Aha!'' He straightened, grinning in the garish red glow as he held up a limp hunk of fabric. ''Found them.''

''Good.'' She snatched the shorts from his grasp, tossed them over her shoulder into the darkness on the other side of the bed.

''Hey, I'm hungry!''

''As am I. But there's breakfast—'' she yanked back the bedclothes, batted her eyes and struck a sexy pose so ridiculously exaggerated that he rumbled with laughter ''—and then there's *breakfast*.'' She punctuated the ribald suggestion with a purring sound deep in her throat. "What do you say, handsome? Coffee, tea or me?"

"No contest." Leering, he leapt into bed with enough force to roll his giggling bedmate into his arms for a deep, sweet kiss. "Wow," he murmured. "Talk about room service."

"Mmm." She nestled against his chest, tracing the manly contours with her lips. "Better than flapjacks, is it?"

"Oh, yeah. But if you're talking ham and eggs with mounds of crispy hash brown potatoes, it's more like a toss-up. Ow!" He rubbed the nipple she'd just nipped playfully. "Okay, okay, ham and eggs comes in second."

"And what might be first?"

"You know what's first."

"True, but a woman likes to hear such things out loud."

He smiled then, a warm, glowing smile that squeezed her heart. Cupping her face with his palms, he dipped his head, kissed each corner of her mouth. "You," he whispered against her lips. "You are first."

If happiness was fatal, she'd have expired on the spot. "Good answer." Sighing, she snuggled in the crook of his arm. "To be cherished above a hearty breakfast, well, a woman couldn't ask for anything more."

She didn't have to look up to know he was smiling. It warmed her from above, shone through the darkness like the golden glow of a candle flame. Ethan was happy, perhaps happier than he'd ever been. She knew it, felt it, was enveloped by it.

A day of success, a night of incredible love.

Only one thing would have made life perfect. "I wish the twins were here," Deirdre heard herself murmur. "I miss them."

"I do, too." Ethan stroked her hair, brushed it with a kiss. "Twice a week isn't enough time."

"No, it isn't." She held her breath, waiting. They hadn't discussed the custody issue for several days, not since Ethan's anguished confession that he feared himself unable to properly support his children, to be the kind of father they deserved. From Deirdre's perspective, Ethan was a perfect father, one who loved his children desperately, enough to put their needs above his own. But it didn't matter what Deirdre believed. It only mattered what Ethan believed, and if his faith in himself had been, or could be restored.

He cleared his throat. "I'm going to ask that the visitation time be increased."

"Are you now?" Her heart motored happily.

"Yes." He shifted, propped his chin atop her head. "I want overnights, too." He paused a beat. "I want my kids, Deirdre. Maybe it's selfish, maybe it's wrong, maybe I'll never be as good a father as they deserve, but I want to try. I want my boys with me all the time. I want—I want—" He coughed away a catch in his voice. "I want what Manuel Rodriguez has."

The breath she'd been holding slid out all at once. She understood what he meant. They'd spent the evening with the Rodriguez family, sharing a modest meal served with graciousness and with love. The money they'd delivered would make life easier for the family, but it had little to do with the sheer happiness permeating their humble home. That emanated from deep inside, from the hearts and souls of each family member, from the chattering children who made the tiny cottage walls vibrate with laughter, to the proud parents whose eyes glowed with the sheer joy of living.

"Did you see those kids run out to greet their father?

Did you see the light in their eyes, the light in his eyes?'' He shifted, tilting her chin up to gaze into her eyes. ''Those kids don't care about living in a mansion. They don't even know that they're poor.''

''They aren't poor, Ethan. They are loved and cherished beyond measure by parents who adore them, and who adore each other. The money they received will make the reality of life easier, but it won't make it better, for they are already blessed by the riches of the heart. It's the only wealth that matters.''

The concept seemed to baffle him. ''Not if your belly is empty and there are holes in your shoes.''

Deirdre laughed. ''When I was a child, I thought everyone cut cardboard for their loafers to keep out pebbles. There were so many of us, after all, that every item of clothing was passed down until it literally fell apart.''

''How did you feel then? I mean, when you were old enough to see that other kids had more than you did.''

She considered the question carefully. ''I won't say there weren't times when all of us didn't fancy something we couldn't afford, nor fight off the green-eyed monster when comparing a friend's shiny new bike with our own rusty, secondhand wheels, but I don't think we ever felt as if others truly had more than we did. It never occurred to us that we were deprived until we grew old enough that our friends told us so, the same friends I might add, who wore all the finest fashions but hung out in the malls after school to fight off loneliness.''

''Loneliness.'' The word was a whisper, thick with emotion.

She touched his cheek, softly, reverently. ''I can't imagine what it would feel like being an only child.''

He shrugged, tried for a smile that wasn't quite complete. ''It was great. I never wore hand-me-downs, shared a closet or fought to watch my favorite TV shows. Nobody ever tattled when I sneaked a flashlight under the covers to read comic books in bed. I didn't have to arm-wrestle to use the telephone, or flip a coin for the drumstick. Santa Claus piled great stuff under the tree every year, and since there was only one stocking hung, it was always stuffed. I got everything I wanted, and never had to share."

"Sounds terrific."

"It was."

"It also sounds lonely."

"Not every kid without siblings is lonely."

"But you were."

He hesitated, allowed his smile to break free. "Yes, I was."

She traced a fingertip along his jaw, down his shoulder to the edge of the gauze bandage that still encircled his right forearm. "You must have been so thrilled when the twins were born, knowing that they will always have each other."

The comment stirred him. "The first thing I did when I saw my sons was the obligatory finger-and-toe count. The second thing I did was to thank God that they wouldn't grow up isolated and alone."

"Like you did."

He shrugged, offered a smile that was slightly nostalgic, a tad forlorn. "Hey, how did this turn into a pity party? I thought we were going to indulge in a little pre-breakfast hanky-panky."

"First we hanky—" she slid her hand low on his belly "—then we shall panky ourselves senseless." He moaned as her fingers curled around him. She kissed his chest, delicately suckled his nipple, thrilled by his responsive shiver, the wild leap of his heartbeat. Silky hairs tickled her cheek. His manhood pulsed in her palm. "I can't get enough of you," she whispered. "You make me shameless."

"You make me pure." He rolled her over, tangled his fingers in her hair. "No coy trickery, no mind games, no hidden agenda—you simply are who you are. Honest and honorable, decent and sincere, beautiful and loving, without a pretentious bone in your body. You give me hope," he whispered, stroking her inner thighs. "Hope that a world with you in it can't be such a cruel and cynical place after all."

Deirdre would have responded if she could have, would have told him that it was he who gave her hope, he who'd taken a heart shattered by grief and healed it with a love so deep, so profound that she could weep from the joy of it. There had been a time in her life that she'd thought herself incapable of falling in love again. Certainly she'd have never imagined the intensity of emotion Ethan evoked in her.

For she did love him. Deeply. Profoundly. With every breath in her body, every fiber of her being. Ethan meant more to Deirdre than her own life, and she couldn't love his beautiful children more if they'd been of her own womb.

The sensation was both exhilarating and frightening. Deirdre had been expected to reconcile the Devlin family, not become a part of it. Yet as Ethan moved over her, whispering sweet words as their bodies intimately joined in a rhythmic dance of love, she realized that she had already become a part of it, because Ethan had become a part of her.

Her body quickened, and she cried out, wrapping herself around him as if she could forever hold him sheathed in her welcoming warmth. For this blissful moment in time, he was safe; he was sheltered. He was loved.

"You found him?"

From her vantage point outside the office door, Deirdre blatantly eavesdropped as Ethan handed in his report. Looking rather dumbstruck, Horace frowned and set about flipping through the pages as if seeking something to criticize. Judging from the stiff square of Ethan's shoulders, he, too, was braced for rebuke, and prepared to meet it head-on.

Horace spoke without looking up. "How do you know it's the right Rodriguez? You could have handed over Svenson's money to some schlub who's already buying drinks for his friends at the local bar and telling stories about the gullible fool that stuffed someone else's check in his hand."

Ethan crossed his arms. "Keep reading."

There was enough edge on his voice to raise Horace's bushy eyebrow a notch, but the older man simply flipped a page without comment and did as requested.

It took a while. The report was lengthy, detailed and amazingly complete. Ethan had prepared it himself on a portable typewriter he'd apparently been lugging around since his college days. Deirdre had read it earlier, when Ethan had first arrived at the office looking as nervous as a schoolboy on his first date.

Ethan's report was brusquely official, devoid of adjectives and littered with law-enforcement jargon that referred to Mr. Rodriguez as "the subject," and much to her amusement, referenced her own presence as "civilian technical support."

Now he stood in his father's office, ramrod straight and slightly pale, less concerned about his report preparation process, she suspected, than the reaction of a man whose approval he had repeatedly sought and never quite attained.

Horace cleared his throat. "Quite an interrogation you performed on Mr. Rodriguez, questioning him about the make, model and color of Svenson's vehicle, grilling him about how he'd unfastened the seat belt in order to hold Svenson's head above water until help arrived. By the way..." Horace angled a glance upward, then returned his gaze to the report lying in front of him. "How did you know the seat belt had been cut with a field knife? That information wasn't in the original police report."

"One of the paramedics mentioned it while describing what she saw upon her arrival at the scene."

"You contacted the emergency medical team?"

"Of course. I also contacted the officers responding to the call. One of them recalled noticing that Mr. Rodriguez's hands were callused, with reddish stains on his fingers. Since the accident occurred during tomato harvest, I presumed that we were seeking a migrant worker who would follow the same crop rotation from season to season."

Horace studied his son. All he said was "I see."

Ethan jammed his hands in his pockets, rocked back on his heels. "Anything else?"

"No." The older man eyed him impassively, then pushed the report aside and turned his attention to studying a legal brief as if it were the most important thing in the universe. "That will be all."

The air went out of Ethan gradually, with a slight droop of shoulder, the subtle waver of his chin. Deirdre felt as if she'd been punched in the stomach. No smile, no praise, no gratitude. Just a curt dismissal, as if Horace was speaking to an office lackey instead of to his own son. She wanted to cry, she wanted to scream, she wanted to rush in, yank the damnable legal document out of Horace's hands and beat him on the head with it.

Ethan simply spun on his heel and walked away.

As he reached the doorway, Horace's swivel chair creaked. "One more thing..."

Pausing, Ethan glanced over his shoulder while his father laid down the legal brief and slowly, deliberately rose from his chair.

When Horace spoke again, his voice was soft, choked, raw with emotion. "Good job, son. Damned good job."

Ethan's Adam's apple bobbed. He acknowledged the compliment with a curt nod, but his eyes were moist. And he was smiling.

Chapter Thirteen

"Gwamma, Gwamma, we—we—we went on a mewwy-go-wound!"

"Gamma, Daddy bought us moose hats!"

Wearing matching caps adorned with adorably silly stuffed antlers, the twins scampered through the patio entrance buzzing with excitement from the weekend adventure, not to mention a sugar high from cotton candy, gooey cinnamon rolls, candy bars and assorted sodas. Deirdre had gently warned him, but Ethan hadn't been able to deny his sons anything they'd asked for.

Finding the kitchen deserted, the children disappeared into the living room, hollering for their grandmother while Deirdre hauled a duffel stuffed with toys, tiny eating utensils, toddler cups, matching toothbrushes, their favorite bubble-gum-scented shampoo and other sundries onto the kitchen counter. Ethan dropped the suitcase packed with toddler clothes, snagged her arm and spun her around.

She stumbled against his chest, laughing. "Ethan! Your parents are in the other room."

"Shall I call them to watch?"

"Umm, that depends on what you have in mind."

"This," he murmured against her sweet mouth. With a sigh, she melted against him, parting her lips for his kiss, trembling as he accepted her invitation to taste so deeply, that fire burst through his belly and his knees went limp.

With some effort he allowed her to step away, which she did reluctantly. Her breathing was fast and shallow, her eyes glazed with the same desire that pulsed like liquid fire through his blood.

"You are beastly," she whispered, tracing the outline of his lips with her fingertip. "After an entire weekend of forced celibacy, kissing me like that...well, 'tis cruel and unusual punishment to be sure."

"We didn't *have* to be celibate." He sucked her fingertip into his mouth, watched her shudder with delight.

"The wee ones were sleeping in the next room. What if they'd awakened and found us, ah, otherwise engaged?" She eased her fingertip from between his lips, then smoothed his hair in an intimate gesture a woman uses to claim a man as her own. "They're a bit too young for a lesson on human sexuality, don't you think?"

"If people stopped making love because there were children in the house, world population would plummet." He nuzzled her throat. "We'll be alone tonight, you know."

"I can't wait." Her voice was low, husky, erotically charged.

He shivered with electric anticipation. "Neither can I."

In the two weeks since they'd located Manuel Rodriguez, their romance had blossomed into something so deep, so exquisitely intense that Ethan dared not examine it too closely. There was a fever in his blood for this woman, emotions powerful enough to be troubling. When he was with her, he couldn't think beyond the bliss of the moment. When they were apart, he couldn't think beyond the moment they'd be together again.

He was consumed by her, by thoughts of her, by feelings for her. At some level he feared that, feared the loss of control it represented. Yet he couldn't deny the depth of sheer happiness she brought to him, a happiness beyond his experience. A part of him warned that it couldn't last. For Ethan, happiness had always been a fleeting thing, something elusive, a beautiful butterfly fluttering for a moment then flitting away forever.

"A tuppence for your thoughts."

"Hmm?" He smiled at her, lifted her hand from his cheek to reverently kiss her palm. "I was thinking about how happy you make me."

Her eyes widened, glistened with moisture. "You make me happy, as well, Ethan. You and the boys. I—" she flushed, swallowed hard "—I care deeply for you all."

Wariness tightened his back, slipped a chain of caution around a heart swollen with emotion, fragile with fear. There was something in her voice that touched him. This was an extraordinary woman, a woman who deserved the moon and the stars and all the beauty of the earth wrapped in gold and arranged at her feet. Was he the one who could give that to her? He saw the question in her eyes.

It terrified him.

"Oh, excuse me!" Nettie chuckled as they sprang apart, her busy hands alternately covering her tickled grin and hovering midair as if conducting an invisible orchestra. "The boys wanted to say good-night. When you're through, of course." Flashing a delighted smile, she hustled back the way she came, and her whispered voice filtered into the kitchen a moment before footsteps echoed from the stairs. Ethan knew his mother had been speaking to Horace. She reported everything to her husband.

It neither concerned Ethan nor amused him. It simply was the way things were between his parents. He accepted it.

Deirdre, however, was clearly embarrassed about having been discovered in such an intimate embrace. She stepped away with a guilty laugh. "Well, looks like our secret is out."

"So it seems."

She tilted her head, regarding him with glowing eyes. "It was a wonderful weekend."

"Yes, it was."

"The children had a lovely time."

He just stood there, feeling oddly disoriented. Her smile wavered.

When he didn't respond, she rubbed her palms on her slacks. "Well, I guess we should tuck them in."

"I guess so."

She eyed him quizzically, offered a thin smile. He followed her out of the kitchen, had just reached the landing of the stairs when Horace stepped out of his study. "A moment of your time, Ethan."

He paused, then glanced at Deirdre, who'd hesitated halfway up the stairs. He saw confusion in her eyes, along with a touch of worry. That didn't surprise him. Although his relationship with his father had become increasingly civil over the past couple of weeks, the underlying tension remained. "I'll be up in a moment," he told her, then joined his father in the study.

Horace settled into a scuffed leather chair adorned with brass upholstery tacks. "Your business is doing well."

"I've had a few referrals." Ethan perched on a love seat upholstered in the same burgundy leather, but not nearly as worn as his father's favorite chair. "Not many."

"You're trying to locate a witness to a traffic accident."

He shrugged, not even bothering to ask how his father had acquired such insight. "A friend at the highway patrol office asked me to check into it. He doesn't believe the accident occurred the way the surviving driver described it."

"Any leads?"

"A few."

"You have other cases, as well?"

"A few."

"So many that you can afford to turn some clients down?"

Ethan shifted, realized that his father had been following the progress of his newly established investigative venture with more interest than he found comfortable. "I'm not into spying on a cheating spouse to provide the offended party a bigger slice of marital pie, if that's what you mean."

"Divorce can be quite lucrative."

"Only for lawyers."

"And private investigators."

"Domestic cases don't interest me." The statement

was brusque, challenging. Ethan expected an argument, a lecture about how success in business requires following the money.

Instead, Horace shifted his girth, propped an ankle on his knee and asked, "What does interest you, Ethan?"

The question took him by surprise. His father rarely reflected interest in any opinion beyond his own, and was more prone to issue orders than make requests. Ethan gave due consideration to a response. "I'm not certain, actually. I know that when I handed that check to the Rodriguez family, I felt good inside, as if I'd actually done something worthwhile. It was an entirely new experience, searching for someone who was pleased to be found. I know it wasn't a big thing on the scale of world events, but it was a big thing to them. Turns out it was a big thing to me, as well."

Horace regarded him. "The transformation from chasing ruffians and thugs to making life better for decent, hardworking folks must have been somewhat enjoyable."

Surprised to have his feelings so accurately described in a succinct nutshell, Ethan shifted, shrugged, managed a nonchalant nod. "Yeah, I suppose."

"That can be arranged." Horace reached into an open briefcase on the table beside him, extracted several manila folders. "These files are similar in nature to the Rodriguez case. Your fee will be as stated in the contract." He paused to riffle through the briefcase and remove what appeared to be a legal agreement. "I think you'll find the terms agreeable."

Frowning, Ethan leaned forward to accept the document, scanned it, handed it back. "I don't need charity."

"It's not charity. I need dependable investigative service. You can provide it. A business deal, pure and simple."

"A hundred and fifty dollars an hour plus expenses is charity."

"You don't think you're worth that?"

"It's thirty percent higher than the going rate."

"Then you'll have to be thirty percent better, won't you?"

He laid the contract in his lap, tapped it with a fat finger. "Unless you don't think you can hack it. Is that it, boy? You don't think you're good enough?"

Ethan swallowed his anger. He knew this man, knew his motives, knew his methods, had lived with them all his life. "I charge ninety-five dollars an hour, plus expenses, and I retain right of refusal for any case, for any reason, with no drop fee. End of discussion."

Horace tossed the document aside with a dismissive flick. "Fine. If you don't think you're worth more, you're probably not. Sit down," he said as Ethan rose. "We're not through."

"Yes, we are."

"No—" he thrust another document into Ethan's hands "—we're not."

This wasn't a service contract, it was a court petition. One with his parents' names beside his own. Stunned, Ethan sat back down in disbelief. "You're dropping the custody suit?" A troubling jitter in Horace's gaze was lost in a flood of sheer relief. "I'll have my children back?"

"Mother thinks it best." Horace shifted, unwrapped a hard candy from a filled bowl beside his chair. "There are a few conditions, of course." He popped a candy into his mouth, angled a glance at Ethan, who tensed slowly.

There were always conditions. He should have been prepared for them, shouldn't have let joy make him vulnerable. Pasting an impassive expression on his face, he laid the precious petition on the worn leather, draped an arm across the back of the love seat in as cavalier a fashion as he could muster and waited.

Horace tongued the melting candy into his cheek. "The transition must be made slowly, at the children's pace. Weekends at first, then overnights during the week until the boys are completely settled."

Ethan wanted to shout, *Yes!* but merely nodded.

"You will, of course, stay in Santa Barbara."

Ethan felt his fist clench, opened it slowly. "No."

Horace's head snapped up. "You can't return to Los Angeles."

"I can if I want to."

"And do you?" The older man settled his expression, calmed his harsh tone. "Want to, that is."

"Not at the moment, but I'll not have my future movements dependent on your discretion or approval. I'll live where I wish, and my sons will live there with me."

A vein pulsed at Horace's forehead. "I will not have my grandchildren taken away."

"Then I'll see you in court." He leaned forward as if to rise, settling back only when Horace raised a palm.

"Mother and I want fair and reasonable visitation. Two weekends a month, birthdays and holidays."

"One weekend a month, invitation to birthday parties held at whatever location I choose and shared holidays at my discretion." Flexing his fingers, he paused a beat. "That means I decide when, where, with whom and for how long."

Horace's eyes narrowed. "Plus the boys spend one month in the summer with us."

"One week."

"Two weeks."

"Fine." Ethan's heart was hammering. This was it.

They'd come to an agreement. He'd have his children home soon. Everything he'd ever hoped for, everything he'd dreamed about for so long was within his grasp. "Include those terms in the court petition, and we've got a deal."

"I'll see to it in the morning. Oh, one more thing." Horace spoke without looking up. "All terms will be implemented only upon the establishment of a stable, two-parent home."

Ethan's breath rushed out as if he'd been punched. "What?"

"Surely you don't expect me to allow my grandsons to be raised by day care centers and nannies. It shouldn't be that difficult for you to find an acceptable wife."

"Acceptable?" For a moment, Ethan thought he might explode from the shock. "Acceptable to whom?"

"Hopefully to both of us. However, since your previous attempt to select for yourself was a resounding failure, I presume you'd be amenable to suggestions on the matter."

Ethan simply sat there, stiff with disbelief. "Let me get this straight. I can have my children back, but only if I marry a woman of your choosing?"

Horace shrugged, helped himself to another candy from the crystal bowl. "My requirements are relatively simple. She must be domestically inclined, of course, a women willing to relinquish her career to devote herself to her family." As he spoke, he unwrapped the candy, tossed the cellophane aside. "She must be a woman of honor and spirit, a woman who'd love the twins as if they were her own. A woman like...say—" he popped the candy into his mouth and spoke around it "—Deirdre O'Connor."

It would have been kinder if his father had pulled out a pistol and shot him in the heart. Ethan swayed, struggled to breathe. So that was it—his father's trump card. Emotional extortion, the final hand of yet another manipulative charade.

And Deirdre had been a part of it.

Betrayal shattered inside him, a pain so sharp it nearly doubled him over. Slowly, stiffly he managed to stand, thankful his knees hadn't buckled. "I should have known."

Horace blinked as if sincerely baffled. "Known what?"

"It must have cost you a bundle. Women like Deirdre don't come cheap."

A crimson flush stained his father's fat cheeks. He sputtered as if choking. "Now see here—"

"Don't even try it," Ethan growled. "You've tainted every pure thing in my life, defiled everyone who ever meant anything to me. This time you've gone too far."

Furious, Ethan turned toward the doorway, and froze. There stood Deirdre, pale, stunned, obviously shaken. She touched her throat, her wounded gaze darting from Ethan to Horace and back again. Something cracked inside his chest. He knew she'd betrayed him. He knew she'd conspired with his father. God help him, he still wanted to sweep her into his arms, whisk her away from this madness and never look back.

He wanted to, but he wouldn't. Instead he met her soulful gaze with one of steely determination. "Sorry, babe, but that was a deal-breaker. Better luck next time."

Then he brushed past her without a backward glance, and slammed out of the house.

"How could you?" Having overheard the final segment of the conversation, Deirdre marched into the room to fling the court petition into Horace's shocked face. "How could you do something so vile to your own son?"

The man looked positively bewildered. "Is it wrong to want my son to be happy, my grandchildren to be well cared for?"

Everything made sense now—all the furtive glimpses, the self-satisfied smiles, the coincidental and the happenstance, all part of a carefully orchestrated lie. "You never intended to take custody from Ethan at all, did you? The lawsuit was nothing more than a ruse to manipulate him, force him to accept your terms."

Horace didn't deny it. "Ethan needed to shift his priorities from the past to the future. A swift kick in the pants got his attention."

"You cannot blackmail people into being happy."

"Blackmail?" His tiny eyes widened. "Now that's rather a harsh term, don't you think?"

"Not harsh enough for what I just heard. How could you do such a despicable thing?" Her voice cracked, her vision blurred with gathering moisture. She was furious. She was heartbroken. She was terrified by the expression on Ethan's face. He'd looked at her as if she was the enemy, as if she meant no more to him than a speck of dust clinging to his shoe.

And why not? After years of pain, heartbreak and betrayal, Ethan had been on the verge of trusting again, of repairing old wounds and unlocking the door to his own battered heart. Now that had all been destroyed. Ethan probably thought she'd been in cahoots with Horace all along.

Huffing his displeasure, Horace bounced from his chair like a fat ball, snatched up the petition and shook it like an angry fist. "Wasn't it despicable for Ethan to turn his back on his family, to choose a life-threatening job and allow a selfish shrew of a woman to bear *my* grandchildren simply to spite me?'' Purple with rage, Horace threw the document on the floor and kicked it. ''None of this would have been necessary if you'd done your job right in the first place.''

''My job?'' Deirdre felt the blood drain from her face. ''Sweet Mother of God,'' she whispered. ''That's it, isn't it? I wasn't brought down here to manage your office or help care for the babies. That was just another ruse, another devious scheme to get your own way.'' She stepped forward, her fists clenched at her side. ''How long have you been auditioning prospective daughters-in-law, Mr. Devlin? Surely I'm not the first. But since you're clearly the producer of this tawdry little soap opera, do tell me.... Did I get the part?''

Horace's anger faded into a bland shrug. ''That depends on how badly you want it.''

''You're offering me a choice? How truly enlightened of you.''

''Come down off that hypocritical high horse, Deirdre. I didn't force you to fall in love with my son.''

She gasped, curled her hand over her heart.

''You are in love with him, aren't you?'' When she didn't respond, Horace heaved a sigh, rubbed his expansive forehead and pinched the bridge of his nose. ''I provided the opportunity, that's all. What was done with it was always up to the two of you.''

''You lied, you manipulated, you brought us together under false pretense.''

Horace regarded her strangely. ''And that offends you?''

''Of course it offends me!''

Stroking his chin, he contorted his mouth in the semblance of a shrug. ''How peculiar, considering the assistance you've provided Clementine in perfecting her myriad matchmaking schemes.''

"That's...different.''

"Is it?''

She steadied herself against the love seat while beads of moisture chilled her upper lip. All the plans, the schemes, the manufactured opportunities to reunite families, or to create new ones. For the children, of course. Always for the children.

That's why Deirdre had come to Santa Barbara in the first place. She, too, had a clandestine motive, a steely determination to repair the splintered Devlin clan, to bring father and son together using their shared love of the children as a lever.

Had it been so different, what she and Clementine had done over the years? Had their methods been less sinister than Horace's, their motives more pure?

It was a heartbreaking epiphany.

Ethan never came home that night. Or the next night, or the night after that. Deirdre left messages on his machine; she paged him repeatedly. She camped by her living room window, stroking her kitten and watching for telltale headlights that never appeared to pull into a driveway that remained bleakly dark. She paced, she prayed, she ranted and she wept.

By the following weekend, she finally accepted that Ethan would never return. It was over between them. Deirdre knew what that meant, knew what had to be done next.

So she did it.

Chapter Fourteen

It was nearly sundown when Ethan pulled into the duplex driveway. Tired to the bone, he brushed the last of the Arizona sand off his jeans, hauled a dusty duffel from the trunk and dragged himself up the porch steps. His eye wandered to the neighboring window. No feline face peered through the closed damask drapes, no perky ears twitched at his homecoming.

He paused, dropped the duffel in front of his door and found himself knocking on the other. He didn't know what he'd say when she answered. He knew only that he was compelled to see her.

"It's about time."

Startled, Ethan spun around, faced the man huffing up the peeling porch steps. "I see your bloodhounds have kept you informed, as usual."

"Mother was worried." Horace pulled a handkerchief

from his coat pocket to mop his forehead. "You look like hell."

Ethan knew that. His eyes were sunken, purple rimmed, red with fatigue. A two-day stubble shadowed his jaw. His clothes were rumpled and stale. So was his body. He needed a shower. He needed sleep. "Thanks."

Wadding the handkerchief in his fist, Horace glanced aimlessly toward the street as if fascinated by the occasional vehicle thrumming past. "Did you locate your witness?"

"You tell me."

"My sources say only that you traveled from Barstow to Las Vegas, then down to Phoenix. I presumed you were on a case."

Ethan made a mental note never to use credit cards when he didn't want his movements traced. "I found the witness."

"Of course you did." A proud smile touched the corner of his mouth. "You're good at what you do, Ethan. Damned good."

That was twice Horace had expressed approval—twice in a lifetime. That may not seem like much to most people, but it was music to Ethan's ears. Swallowing a lump, he shrugged, poked his duffel with the toe of his boot. "Yeah, I am."

From the corner of his eye, he recognized a gleam of approval in his father's eyes. "It's about time you realized that."

Ethan met his gaze. "It's about time *you* did."

Horace blinked once. "I've always known it, son. I have always recognized your talent, your potential."

"Could have fooled me."

"Why, because I didn't want you to squander your future?"

"You didn't want me to have a future."

Horace wobbled back a step. "That's not true. I wanted only the best for you."

"You wanted me to be you." Jamming his hands in his pockets, Ethan glanced away. He took no joy in his father's pain, no pleasure in having caused it. "All my life, I've known you wanted me to follow in your footsteps. I wouldn't, because I couldn't. I didn't want to be you." He took a ragged breath, faced his father without cringing at the hollow hurt in his eyes. "I didn't want to be the kind of man who had to control the lives of others to make himself feel big."

Horace quivered as if struck, but his gaze never wavered. "When I was a boy, my father made all my decisions for me. He taught me right from wrong, chose my career, chose your mother to be my wife, drew a road map for my life and instructed me how to follow it." He paused, pursed his lips reflectively. "God knows, I resented him for it."

Whatever Ethan expected to hear, that wasn't it. He straightened, swayed, removed his hands from his pockets and folded them tightly across his chest.

"Do you recall Maury Goldberg? You met him once, when you were about six." When Ethan shook his head, Horace sighed. "Maury and I grew up together. He was my best friend. We were inseparable, actually. His father died when he was just a pup, and his mother never remarried. He grew up without a man in his life, without guidance, without expectation." Horace tucked the wadded handkerchief back into his pocket. "I envied him."

Shocked, Ethan couldn't think of anything to say.

"Maury made his own choices in life, developed his own value system. He never had to win his father's approval, and his mother... Well, mothers are nurturing by nature, so in her eyes he could do no wrong. I would have given anything to be like him.'' He angled a sad glance. ''I presume you can understand that.''

Ethan reluctantly allowed that he could.

''To make a long story short, Maury and I lost track of each other after high school. I headed off to college to become the lawyer my father wanted, and he shuffled off to see the world. I still envied him, until he showed up at my door years later, ragged, broke, alone, a thirty-year-old drifter with a felony record and no clue how to survive in a world no one had ever explained to him.''

Puffing his cheeks, Horace rocked back on his heels, gazing into space as if reliving every nuance of that moment in time. ''Seeing him again after all those years had a profound impact on me. I saw a man without purpose, without values, without the vaguest sense of responsibility because no one ever taught him that honor and accountability were important.''

Trying to digest the crux of his father's story, Ethan sought clarification. ''Is that what you see when you look at me? A man without honor and accountability?''

''No, no.'' Clearly frustrated, Horace palmed his face, squared his stance and tried again. ''What I'm saying is that Maury's failures made me take a hard look at my own life. There I was, happy, successful, married to the most wonderful woman on earth and with a son who was the center of my universe, all because my father had dragged me kicking and screaming down the right path. Yes, I resented his intrusion but dammit he was right. Because I listened to him, I had everything I'd ever wanted.''

''And everything you wanted for me.''

''Exactly.''

''So you handcuffed my options because you feared

I'd turn out like your felonious friend? Or was it just payback time because Grandpa made your life so miserable?''

"My father didn't make my life miserable. I resented his authority at times, but I never lacked respect for him, or believed he had anything less than my well-being at heart. I never defied him the way you defied me." Horace glanced away, had the grace to look embarrassed. "Of course, I was never as independent as you were, nor as fearless. I would have been terrified to question my father, but you…you had this annoying habit of asking why, of demanding explanation, refusing to accept anything I said without proof. I found it disrespectful and insulting."

"I meant it to be."

"I know you did."

Ethan rubbed his eyes with the heel of his hands, then lowered them to peer over his fingertips. "I was one hell of a brat, wasn't I?"

"Yes." Horace pocketed his hands, toed a loose board in much the same way as his son had earlier poked at the duffel. "And I'll confess that I wasn't as talented at fatherhood as your grandpa was, or as you are."

"Me?"

"You're wonderful with your sons," he said quietly. "They adore you. When I see the love in their eyes when they look at you, it makes me realize how long it's been since you looked at me that way." He coughed, swallowed, glanced away. "I know I've been hard on you, perhaps too hard. Mother thinks so. As does Deirdre."

The sound of Deirdre's name made Ethan's pulse leap. He glanced at the door upon which he'd been knocking. He'd done a lot of thinking over the past two weeks, a lot of soul-searching. It was time, he decided, to share the results.

Horace read his thoughts. "Deirdre's gone, son."

A chill slipped down his spine, numbing his limbs. "What do you mean 'gone'?"

"She handed in her resignation the day you left. A week later, I got a call from the duplex landlord warning that he intended to enforce the terms of the lease even though she'd moved out, lock, stock and barrel."

Ethan swallowed hard, tried to look like he hadn't been emotionally eviscerated. "Where did she go?"

"I don't know." The older man moistened his lips, blinked rapidly. "Everything that happened was my fault. Deirdre didn't have anything to do with it."

"Yeah, I figured. Deceit isn't really her style." From the corner of his eye, he saw his father flinch. There was no need to say anything further. Both men knew that deceit was not only Horace's style, it was his stock and trade.

"What are you going to do?"

Ethan gazed toward the duplex door behind which he'd found so much happiness. "I'm going to find her, of course."

"Of course." Licking his lips, Horace wiped his palms together as his son shouldered the dusty duffel and un-locked his front door. "I was there, you know."

Ethan glanced over his shoulder. "Where?"

"At the hospital, after your accident." The older man licked his lips, blinked rapidly. His eyes reddened, shone too brightly. "I never left, just sat by your bed day and night for weeks. After you woke up, I thanked God for having answered my prayers, and made up my mind that I would never allow you to be hurt like that again."

Slowly, almost painfully, Ethan slipped his keys back into his pocket. "Why are you telling me this now?"

"Mother thought you should know." Horace shrugged, stuffed his hands into his pockets. "She seemed to think it would be important to you."

"It is." A deep breath, exhaled slowly. Ethan fought the telltale prick in his own eyes. His father had been there. He'd cared, he'd really cared. The revelation touched him to the marrow.

"I suppose I should get back to the office," Horace said finally. He made no move to leave. Instead he gazed into the duplex with peculiar longing. "Unless you'd like to invite me in for a beer."

"Sure, why not?" Ethan pushed the door open, stood back while his father ambled inside. "By the way, that Maury stuff was pretty much a crock, wasn't it?"

"Pretty much."

"You haven't lost your touch, Pop."

Horace smiled.

"No, no, bad kitty!" Swiveling around the huge bed that took up most of the tiny one-room flat, Deirdre rushed to the miniature counter where Dublin happily lapped cake batter out of a mixing bowl. The cat waited until the last second, then leapt softly to the floor and sat there, smugly washing his face. "Have you no manners? Shame on you."

With a blob of yellow batter beading his whiskered chin, the kitten paused his personal grooming long enough to slide her a bland look.

"I'll have to throw it all out. What a terrible waste."

Dublin mewed.

"That you didn't eat much isn't the point. How would

you like it if I stuck my tongue in your dinner before I served it?"

The animal blinked twice.

"That's what I thought." Frustrated, she fingered her limp hair, glanced around a kitchen still cluttered with moving cartons. Inside, her favorite tape played on a tiny portable stereo propped beside the nightstand. Outside the small window, a foggy mist shrouded the view of neighboring apartment buildings. It was always foggy in San Francisco this time of year. She used to enjoy the misty ambiance. Now it just made her sad.

As if sensing her discontent, Dublin meowed again, twitching an agitated tail.

"'Tis dreary, I know." The sublease on her old apartment was not up for a while, forcing her into a bleak motel room with a cramped kitchenette. "We'll find a better place soon. When Clementine returns from Hawaii, the St. Ives law firm will reopen for business, I'll return to work and everything will be back to normal."

As if anything could ever be normal again.

A lump of pure misery lodged in her throat as she hummed along with the music.

She moaned as the doorbell rang. "Oh, heavens," she muttered. "Not again." Heaving an irked sigh, she sidled between the sofa and the bed, which were the only pieces of furniture that fit in the small quarters, and turned off the tape player.

"Yes, yes," she called out. "I know the music is bothersome to one who sleeps all day to recover from the strain of tormenting that delightful metallic guitar until 4:00 a.m. I do so apologize for having disturbed you."

Expecting the tattooed creature who lived next door to grunt and leave, as he usually did, she was surprised when the bell rang again. Dublin sniffed the draft emanating around the doorway, and issued a series of thrilled mews. In response, Deirdre peered through the fuzzy peephole, saw the back of a man's head.

Since the head in question was not partially shaved and bristling with spiked green hair, it clearly didn't belong to her musically tortured neighbor. She spoke through the closed door. "What is it you're wanting?"

"Delivery" came the muffled reply.

Since Deirdre was expecting a parcel from Clementine, she tightened her robe sash and turned the doorknob with a peevish mutter. "Where do I—" she nearly fainted when he turned around "—sign?"

"Anywhere except my forehead," Ethan replied. "The word *stupid* is already written there."

She steadied herself on the jamb. "What are you doing here?"

"Looking for you."

A horrible thought struck her. "The children?"

"They're fine. They miss you," he added when her breath slid out in relief. "I miss you, too." His exquisite eyes glowed softly, broke their hold on her only when he smiled down at the thrilled animal curled around his ankle. "Dubby, my man!" He scooped the kitten up, cuddled it in his arms. "Chased any good trains lately?"

Deirdre's heart pounded madly. Ethan had missed her. He was here, and he'd missed her.

His smile was tentative, his gaze uncertain as it flicked over her robe. "I thought... That is, I'd hoped we could talk. If you're not too busy, that is."

"I, ah, I was just getting dressed," she lied, rubbing a self-conscious hand through her hair. She wished she'd applied a modicum of makeup. "I must look a fright."

"You're beautiful."

"You always say that."

"It's always true." He shifted the kitten in his arms. "Are you going to invite me in, or do I have to hold your cat hostage?"

Since the "hostage" in question was nuzzling a furry head against his captor's cheek, Deirdre smiled, stepped back to allow him access. As soon as he entered, the kitten jumped down to bat at the tail of Deirdre's robe sash.

"Not bad." Ethan glanced from the shabby sofa to the large, unmade bed. "Cozy, in fact."

"The furniture came with the room. My belongings are in storage." Her skin heated with embarrassment. "Adequate accommodations are difficult to find in San Francisco. There's a housing shortage, you know."

He issued a sage nod. "Lots of houses in Santa Barbara. Three or four bedrooms, huge kitchens, massive backyards with plenty of room for kids to play."

Her throat went dry. "Sounds like you've been house hunting."

"I have." He wandered into the kitchenette, which was little more than a corner of the room with a miniature refrigerator, a two-burner hot plate atop a diminutive oven, a tiny sink and a three-foot square of counter space. "The boys will be living with me soon. We'll need more room."

"That's wonderful, Ethan."

"Business has been pretty good, too. I have more referrals than I can handle." He peered into the batter bowl. "Looks good. Mom used to let me taste cake batter when I was a kid." He tapped a finger on the rim, and questioned her with a look.

"Help yourself," she said sweetly. "Dublin certainly did."

He snatched his hand back, jammed it into his pocket.

"There's this place on the bluff," he murmured, eyeing the batter bowl as if it had been poisoned. "It needs a little work, but it's in a good school district and has a gorgeous ocean view. Great sunsets. Big kitchen, too. Lots of counter space, with a nifty little work island in the middle. Perfect for someone who likes to cook."

"Sounds lovely."

"It is." He clamped his lips together, ballooned his cheeks. Air slid out slowly. "I thought maybe you'd, you know, like to take a look at it."

"Why?"

"Because I was hoping you'd want to live there. With me. With us."

It took a moment to sink in. "You want me to care for the children again?"

"Yes."

"As their nanny?"

"As their mother." He took a step forward, swept her into his arms. "As my wife."

"Your wife." The whisper slipped out a breath.

"I don't deserve you," Ethan said, "I know that. If you laugh in my face, I won't blame you. If you tell me to leave, I'll go. Just hear me out first, please."

Somehow she managed to speak. "Is this your father's wish, Ethan, or yours?"

"I can't deny that my father adores you, honey. So does my mother, and so do my kids. But this is from me, from my heart. It's what I feel."

"What do you feel, Ethan?"

"You know."

"I want you to tell me."

He licked his lips. "I feel... I feel..." A flicker of panic dissipated into serenity as he gazed into her eyes. "I feel empty when I'm not with you, as if a part of me has been surgically removed. I can't eat, I can't sleep, I can't think. I close my eyes, and I see your face. I hear your voice in a crowd, smell your scent on my pillow. You are a warmth in my heart that never cools, a sweetness in my blood, the essence of all that is pure and good.''

Stunned, Deirdre remembered those words as her own, a portion of the answer she'd given when he'd asked her what love was. A swell of moisture gathered in her eyes. One tear slipped down her cheek.

Ethan gently thumbed it away. "You are that one precious person who enhances and enriches my life. You complete my soul, glorify my goodness, forgive my failures.'' He paused for breath, trembled against her. "You—you make me better than I am, Deirdre. And I love you.''

Dizzy with joy, her vision blurred with happy tears, she stroked his cheek. "That's the most precious thing I've ever heard.''

"Then say that you'll marry me.''

"You know that I will.''

He dazzled her with his smile. "I'll make you happy, honey. I promise.''

"You already have, my love.'' She kissed him softly, sweetly. "You already have.''

Epilogue

Horace pronged the sizzling patties with a fork. "These burgers are done."

Elbowing his father aside, Ethan plucked the fork from his hand. "They're too rare."

"I like rare burgers."

"The FDA says hamburger must be thoroughly cooked for safety."

"You're burning the damned things!"

"Tough." He hooked a thumb inward, resting the tip on his own aproned chest. "It says I'm The Cook. Read it and weep."

Horace scowled at the print-screened cotton. "Looks like something Deirdre would buy."

"Yep." Proudly smoothing the crisp cotton, Ethan grinned down at himself, pleased as a kid at Christmas. "It's a present for my first Father's Day barbecue."

"She should have bought you a blowtorch," Horace

muttered, stepping around the curious cat peering up at the fragrant smoke wafting from the barbecue. "You're determined to blast decent food into charcoal." The older man angled a glance to the utility table beside the smoking barbecue. He faked left, shifted and grabbed for the spatula.

Ethan was faster. "Aha!" Gloating, he waved the confiscated utensil like a sword of victory just as the twins scampered over.

Timmy hovered a safe distance away, while his boisterous brother muscled between the bickering men. "Daddy, Daddy, I—I—I wanna *big* hamburger!"

"Okay, son, just as soon as they're done."

Ethan slid a narrowed gaze at Horace, who huffed right back at him. "They *are* done."

From her vantage point on the patio, Deirdre watched the quarrel with more than a little amusement. Fathers and sons, three generations of Devlin men gathered to celebrate their maleness. It was a day to cherish.

She carried two tall glasses of lemonade across the patio to the lounge chairs overlooking the bluff. Dublin scampered over, waiting patiently. Nettie accepted one of the glasses with a smile. "Such a magnificent view."

"The sunsets are breathtaking." Deirdre settled beside her mother-in-law. Dublin leapt into Deirdre's lap as she gazed out over the ocean. "I love it here."

Nettie patted her hand. "I know you do, dear. I can see it in your eyes."

"You'd see the same thing in my eyes if we were sitting on tree stumps in front of a cardboard shack."

"I know that, too. It's love I see shining there—a woman's love for her husband and her children." Smiling, Nettie sipped her lemonade, glanced toward the smoky barbecue. "The boys are still fussing at each other."

"The big boys or the little boys?"

Nettie chuckled. "Do you need to ask?"

"Not really. The twins play considerably better together than do their father and grandfather." The tart drink cooled her throat. Smacking her lips, Deirdre absently stroked Dublin, angled a glance toward the heated discussion and smiled. Old habits died hard. Her father-in-law was still a bully, and her husband was still a rebel. Their squabbles were legendary, but beneath the chest-thumping jostle for position, they loved and respected each other.

Nettie spoke without taking her gaze from the glorious view. "Who's winning?"

"Ethan. He has the home team advantage, not to mention sole possession of the spatula."

"Good," Nettie murmured. "I've always despised rare hamburgers."

"Then you should speak up for yourself." Deirdre gazed proudly across the manicured yard. "As your son does."

Smiling, Nettie held up her glass. "Men. What frustrating and exquisitely lovable creatures they are."

"Indeed." Deirdre clinked her glass in a toast. "The fatherhood factor. Long may it drive the women of the world to delightful distraction."

"Hear, hear," Nettie said. "And may a hundred generations of Devlin women be as lucky in love as we are."

"I'll drink to that." Smiling, Deirdre leaned back in the chair, thrilled by the comforting sounds of childish laughter and grumbling grown-ups. All was well now. All was as it should be, as Clementine had known that it should be.

Ethan was Deirdre's heart, her soul. She loved him beyond measure.

Deirdre and Ethan had gone from lingering loneliness to a lifetime of love, thanks to a certain wily, white-haired matchmaker. As Deirdre tipped her glass toward the sunset, a remembered lilt of Irish laughter floated back with the breeze. *'Tis welcome you are, child. Be happy.*

Deirdre was happy. Supremely happy. That, too, was as it should be.

Sunshine peeked through the Irish lace, bathing the old Victorian in summer warmth. The rocker creaked, the fat tomcat purred. Clucking softly, Clementine scanned another stack of client files. More families in crisis, more children to be nurtured, more lonely people looking for love. Bringing them together was what Clementine did, what she would continue to do while there was breath in her body.

'Tis for the children, of course. Always, for the children.

*   *   *   *   *

Diana Whitney's next Special Edition will be part of the wonderful new promotion SO MANY BABIES. *This new mini-series begins in April 2001. Diana's book features a bouncing baby left on the doorstep.* WHO'S THAT BABY? *will be available in May 2001. Be sure to catch all these terrific stories in Special Edition*™.

Silhouette Stars

Born this Month

Born this month: Gloria Estefan, Chrissie Hynde, Peter Sellers, Jesse Owens, Maria Callas, David Copperfield, Greta Garbo, Stirling Moss, Fay Weldon, Michael Douglas.

Star of the Month

Virgo

The coming year will be one of great highs and lows. You should, however, make progress in many areas of your life if you allow yourself to learn from past mistakes. Mid-year there is an exciting new project which enables you to improve both your financial status and your working environment.

SILH/HR/0009a

Libra

A romantic month in which you may form a new and fulfilling relationship or make a greater commitment to that special person. Career matters are also well aspected, adding to your blossoming confidence

Scorpio

You may have to choose between keeping the peace at home and your work commitments. Good can come out of this situation if you are prepared to discuss and reach a new understanding. An invitation lifts your spirits late in the month.

 **Sagittarius**

This month's aspects are focused on romance and you should enjoy a sensational few weeks in which you could meet the partner of your dreams or rekindle an old flame. Towards the end of the month you need to be careful what you say and to whom.

Capricorn

You don't like to take risks, but there are times when you have to. What's on offer this month is too good to turn down and although the consequences will be disruptive, the results will be brilliant and worth the risk.

 **Aquarius**

The planets are firing you up and you feel impatient to get moving. Don't worry, life will soon be in the fast lane. A friend proves invaluable and renews your faith in people.

Pisces

Honesty is the best policy and you must tell those close to you exactly how you are feeling as they may want to help and may even have some answers. Mid-month a financial windfall could set off a spending spree.

Aries

Ties and attachments you make this month will influence your life in the long term. Although you prefer to work on your own, joining a team could bring far reaching benefits.

Taurus

Travel is well aspected, especially to faraway destinations, as you need to take time out to absorb recent changes and rejuvenate your spirits. A promise made long ago may come back to haunt you.

 Gemini

You may be in the mood for travel and adventure although you might be limited by work demands and financial pressures. Don't allow resentment to build up. Try to find alternative ways of letting off steam which will be equally beneficial.

Cancer

Ambition is the key to success and you will need to talk yourself into a positive frame of mind in order to see all that is on offer. A friend needs help and you could be flattered that they turn to you.

Leo

A happy-go-lucky month with lots of social happenings to put you in a good mood. Around the end of the month an opportunity presents the chance to change an annoying aspect of your life.

▼™ SILHOUETTE
SPECIAL EDITION®

AVAILABLE FROM 22ND SEPTEMBER 2000

SUDDENLY, ANNIE'S FATHER Sherryl Woods

That's My Baby! & And Baby Makes Three

Slade Sutton might never have thought of himself as a father but his
young, motherless daughter did. Slade needed help and Val Harding
was in just the right place...

CINDERELLA'S BIG SKY GROOM Christine Rimmer

Montana

Everyone was talking about how schoolteacher Lynn Taylor had ended
up in sexy lawyer Ross Garrison's bed—until Ross decided to protect
her honour and claimed Lynn as his bride-to-be!

HUNTER'S PRIDE Lindsay McKenna

Morgan's Mercenaries: The Hunters

Rugged mercenary Devlin Hunter thought Kulani Dawson was far too
pretty to be his partner! But after nights filled with danger and passion,
Dev's real battle was preventing his partner from stealing his heart!

THE NO-NONSENSE NANNY Penny Richards

Fiery, beautiful Amber Campion was back in town, but no one was
giving her a chance—until rock-solid sheriff Cal Simmons asked her to
look after his niece and nephew. Cal had always had a soft spot for
Amber...

MY CHILD, OUR CHILD Patricia Hagan

New York Times Best-selling Author

Jackie Lundigan hoped to convince strong silent single dad Sam
Colton that his home, his child—his heart—were meant to be shared—
with her!

COWBOY BOOTS AND GLASS SLIPPERS
Jodi O'Donnell

Who would hire an ex-countess with no experience? 'Iron' Will Proffitt
would; he gave Lacey McCoy, 'America's Cinderella', all his dirtiest
jobs. But Will was no Prince Charming, was he?

River Deep

An amazing new 12 book series where power and influence live in the land, and in the hands of one family.

The McKinneys are a dynamic Texan dynasty who are determined to nourish old fortunes and forge new futures.

Join us as we cross the water to follow the lives and loves of the ranchers.

Book One
FREE

Look out for the new titles every month

Deep in the Heart by Barbara Kaye
23 June 2000

Cowboys and Cabernet by Margot Dalton
21 July 2000

Amarillo by Morning by Bethany Campbell
21 July 2000

White Lightning by Sharon Brondos
18 August 2000

Even the Nights are Better by Margot Dalton
18 August 2000

After the Lights Go Out by Barbara Kaye
22 September 2000

Hearts Against the Wind by Kathy Clark
22 September 2000

The Thunder Rolls by Bethany Campbell
20 October 2000

Blazing Fire by Cara West
20 October 2000

Stand By Your Man by Kathy Clark
17 November 2000

New Way To Fly by Margot Dalton
17 November 2000

Everybody's Talking by Barbara Kaye
22 December 2000

RD/RTL/1b

FREE
2 BOOKS
AND A SURPRISE GIFT!

We would like to take this opportunity to thank you for reading this Silhouette® book by offering you the chance to take TWO more specially selected titles from the Special Edition™ series absolutely FREE! We're also making this offer to introduce you to the benefits of the Reader Service™ —

- ★ FREE home delivery
- ★ FREE monthly Newsletter
- ★ FREE gifts and competitions
- ★ Exclusive Reader Service discounts
- ★ Books available before they're in the shops

Accepting these FREE books and gift places you under no obligation to buy; you may cancel at any time, even after receiving your free shipment. Simply complete your details below and return the entire page to the address below. **You don't even need a stamp!**

YES! Please send me 2 free Special Edition books and a surprise gift. I understand that unless you hear from me, I will receive 4 superb new titles every month for just £2.70 each, postage and packing free. I am under no obligation to purchase any books and may cancel my subscription at any time. The free books and gift will be mine to keep in any case.

EOZEC

Ms/Mrs/Miss/Mr ....Initials..

BLOCK CAPITALS PLEASE

Surname...

Address...

....

....Postcode ....

Send this whole page to:
UK: FREEPOST CN81, Croydon, CR9 3WZ
EIRE: PO Box 4546, Kilcock, County Kildare (stamp required)

Offer valid in UK and Eire only and not available to current Reader Service subscribers to this series. We reserve the right to refuse an application and applicants must be aged 18 years or over. Only one application per household. Terms and prices subject to change without notice. Offer expires 31st March 2001. As a result of this application, you may receive further offers from Harlequin Mills & Boon Limited and other carefully selected companies. If you would prefer not to share in this opportunity please write to The Data Manager at the address above.

Silhouette® is a registered trademark used under license.
Special Edition™ is being used as a trademark.